GRANDMOTHER WOLF

GRANDMOTHER WOLF

Patricia Tyrrell

Weidenfeld & Nicolson
LONDON

First published in Great Britain in 2005
by Weidenfeld & Nicolson

A CIP catalogue record for this book is
available from the British Library

ISBN 0 297 84896 8 (hardback)
ISBN 0 297 84813 5 (trade paperback)

Typeset at The Spartan Press Ltd,
Lymington, Hants

Printed in Great Britain by
Clays Ltd, St Ives plc

Weidenfeld & Nicolson
An imprint of the Orion Publishing Group
Orion House, 5 Upper St Martin's Lane,
London WC2H 9EA

www.orionbooks.co.uk

GRANDMOTHER WOLF

I

So I told Chehab to send the boy here – to Beirut.

Old Chehab, the same age as me but he's always been poky, a turtle crawling within its mottled shell. Nowadays he's an Americanised turtle waving slow flippers across his desk in Seattle, USA. Of course my phone wasn't working when he tried to call (this *is* Beirut) but the bank's unofficial fixer had performed an illegal miracle for them earlier in the week, twining rooftop cables, so they were temporarily in touch with the world. They sent a minion by taxi to fetch me; as the widow of the bank's founder I'm privileged.

'What does Chehab want?' I asked. I so rarely go out these days. The minion murmured soothingly about the tranquil afternoon with no shooting and the sky undisturbed blue. That was irrelevant, because there's never any point in being afraid. Some militiaman's radio several streets away thumped a rock beat, dah-dah-*dah* miss you, dah-dah-*dah* need you. 'What does Chehab—' But the minion didn't know.

This youth is elegant though, in his purplish-blue junior-financier suit. 'From the Pierre Cardin boutique,' I say (not a question). He nods proudly. Beyond his sleek head, while we ride, the city which I'm deliberately ignoring suddenly forces on me the gaze of its many burnt-out windows, dark eyes which scorch through the afternoon's glare. I look away from them and speak polite idiocies to the youth. Finally we arrive.

The thickly carpeted sixth-floor room crackles with

machines; in a hushed sanctum beyond, with a part-shuttered window, the branch manager receives me. His pudgy gesture makes the waiting phone a god we must both worship because it has kindly agreed to function. 'Calling from Seattle,' he says, 'Monsieur Chehab.'

Out of the receiver crumbs of politeness fall; after our twenty-year silence Chehab could have spared me those. His voice sounds crustier than ever, but I watch our city past the shutter – our bony lovely ruined city – and I grin. Present-day Beirut would soon crunch through his shell. We two speak in French, of course (it's the only civilised language), but he's acquired an American twang which distorts his formal phrasing. 'My dear Madeleine, Etienne's son has become a problem. No interests except unfortunate ones, and his recent suicide attempt—'

Something twitches in Chehab's voice at this; can he possibly care about the boy? Why should he? It's not *his* grandchild. And I, the relative involved, find no emotion in myself toward this unknown youth except boredom at being summoned to the bank on a hot afternoon when there isn't even any fighting. Not that I'm hungry for more bloodshed, but weren't the militiamen playing cards and drinking 'araq when we passed the Line checkpoint? An insulting nonsense. 'What do you expect me to do at this distance?' (Or at any distance or closeness.) I speak sharply, on purpose.

'Madeleine, please!' Begging, he sounds much older than me. 'I'm at my wits' end.' (His wits like tiny frayed ropes, himself dangling.) 'The boy's . . . episodes . . . have made headlines here. That isn't good for the bank, nor . . .' The phone winces and fades as Beirut loses contact with the world, then recovers it. 'Are you there, Madeleine?'

Damn you, yes.

'So I thought . . . get him out of the States for a while

till matters quieten down . . .' Elephants dance on the line and his voice falters between their crashings. '. . . You agree?'

To what? Send the boy anywhere you wish. Etienne, my eldest, was the most unsatisfactory of my children. Not tough but a stick-insect living within the narrowest limits. My husband sent him from Beirut to the Seattle branch; he worked dutifully and died prematurely there; the morticians performed their barbarous laying-to-rest rites; I sent a large wreath, non-mourned and have forgotten. Also he's been dead five years. 'Send the boy where?' I say in an old-woman drone; not tired, merely bored.

The phone blares, startling me and the manager who hovers discreetly just inside the door. 'Why, to you in Beirut! Haven't I just said—' More elephants; past them his alarmed voice rises. 'You're his only relation . . . the reputation of our bank in nationwide financial circles here requires . . .'

My husband and every other bank official always spoke with this awed tenderness of the bank's needs. A sensitive plant, which closes its leaves at any breath of gossip. But, 'What would I do with a troublesome teen-ager?' Against this my head defends, Might be an amusing experience. But I'm – not too old, only can't be bothered.

Between the elephants the voice blares, 'It's not unsafe there now, surely? The fighting's stopped.'

A universe of innocents. No news from Lebanon in the papers today? Fine, their problems must have been solved. The manager's face mirrors my own. I defy us both and astonish myself by saying, 'No fighting at present, no. And there are other foreigners in the city . . .'

There may be, and not only hostages or the reporters who scurry from one incident to another. I did hear that the American University is functioning, after a fashion;

whose fashion one doesn't care to speculate. Meanwhile the various militias seethe or play cards in their ratholes, giving off a variable hum like insect colonies and building up to the next phase.

Through my straying thoughts the hard-surfaced voice says, audibly relieved, 'Discipline, that's what the boy needs. A firm hand. And, Madeleine, you always did—'

Didn't I though? And perhaps still do; at least Brigitte and Georges seem to think so. They're fully adult in age, yet they rebel so innocently, in such unimportant ways, and in the big matters they remain almost wholly within my orbit. Their attitude to me quite disconcerts me at times: they're bitchy or tender, but always full of filial respect. An unexpected pleasure. Perhaps they'd like to be involved in this decision, which now hangs in the balance. No, *my* house. I'm invariably firm about that. And only Brigitte still lives there with me. Brigitte and myself and this problem boy: plenty of room. 'Send him along,' I say, suddenly gleeful, foreseeing shoals and reefs ahead (life has been dull lately). 'I'll lick him into shape.' I hang up the phone and at once regret the bother, upheaval – the responsibility? But I've promised; that's final.

2

The oldest trustee of his father's estate called him in for a bare scrappy interview. Rick was uptight anyway because the bank's limousine and a couple of minders had showed up unannounced at the hospital a half hour before his discharge time. He'd planned to hire a fast car as soon as he got out and head for some backwoods motel where he'd be alone to figure out what to do next, but the chunky black-clad minders – like in a fourth-rate Mafia movie – insisted and started putting their hands on him, and everyone in the lobby gaped. So after he'd shaken off their fingers and explained loudly that he was his own boss, he agreed to go along with them this one time; in future he'd arrange things so these people wouldn't get a chance to bully him. Meanwhile their limousine rushed him to head office where, in a penthouse room all glassy dazzle and acres of pale grey carpet, old Chehab like some alien-world wrinkly presided.

Rick let the expected harangue drift past. Chehab's grey suit merged with the background; only the wrinkly's eyes and mouth lived. Rick had dressed specifically for the only sort of future he could contemplate and, while the formal phrases clicked out, his gaze travelled down his battered jeans, along his scuffed sneakers and beyond the window to where the highrise cluster of Seattle glittered in the February sun. Chehab was saying, 'The publicity from your activities has been – you understand? – bad for the firm. Financial institutions that handle large sums—'

Thirty floors below, mist sheened up from the Sound. Rick said, 'First time I've heard a try for suicide described as an activity.'

'That and your other—'

Rick took his eyes off the city and transferred them to Chehab, though he sensed it was useless. 'Look,' he said, 'won't you please do as I suggested – split my dad's estate between the four trustees and leave me out of it?' He managed a wry grin. 'Or hand the money over to charity if you feel it's tainted.'

'No question of "tainted".' Chehab flushed. 'A family-run bank is a perfectly respectable business. And we can't rescind the terms of your father's bequest even if we wished. So you already receive a substantial income, and you will certainly inherit the trust fund plus his shares when you reach twenty-five, seven years from now.'

Below, in the miniature world of city and Sound, a helicopter curved down toward the Medical Center landing-pad and from the ferry terminal a green-and-white Bainbridge Island chugger crawled out on the plum-dark water. Rick thought, If this window were openable would I have the guts to jump, even if I shove myself with the reminder that Josie's wedding is Friday? Goddam it, that one botched try has made me jittery about chucking blood around on my hospital-scrubbed body and this super-clean city. He said, 'How can I get it through your head that I don't *want* the blasted money or the bank? I plan to make my own way.'

'With what and in what direction?' Chehab picked up a gold-ribbed pen and began tapping it on the desk. 'Your scholastic record is terrible.'

'Schools teach such unnecessary crap.'

The pen tapped faster. 'Outside of school can you name one useful interest you've ever pursued?' The wrinkles deepened. 'A lack of drive—'

'Hell!' Rick said, stung because the truth was the opposite: all the things a person might do with a life surged through him continually in great colourful waves. Surely the future was a matter of surfing these urges till the strongest and most persistent of them won out. He crossed his ankles so that his worn sneaker toes lined up defiantly at Chehab, and ticked off on his fingers the legitimate ways he'd recently spent time. 'Swimming and rowing and reading' – Thoreau and homesteading books passionately on top of the pile, but you couldn't explain that to this shrivelled old urban type – 'and year before last I spent time in the Junior Helpers, that citywide thing where you go around running errands for old people and learn first aid and such—'

'Praiseworthy.' Chehab's tone curdled. The flashing gold pen meant everything Rick longed to avoid: strait-jacket responsibility and a tedious routine where people would gawp up to him because he had money and was officially the boss. And his private fortune increasing all the time without him needing to lift a finger; that'd be indecent. Chehab went on, 'No qualifications, no serious application toward the future. And your other recent activities—'

A grilling, as if Rick were a spitted fish. He jumped up and began to pace. 'Okay, so I've gotten drunk and had girlfriends and wrapped a car off the road. And spent money other ways, like every kid in the States whose parents have dumped an inheritance on him.' He turned abruptly. 'I've been feeling my way. Isn't any kid allowed that?'

'We are not discussing the morals or customs of this country. You are Lebanese.'

'The hell to that. I'm American-born.' The pen waved itself at him like a tormenting little penis; yes, there was that angle too. Nights spent with Josie who, two years older than him and very conscious of her experience, had finally said . . . He burst out, 'Why won't anyone give me time?'

Chehab's gaze hit the wrists where scars glared, as if he were asking, How much time did you give yourself? And yet it hadn't felt that way at the moment of slashing, only that Josie had suddenly proved to be violently opposed to their shared dreams and to him. Her rejection of him personally, plus his horror at the business career that the bank trustees would try to force him into, had sheared him away from hope.

'I'll tell you one thing,' he said, 'I'll never ever join your bank.' He paced back to the desk and leaned across it at Chehab. 'I aim to live poor and—'

Chehab grunted ferociously. 'What do you know about poverty? You've always been extremely rich.'

From this height the city was soundless, as unreal as the whole world had seemed in that moment of slashing. Rick sat down and straightened his shoulders resolutely, but Chehab's words had planted the feel of unreality inside him too. The two of them stared at each other, then Rick started talking to drive away the echo of Chehab's last words. 'This dumb plan you've cooked up – if I refuse to go to Beirut, what's the alternative?'

A sardonic flicker crossed Chehab's wrinkles. 'You're not free to refuse.' The pen made regular circles. 'Personally I'm convinced you're sane. As for that suicide attempt, no doubt you were feeling emotional over your car crash or a girl. And wasn't there talk of gambling?' The dark eyes pierced.

'I paid my debts' – sullen because he felt spied on; how had they found out else? – 'and quit. Gambling scares me.' This was true. Sitting beside the roulette wheel, losing money, had brought a warm relief till he realised he was losing control of himself too; his willpower and ability to make decisions were spinning out of reach along with the spinning ball. He was sure he could handle poverty, but not this loosening, this dissolving. 'As for the Thunderbird, I told the body shop man to keep it for himself when he'd fixed it, or to sell it if he'd rather and keep the money.' (The flash of pure delight on the man's face had almost, in that moment, compensated for owning a fortune. But only almost.) 'And the girl – that's strictly my business.'

But Beirut did sound like a messy place where any sort of behaviour went. Maybe if you decided the future was a zero you could chuck your life away fast and unnoticeably there? He repeated, 'What's the alternative?'

'Ah.' Chehab laid down the gleaming pen. 'As I said, I personally regard you as sane. But no doubt some psychiatrist could be found who would agree with the board of trustees that you need a long rest in some . . . supervised clinic.'

Rick's hands tightened. 'That's blackmail.' The helicopter had landed; the ferry headed out distant across the Sound.

'I care about this firm,' Chehab said. 'You may have no loyalty to your father's memory or to the business that his family built up, but the four trustees do. And our employees do also.'

'Cosy,' Rick said.

Chehab picked up the pen and reading-glasses and drew a memo pad toward him. 'Rick, I believe you're a good boy at heart, but you're no use to us in your present condition. What with your father's premature death and your late mother's rather . . . erratic . . . personality, you haven't been correctly moulded. Your grandmother Madeleine is competent and sensible; she'll help you grow up.'

Rick said, 'You leave my mother out of this.' When his heart quit banging around he opened his mouth to say, I refuse, you can't make me go. But these old men were his legal guardians and till he came of age they'd got him strung over all the barrels there were; the glare of Chehab's glasses brought to mind what would happen if he refused. A supervised psych cell on a locked corridor, with tranquillising shots if you spoke up – no. He'd heard the experiences of other kids in his class at school. And the prospect of meeting his grandmother in Beirut did slightly intrigue him. Only slightly though, because his parents had rarely mentioned her, and the formal cards he'd received from her at long intervals, transmitted through Chehab, had made her seem dry, crusty, not really a relation at all. But technically she was family. Chehab said she didn't write oftener, or call Rick, because of communication difficulties due to the Lebanese civil war. Rick thought savagely, That may not be the only communication problem she and I'll have if she's got the same mindset as Chehab. But he could most likely get out from under her thumb in Beirut easier than he could get out from under Chehab in Seattle.

He said, 'If there's really no choice . . .' and Chehab was already writing in lacy script on the memo pad. Anger at having been out-manoeuvred forced Rick's next words to the surface. 'But as soon as I get there, you know what I'll do?' His mind condemned the threat as childish.

Chehab tore the sheet off the memo pad and fingered it; his eyes were flat and abstracted. He said, 'In Beirut you may not need to take any initiative toward suicide. The fighting has stopped and Madeleine agrees with me that the city is perfectly safe, but if you're as reckless and foolhardy there as here, you may find some leftover lone gunman who'll dispose of you.'

Rick said loudly, 'I'll be glad.' He got up and went to the door; in the corridor his minders waited. He said, 'Are these guys necessary?'

The old man, tidily folded into himself beyond the big desk, said, 'I intend that you shall reach Beirut intact. I have great faith in Madeleine's power to transform you.' In a voice as quiet as the husk of that other-world alien he added, 'Your father trusted me with the responsibility of you. I respected and cared deeply for your father.' The door shut on Rick's unwary spurt of pity.

Within days he was ready to go; the haste of these elderly grey men seemed to him indecent. But he did pack his own suitcases, thank you; no minder was going to mess around with his clothes. Old Chehab in a cryptic note told him to take only used items. You won't, said the delicate curly script, need good city clothes there. Jeans and shirts and sweaters and a jacket, that's all.

This fiat sent Rick to the big atlas in his father's study and then to the public library. He emerged from the stacks thoughtful, not scared exactly but with his adrenalin surging, caught the eye of his current minder (who lurked a few yards away) and said to him past the culture-dabbling city matrons, 'What's going on there *now*? These books are all three or four years behind.' He wanted to add, How about this hostage bit? And barricades and rooftop snipers? Because I've got a right to know what I'm getting into. But the minder only stared and said, 'Excuse, excuse – no can—' The librarian shushed the pair of them, so Rick marched outside, minder in tow. A couple of jet fighters shrieked overhead, leaving scribbled white airstreams on the blue, and Rick thought, The local types can't do any worse than shoot at me.

3

Anyway, how much bother can one eighteen-year-old cause? Yesterday (the day before his due arrival) I told Seraphite to get the spare bedroom ready. She's worked for me a long time and knows better than to argue, but the clatter of her broom and swish of her skirt said, What're you planning now? This morning I informed Georges when he made his usual short before-breakfast visit; he grinned past his beard, raised an eyebrow and his rifle in salute, and left. And I told Brigitte when she strolled down to her usual late breakfast; that was soon enough. It's not a matter for her decision, so she didn't need time to reflect.

She looks her most delectable at breakfast; if I were a man I'd fall in love with her then. The dark long hair drifting, the gaze melted with sleep. (I wonder what she dreams of. But I'd never ask; God knows what farrago of horrors she might produce.) Her peignoir – an old turquoise silk Dior of mine – drifts too. But she'd better hurry to accept some man; during a woman's thirties the ineradicable mouth-lines, the significant wrinkles, arrive overnight. This morning she plunges into her coffee and pita bread as luxuriously as if they were sleep itself. I've stayed waiting at the table with my prepared question: 'How much bother—'

'Really, Maman!' (I've often asked her to call me Madeleine as Georges does, but she refuses; no doubt she enjoys emphasising my age.) 'These abstract speculations at breakfast—'

'Not abstract.'

We always eat in the upstairs kitchen of my house, overlooking ruined back yards; concrete-dust and an echoing silence surround our meals. Seraphite turns from the stove with more coffee; her glance at me is penetrating but amused too, as if she enjoys my manoeuvring. She's Arab from beyond the Line. By all the rules Georges should be hefting his gun at her and she spitting the ashes of us French-speaking Christians from her lips, but there are no unbreakable rules in this city. Thirty years ago I took her on as maid, gave her a French name instead of her barbarous Arabic one . . . and here, six days a week, despite the pragmatic logic of guns and grenades, she still works; I've better sense than to ask her why.

'The boy will arrive,' I tell Brigitte with unholy irrepressible glee, 'this afternoon. You'll need to take time off from your so-called studio and go with me to the airport.'

She sets down her cup and slab of bread; her eyes leap awake. 'Maman, what have you been up to? You can't have invited someone *here*.'

'Family,' I say. 'A special request; there wasn't much choice.' But she's too smart for that.

'All the choice in the world. "Spend your holiday in lovely Beirut" . . .' This grinds my heart because the pre-fighting travel posters did say that. 'Who the hell have you inveigled into—'

'He's got problems, needs a change of scene, and his scene needs to lose him for a while. But he's part of our family. Etienne's son.' It sounds acceptable.

'Etienne's son – foreign-born – are you insane?' She throws her half-full cup in a long perfect curve of pure fury; it smashes against the far wall and Seraphite, tight-lipped, takes a mop to the tiled floor. Brigitte hasn't done that since childhood; in those days I was always glad when my work as an anthropologist took me abroad away from her tantrums. Never a meaningless rage but tightly rational. She rises and stands over me in a beautiful ferocious turquoise arc. 'A *foreigner*?'

'He has dual nationality, I suppose, but Chehab will sort out his passport.' The turquoise arc leans pulsing at my face, but I refuse to be intimidated. 'Danger?' I let my old-woman voice maunder on, 'Oh, I don't think you need worry. The city's quieter than it was.' Beneath the maunder I'm delighted that Brigitte can still surprise me; it's worth having the boy here, to discover that.

'I don't care if the fool gets bumped off as soon as he arrives at the airport,' – she must have been watching old films with one of her numerous men-friends; that 'bumped off', spoken in English, has precision – 'but he's a young hothead, foreign, rich, naive, and of course doesn't speak French or Arabic.'

Now she's provoked me where it stings. 'You're well aware that I've forbidden the speaking of Arabic in this house.'

My cold anger rebuffs her fury; she sits down and sips the fresh coffee that Seraphite has poured. 'All right,' she says slowly, 'we'll excuse his lack of Arabic temporarily despite the fact that everyone in Beirut uses it except my fanatical mother.' I can feel her mind poking around my edges, testing every approach to undermine my pleasure in this visit. 'Damn you,' she says, 'you're enjoying this, aren't you? Bringing in this young fool unknown and stirring us up to fear and suspect and to wonder what future you've got in mind for him—'

'No special future.' I put my hand over my cup to reject Seraphite's approach with the coffeepot, then I lean back and grin at the pair of them. 'As you're aware, Brigitte, my money is tied up in trust funds for you and Georges and Helene,' – the forgettable daughter in Paris – 'so I couldn't—'

'Blast the money.' She sets down her cup and something more profound than china-smashing moves in her voice. 'Do you never think of anything but money and power?'

'Not much.' Her words hurt although my smile remains; I hadn't realised she might *hate* me. Irritable bickering is all very well, and cup-throwing once in a while if she must, but *hate*? 'This boy won't interfere with any plans of yours.'

'Oh, plans!' She shakes her head at me, but she's calming down; the line of her mouth relaxes. 'How long will this creature stay?' she asks. I lean easier in my chair and Seraphite gives a little sigh; the three of us are a linked household again. Cursing, fighting, often quarrelling, but a real household.

'Chehab didn't say. Not long, I imagine – a month or two?'

'And you've waited till the day of his arrival to order me to take time off from work?'

My lips twist in a grimace of rueful confidence.

'Yes,' she says, 'you would. Maman, if I didn't love you so, I'd find you intolerable.' But she smiles at me, she smiles warmly.

'You can spare the time though?' I say.

'Surely that's not a question? You never make requests.' But when she reaches for the dish of peach confiture, her fingers amble tranquilly. The studio recognises her worth – she's taken some astonishing photos for them – so she'll demand this afternoon off and they'll agree. 'How old,' she says, 'is the boy?'

'Eighteen. And – you realise? – he's my only grandchild.'

'Too young.' She's shaking her head. 'You'll make mincemeat of him.'

'That's absurd. My only grandchild—'

'Isn't it rather late in life for you to develop a sense of

family?' Her ironic tone underlines the words; she can't possibly mean them literally, but what does she mean? 'My dear,' she says, 'you've never been notable for helping lame ducks before, or problem children.'

And I remember, as in a troubling dream, that Brigitte only calls people 'my dear' when she's really annoyed with them.

Afternoon: Brigitte and I go by taxi to the airport. The driver, a fortyish swarthy man, has a Turkish-style curled moustache but, since the fighting started, one doesn't ask about people's origins; Brigitte has warned me that taxi drivers will discuss the weather, their young children, and nothing else. A thin late-winter rain falls, a grey skin beneath which the ruins breathe.

Brigitte wears a white clinging coatdress and I my black-and-grey Chanel suit from before the fighting. Together we resemble a sketchy attempt at a chess set. With her expert make-up and shapely figure she looks expensive, sexy, slick; the elegant bones and piled dark hair make an effect. I'm absurdly nervous about the boy's arrival, so I goad her. 'He's only eighteen,' I say meaningfully, 'and your *nephew*.'

'You bitch.' But she takes my arm and squeezes it in our familiar way. As I said, a tender filial respect; surely I couldn't be wrong about that.

The airport road; how strange that Beirut retains anything so normal as an airport – and functioning most of the time, too. I've not driven this way since the last of Helene's visits, those blank sheets of paper between the scrawled pages of our lives. 'Your sister,' and I chuckle because if you don't laugh at people like Helene, what *can* you do with them? 'How long since she's visited?'

'A million years.' Between me and the rain (and the scarred buildings, which I'm carefully not looking at) Brigitte's wide smile reappears. 'She's sensible.' I relish

this scorn; we who've stayed can count ourselves survivors.

'Do you suppose the boy's afraid of Lebanon? After all,
he's being banished here, and the worldwide news
reports—'

'So scared that we'll have to send him straight back.' A
hint of steel flickers behind her smile; she does resent
his coming. So my decisions do still make an impact? The
taxi swings onto the wide boulevard heading south, and
to avoid noticing the buildings I keep my gaze on the
central strip. Grass grows tall there, tangled winter-
brown grass not mown for years; why should they cut
it? How could they? Into my fantasy of a mowing-
machine crisscrossed with bullets Brigitte says (and this
time her tone holds genuine interest), 'Chehab claimed
that this boy's got problems? In addition to having no
parents, which is of course survivable.'

Among those elephant-lurches on the phone, how can I
be sure what his problems are? 'Something about a car
crash and big gambling debts, perhaps some disastrous
love affair.' Our taxi swings off the boulevard to the
airport gates and now I can't help noticing: militiamen
stand around with pistols or rifles at the ready, and barbed
wire bristles at the gates, the approaches, the doors of the
terminal buildings. Between the airfield and the sea lies a
wilderness of sand dunes; my husband and old Chehab
used in boyhood to shoot wild doves there. I tell Brigitte
this and she says with grim pleasure, 'Kids from the city
still do, between incidents.' Of course they would.

Our taxi draws up near the door of the arrivals terminal; rain drums its fingers on the buildings and tarmac.
I say to Brigitte, 'You should know what to expect of this
boy; don't you spend your evenings watching American
films?'

'A tearaway,' she says with Hollywood accent, 'a
young rip, a hoodlum.'

'Then he's come to the right country.' Clearly she plans to invest a lot of energy in hating him.

'Stay in the taxi,' she says, tender and filial again. 'I can meet him when the plane lands. You mustn't get wet.'

'I'll melt?' I love her concern but no one shall spoil me; I push her detaining hand aside and climb out. A militiaman (whose uniform, like Georges', takes the cedar emblem of Lebanon in vain) halfway assaults us, but Brigitte whispers to him and he lets us pass. Did she say, 'This is Georges' mother' or, 'She's old and loyal' or simply, 'Tonight'? It's a mess; I detach my mind from her responses but there's pain. I say, 'The weather is clearing,' and on cue it does; Brigitte furls her black-and-white umbrella.

Over the city from the north the plane drifts down. It floats gentle as a pre-war surfer, and its descent meticulously follows the straight line of the city's demarcation zone. A pity that the foreign boy's first sight of Beirut must be that evil scab . . . The plane sees us and shrieks in annoyance, in disbelief that the airport is open and we alive humans are waiting; it lands.

A hoodlum? A young tough? Surely someone's guess slipped up? My first stunned thought is, How like his docile mother! Anonymous clothes – his choice perhaps but also a sensible precaution. Blue denim shirt and jeans, bulky socks, scuffed sandals; he has the dark thick hair and upright stance of our family but there's much of Gabrielle about his face – a wide-openness. That quiet girl who I swore was the right wife for Etienne . . . Brigitte leaves me in a corner of the arrivals hall (my legs have suddenly become absent-minded) and when he finishes with customs and passport examination she says to him loud and distinct, 'Bonjour, Rick.'

An awkward name like a jaggedly broken stake. There's no danger to the boy, I'm sure there isn't, but his wide-open gaze makes him seem like some plain or sea, waiting to be the site of battles; we Lebanese are much more private and hence safer. So surely Brigitte oughtn't to call him by that very foreign name amid all these jostling watchful local men; surely she ought to wait till we're in the taxi? But she goes ahead, she repeats it. He glances hazily behind him, then answers her in English with an American drawl, 'Aunt Brigitte? I did have a minder . . .'

Silent nondescript men who might be paid minders scurry in and out of the hall. Brigitte looks bewildered – by this or by the ageing he's conferred on her with that 'Aunt'. My legs recover, I go forward and say, 'He's probably vanished; his duty's done.'

'Yeah, I guess so.' I never watch films nowadays, so I'd forgotten how languorous and drowsy Americans can sound. 'Grandma.' He offers me his hand, and the word makes ten thousand years of caresses. Then that guilty glance behind him again, as if he's already failed some test of ours. 'They didn't trust me,' he says, 'to stick around till departure date and get myself onto the plane, so that guy's been dogging me ever since Chehab called you.'

Brigitte finds her voice. 'A friend?'

'Hell, no!' An easy perfect-toothed smile. 'An okay sort, but we didn't have a whole lot in common. Like . . .' He stares around and his voice fades; perhaps he's realising that the minder's homeland is his too.

Brigitte pounces on this. 'Your country.' Her fingers thrust at the flaking paint, the grimy chipped floor, the bullet-pocked walls. This cavernous space smells of plaster-dust and fear, but there'd be no point in wondering how many incidents have happened here, how many people have been killed within this cubic footage.

'Your family. And,' Brigitte continues, 'you will please remember that you may speak English in future only within my mother's house. My mother and I will speak

English with you there, but elsewhere you must, for safety's sake, speak French. You understand me? Now, your taxi waits.'

He winces as if in excessive guilt; the three of us go outside.

Brigitte with exaggerated care helps me into the taxi, and at my ear she murmurs, 'Mincemeat.' Yes, that's what I'm supposed to do to him. But my feelings toward him have lost their focus, they're groping disoriented – because I, like Brigitte, had expected a young rip, a tearaway, not this drifting uncataloguable type.

Our taxi swings around and begins the return journey: past the guarding militiamen, the wire-festooned gates, past a muddy bunch of scarlet paper flowers whose significance no one will ask, and along the boulevard. Beyond the wire, on the airport perimeter, a pack of wild dogs cavorts amid marigold splashes and tall dead grass. The boy stares at the untidy brown grasses, at the smudge of pinewoods on our right, at the Palestinian cemetery with its cracked walls and leaning monuments; he seems not afraid but absent. Our driver jumps the third successive set of lights (the beggars swarm if you stop) and as if this has roused the boy he says, suddenly aggressive, 'What're you supposed to do with me?' As if he automatically rejects any plans we've made for him.

Neither of us answers. He glances from Brigitte to me, then his eyes flicker across the bumpy, glowing scars on his wrists. Brigitte must sense my momentary unease, because she leans at him and in a voice low as the buzz of the taxi she says, 'If, my dear, you do anything to worry or upset my mother while you're here, I'll make sure you suffer for it. Do you understand?'

I laugh at such melodrama and say, 'Really, Brigitte!' Yet her loyalty pleases me. And I must ask the boy soon about his past so as to know what to expect; moreover, what exactly *did* Chehab have in mind? Brigitte's mutter at the boy has set his face glowing like those scars, so I say to him confidentially (I'm going to enjoy balancing the two of them), 'We'll talk later.' ('Discipline' was what Chehab mentioned, but there's plenty of time for that.) 'Then we'll—' His attention slips from me; Beirut has taken over.

His gaze pulls mine with it; I can't avoid staring now. His eyes – receptive, wholly shocked – dissolve my defences. Chehab in those preliminary telephone maunderings said, 'Life must be painful for you, Madeleine, now that Beirut—' And I'd answered him truthfully, gladly, 'My training as an anthropologist comes in handy. I've disciplined myself to have no country any longer, no nationality. The various factions in Lebanon are a bunch of primitive warring tribes like any others; I stand aside and observe them; I'm detached.' But that stratagem doesn't work here, now, next to this innocent's appalled face.

We pass the broken blur – a heap of grey-yellow rubble in the sun – where Sabra camp was razed. Then, all the way to the city centre, the streets are giant mouths full of hollowed rotting teeth. Brigitte says to the boy, with that grim pleasure she used about the dove-shootings, 'You haven't seen anything like this before.'

'Sure I have.' Then he becomes honestly uncertain. 'Not in real life, but photos or movies. The South Bronx maybe, or England in the Blitz. War movies mostly.'

'Yes.' Brigitte's sibilant curls peacefully in the corner of the taxi.

Suddenly I remember to ask him politely, 'You had a good journey?' Michel and I always asked visiting friends this when we met them at the airport; they used to come for the nightlife, surfing, skiing.

Brigitte laughs. 'Maman, you're so late!' But the boy detaches his stare from the outdoors and pulls himself together.

'Oh – yeah, Gran, thanks.' (I insert sourly, 'You'd better call me Madeleine,' at which Brigitte chuckles.) The boy finds a moment of real enthusiasm. 'We switched planes in London; I wouldn't mind visiting there some day. The place looked kind of . . .'

No doubt it did; so would anywhere except here. Through his lit gaze I visualise an hour of tepid cloud-and-showers (mustn't Seattle be much like that?), a mostly familiar language, a northern freshness to the air. Whereas here the rain has fled, deepening the mountains' apricot-and-snow where it passes over them; on an earthen barricade as we approach the Line a militiaman sits playing a flute and the sky burns flagrantly blue. Not much like London.

The Line crossing-point: the boy draws a quick breath and I say irritably, 'There's no *danger*.' Merely a matter of routine. They check our papers and we drive across; no one's fighting today. There's only a network of barricades – some earthen, some wire or burned-out vehicles – and a lounging assortment of militiamen in various uniforms.

I don't glance sideways north or south along the Line; the boy's incredulous eyes can have that charred canyon to themselves. We drive along the museum corniche into Ashrafiyeh, my beloved wrecked quarter. The taxi stops beside a street market and I say to startled Rick, 'We must walk from here.' We pick our way between the striped canvas awnings of the stalls, among piles of smashed concrete and rusty girders; all this is routine, too.

The only way into my house is along the alley and through a ruined cinema; it's a great nuisance not being able to use your front door, but that's the price I pay for living on the Line. The wonder is that the house is still habitable. In the alley the boy wrinkles his nose; he'll soon get used to the unchanging stink of rubble dust and burned and unburned garbage. Inside the cavity of the ruined cinema Brigitte takes my arm to steady me. I don't want a broken bone if it's avoidable; the local hospitals aren't what they were. At the huge hole where the screen once hung, Brigitte pauses and says to Rick, 'Always take the left-hand passage here, not the right.'

He asks with childlike defiance, 'Where does the right-hand one go?' and she gets annoyed, which is silly because there's no question that we're the experts.

'Straight to the Line, my dear,' she says, 'so if you want to get shot . . .' Which is silly too; there hasn't been any shooting on this section of the Line for at least three months. But no doubt she's trying to sound dramatic and impressive. And various militias do still patrol the whole length of the Line, but that's routine also; Georges told me it is. He'd have been notified if anything were brewing for the near future.

We leave the cinema by its back door and cross a series of rubble-strewn back yards; I once had neighbours. Broken half-walls of houses surround the yards, houses built – like mine – of golden sandstone with Ottoman curves and curlicues. The last back yard belongs to me. Here the charred walls stand higher; we've privacy, and against my house wall a precious water tap and pipe, which one of Georges' fixer friends rigged up for me from the only intact water main in the area. My narrow house leans above the tap and us; Seraphite has this afternoon off, so Brigitte unlocks the door. Always I go into my house as into a sheltering womb; if I have any passion left, it's for this. My womb, my tapestried cell, my loved cosy prison.

Brigitte enters, I enter. The boy hesitates – then he too steps inside.

4

Night-time. I go to bed tired because this boy keeps repelling, in the most definite way, all my explorations.

I insisted that Brigitte go out as usual for the evening – she gets scratchy if she stays dutifully at home – and I spent those hours making polite searches to which he responded with an opaque courtesy, but remaining rock-stubborn. Thus, 'We'll keep you busy while you're here. What are you interested in?' Silence. Meanwhile my fingers caress a stone child riding a dolphin, on the table beside me, and I long to fling the statuette at the boy's infuriating monolithic face, but no: I value my sardonically smiling stone child. He's survived Pompeii and the centuries since and the Lebanese militias; I've the responsibility of protecting him and this room's other treasures from damage. So I poke again, more forcefully. 'Georges will take you to such-and-such, and Brigitte—' The silver chains scattered on the table around the dolphin's belly rattle; as if they've fallen apart and freed his tongue the boy suddenly says, 'Gran, I don't want to sound rude,' – meaning he will – 'but to me this month or so here is a sentencing, a time they've insisted I serve. Afterwards I'll go home and stay out of Chehab's orbit and pick up again where I left off.'

So he compares this tall, expensive house, this luxurious room, to prison and myself to a jailer? When I call my house a prison the word almost amuses me, it's satirical, but this boy's cold, disdainful tone for what I love is infuriating. His scorn irritates me so much that I shout, 'Why did you come here if you hated to?'

From the wing chair his face, naked and unhelpful, stares at me past the cut-velvet upholstery; perhaps for once he'll speak the truth. 'Because Chehab told me to choose between this trip and being an in-patient at a psychiatric hospital, locked unit.'

'He could do that?' I can hardly believe it, and anyway Chehab has always, beneath his crusty exterior, seemed averagely compassionate. 'But you're not insane.'

'He was running scared.' His eyes flicker across the scarred wrists as if he fears his own hands' power. 'No, I'm not crazy, only a whole bunch of problems got massive at once.' He painfully, stagily, tucks the wrists away and looks full at me. 'Gran, you don't know the States – those psych units that are run by and for rich people. Anything goes. You've got money and a trouble-some kid? Okay, we'll tuck him away out of sight, calm him down for you. Keep him in a locked room with window-bars, sedate him, the works.'

'That sounds incredible.'

'Like I said, you don't know the States.'

So calm, and his shrug of indifference is just right; I find myself believing him. But first, 'What did you do to make Chehab so nervous?'

He grins, weary yet youthful. 'I got some bad publicity, that's what, dragged the family name into areas he objected to.'

'Such as what?'

His weariness deepens; how many other people has he already been forced to recite this catalogue to, 'experts' from various esoteric disciplines? Do I sense also that their answering murmurs were unhelpful, or is this guess arrogant? 'You really want to hear it all, Gran?'

And does something else underlie his tone, a hesitancy caused by my stooping elderly body, my wrinkles? Better make clear at once that chronology is irrelevant to me. 'You must learn to treat me simply as an adult; I'm a tougher fighter than you any day.'

His face hardens and he leans forward. 'Okay, here's what I did. One gambling episode; I quit in time to pay my debts but Chehab got scared by the report he heard. One car crash – doesn't everybody have those?'

'The other driver?' I insert mischievously, but he solemnly shakes his head.

'Nuh-uh, I was alone on the road at night. Driving kind of fast, sure, but not stoned or drunk. Wrapped the T-bird around a tree.'

'Fools for luck. You walked away from the wreck?'

'Yup. And . . . oh yeah, there was an affair with a girl. Failed love-chase. But doesn't everybody—'

'That was when . . .' I nod toward his wrists.

'Sure was,' he says too smoothly. 'But, like I say, doesn't— hell, most of the kids I know are totally mixed up, the rich ones anyway. Tries for suicide were pretty usual among my classmates.' He watches me. I say nothing (I can't visualise a world where possessing money and never being hungry or shot at could *cause* problems) and after a while he goes on. 'Trouble was, all these damn things – ordinary things – about me hit the Seattle papers inside of a year. Hit on account of the family name, bank's name, whatever. And old Chehab didn't ride them peaceful like most of my friends' families would; he got all shook up and twitchy, decided I was bad for business. Sole heir is unstable, what wild things'll he do when he comes of age and inherits his father's spot?'

That would, in the eyes of a senior bank official, be a reasonable question. Such huge sums of money are involved . . . and this boy's casual jaunty tone brushes aside not only the money but also the security of all the bank's employees. Natural at his age perhaps, but his bravado makes him sound more naive than even I had anticipated.

He shifts in his chair and says, 'Well, maybe I didn't handle my last interview with Chehab too tactfully. In hindsight . . . but I was determined to be honest with him. He called me to his office and instead of saying, Sorry and I'll be a good boy in future – instead I told him what he could do with the bank and the family name. And with all the damn money I'll inherit. I told him exactly what I thought of that and where he could put it.'

'So what do you intend to live on?'

He flushes dusky. 'I'd get a job. Not banking and not necessarily white-collar, but the sort of job I'd enjoy.'

'And what would that be?' He's so open a target that he makes me fierce.

'Christ!' he says. 'How would I know yet? Why won't anyone give me time?' He hauls his long body out of the chair. 'Gran, it's been a busy day. I'd just as soon hit the sack now, if you'll excuse me.' But I've begun to laugh – can't prevent myself – from three remarks back.

'How would you know what it's like to work, to go without things?' I say. 'You've always been extremely rich.'

With his hand on the door he says, expressionless, 'Chehab threw that at me too. You folks certainly do know where to jab and have it hurt. Now if you'll excuse me—'

'Goodnight, Rick.' But he's already gone.

Midnight; I'm in bed but can't sleep. Hadn't realised how a new person in the house takes up space, commands attention, makes noise. A youth too . . . big feet, big clean energetic hands, strong torso, takes deep breaths that seem to use up all the house's air; I'd forgotten how much energy the young have. I lie awake, prodded by one devastating insight after another: how despite

Brigitte's threat to him he might on impulse do something appalling to himself, how if not he'll be bored to fury, will stamp through the house yearning to get into trouble, will require outlets that it hadn't occurred to me to provide. He's eighteen, had at least one serious girl-friend and grieved over her, therefore sex . . . And sports – or something else to use up more of that terrifying energy. *Draining* energy, to me who watches. And he's unconscious of his energy's abundance, its trespassing; this is simply how a young person lives. A rich American person – surely that has much to do with his impact on me. His mind may put up barriers but his flesh bounds with exuberant health. He has never, despite his ideal-istic whimpers, slept in a cellar under bombardments or scraped an existence in a city devoid of milk and bread; he's never needed to wonder where the next thousand dollars or meal or roof would come from. I lie in the dark (an intense darkness because we keep the front windows of the house tightly shuttered) and reflect how odd families are. Michel and I, in some night of pleasant but never world-shaking copulation, begat Etienne; and dry-stick Etienne together with that floaty reticent wife of his, in some night whose details I can't begin to imagine, begat this youth who is so unlike myself and Georges and Brigitte – and yet is our kin. Such a dry stiff father – and this impulsive idealistic boy?

Faces float past my closed eyes . . . then a shutter creaks like all the burglar alarms in the world and in-stantly I'm wide awake. I get up and pull a dressing-gown on. Georges fixed my shutter so that I could open it quickly if necessary; I push it ajar.

5

Midnight, but he couldn't sleep. The rusting gutted cinema and the gutted grey city and Madeleine's treasure-cave of a living room, jammed with silver and marble and watercolours and Oriental rugs – all these tumbled together in his head and bewildered him. He had turned out the little oil lamp (electricity was apparently permanently off) but silence and the room's red silk hangings and the shuttered window pressed at him like shouts. Somewhere there must be a window that would open to the night air and a view less claustrophobic than the cluttered and ruined back yard he'd glimpsed between his own shutters on arrival. Even in Beirut there must be street lights – a street or two away maybe, but *somewhere* – and people walking or chatting in bars and restaurants; hadn't the so-called 'experts' agreed that the fighting was finished and the city returning to normal? Somewhere within sight there must be an urban life that was halfway familiar.

Next to his room on the back of the house was Brigitte's, but she'd gone out for the evening and would be home, Madeleine said, very late as usual. Across the landing, on the front of the house, Madeleine had shown him the doors of her room and next to it a room they didn't use because of a crack in its wall. Surely no one would hear if he crept in there and undid the shutter to look at the city; Madeleine was so old she would for sure be asleep by now. He threw a robe over his nakedness and tiptoed.

The window unbolted readily, but that was the end of

easy predictable things; he gazed out and felt he'd gone one extra step and an unearthly abyss had swallowed him. He wasn't conscious of exclaiming or shifting his feet, but the bolt in Madeleine's shutter slid and her wrinkled face appeared. She said, 'You couldn't sleep?'

'Nuh-uh.' No doubt his wakefulness would annoy her. He stared down at the jagged black gulf and narrow side canyons; finally he found words. 'Chehab told me Beirut is safe nowadays?'

Her harsh little voice said, 'You sound so damned *innocent*, but you've got no right to be innocent here.' Then her tone melted like a fiery metal caught in a glow. 'Don't be afraid,' she said, 'he may be right. There's been no shelling for months and no shooting recently.' She became amused, mocking. 'We intend to return you safe when your time is up.'

'I'm not frightened,' he said, 'only this is so . . . different.' The muttery noises from the black-and-silver gash before him sounded like a backcountry woodland: rustling dry grass, the rasp of branches against each other or against broken walls, and a breeze that rushed from far off. Then an anonymous crash, and Madeleine spoke again with that unexpected comforting tone, like an accomplice.

'A beam or slab of concrete breaking loose,' she said. And when a crooked shadow scampered into the moonlight, 'Only a cat. The ruins are full of feral cats and dogs.'

Could this gash ever have been a city street? And what the hell must she feel like, living next to it? 'Tough for you,' he said, 'having this for a neighbour.'

Her answer was so swift that she must have used it often before, a quick, brief retort about being a trained anthropologist and therefore, Rick gathered, not caring much about anywhere. 'Sentimentality,' she said with distaste, 'a disease spread by droplets.' She switched to lightness. 'But you'll be perfectly safe. Tomorrow you shall meet Georges, my youngest son, and he'll tell you the same. He's a militiaman and picks up all the latest rumours – he's my thermometer for the city's temperature.'

Distant footsteps echoed and she explained in an undertone how they'd be a foot patrol by Syrian or Lebanese soldiers. Rain scurried along the demarcation chasm and Rick wondered what lay beneath these windows. Surely fragments of bone from the years of fighting, and bullet-cases and burned pieces of barricades, and twisted metal street lamps. He must say something in reply to Madeleine; he intended to work at making it true. 'I don't plan on being protected.' What must it have been like to live here with the shells and bullets whizzing and buildings crashing on every side? 'I'd never support violence – there's always got to be a better solution,' – trying to fumble his way into these incomprehensible politics – 'but I wouldn't run scared.' She let his words drop into the dark void, but he wanted to make his position clear, to anchor himself among these weird surroundings, so he went on, 'Gran, I truly meant what I said about not working in the bank. Places like that just aren't my scene.'

He expected she'd react like Chehab – after all, she was the widow of the bank's founder – but she said quickly with what sounded to be glee, 'I couldn't reproach you.'

'Oh.' And, after a long silence, 'But Chehab said—'

'I make up my own mind. Chehab doesn't speak for me.' Far off a torch gleamed and was extinguished; she said matter-of-fact, 'A sentry.'

He said, unbelieving, 'You really accept that people'll want to do their own thing?'

She laughed and said with that gleeful energy, 'What do you want most in the world, grandson? Because that's what you should run after and grab with both hands.

People who try to kill themselves are capable of *caring*.'
He flushed because she and all this city had seen so much
bloodshed; his fussing over the one human life must seem
obscene. Her amused energetic voice echoed back from
the broken walls opposite. 'If you'd done something
petty like doctoring the accounts, I'd have let you stay
seven thousand miles away, but passions interest me:
they can be used. So what do you really long for?'

6

Of course he starts a Thoreauesque babble about how he'll work the land (in a genteel unrealistic manner; there's not much dirt under the fingernails in this dream) and live frugally in close touch with Nature – to which he gives a very big N – without needing to worry overmuch how he'll find enough money to pay the real estate taxes. When I express a mild contempt for this theoretical wishy-washy wholesomeness, he forgets the pacing sentry and a cold splatter of rain and a dog that howls from across the Line; he says with a fierceness that delights me, 'You must have heard what my mother did – how she left us. 'Course I was only eight, and her going hurt, but later I realised exactly why she and my dad didn't get along and what she was looking for.'

He props his chin on a fist. The sentry has gone and the dog stopped howling; the two of us move within that far land of his. The city all shiny metal and glass, a noisy bustling place, and beyond it the green-black waters of Puget Sound and those hilly forests where – if it weren't for lumber companies and fanatical conservationists and Indian reservations and the general practicalities of life – his dream might become real.

'My mom up and quit,' he says, his voice pure with longing, 'she walked out of our house one day and got the local ferry into Seattle, the train south from there, then a Greyhound bus. She found a commune – there were still a few left over from the Sixties – up in the hills inland from San Francisco.' His voice leaps at what is apparently, to him, the wonderful arrogance of her going. 'And she lived up there, fitted in, claimed she was happy. *Was* happy; my dad told me after she'd died that he put detectives on her trail and as soon as they'd established her whereabouts he made the trip to see her. A weird bunch of folk, he said, but my dad was always one for socially acceptable haircuts and tidy suits and regular solid meals.'

That at least is true, but I don't recognise the woman. Etienne's peaceful, quiet, *ordinary* young wife?

He leans toward me and Beirut has dissolved away; there's nothing in the universe except this ferociously caring young innocent and my baffled self. 'If you ask me,' he says, 'my mom was never truly herself till she got into that commune. Otherwise why would I recall her as always being a grey person? Not grey skin or hair, of course, but grey inside.'

I personally arranged that marriage; Michel left such matters to me and I consulted him if I was in any doubt, but with that couple there was no doubt at all. Both young, conventional, not clamouring for anything special; can I help it if she developed this oddness a few years later? 'No,' I say, 'you must be wrong about that.' He peers as if my voice has changed, but truly it hasn't. I add – angrily, because the girl's actions and his defence of them are ridiculous – 'No doubt they lived in home-made tents and ate uncooked beans and spent their time plaiting fancy braids in each other's hair, and she accepted *that* as a perfect life? And that wild place killed her.' (She had been, in her passive way, a beautiful and charming girl.) 'As if Beirut weren't full enough of death,' I tell the vanished sentry and the wild dog – or another – which has begun to howl remorselessly again, 'she was safe in that big sanitary country of yours; did she have to run to such a wasteful early death there?'

'They built huts at the commune,' he says sullenly past

the dogs' obscene chorus. 'My dad said it was cold in those hills but they'd light a big fire and all sit round it. And they ate brown rice, cracked wheat . . . I don't know what. Plain healthy food.'

'And they took drugs.'

'Well, yeah, some of them – but I'm sure she never would. She just happened to get in the way when two of them were lit and arguing.'

'A good clean death,' I say scornful. 'Is that what you want for yourself?'

'Hell no, not like hers – but they were *happy*. Or the main part of them were. In my book that counts for just about everything.'

'You'd like to run off to one of those camps and eat rice and never wash?'

'You sure have an uncooperative way of putting things,' he says, shifting at his window. 'No, communes are out of date and anyway—'

'Anyway you like soft beds and hot showers?'

'Look.' He pushes himself upright from the window and perhaps I've earned the fury in his voice. 'If we two are going to do nothing but snarl at each other I'd much the best go back where I came from. Chehab needn't get to know, I can slip into the States quietly and – why don't I do just that?'

I remember the scars on his wrists: too recent, much too recent. 'Perhaps you'd better, if you're afraid of Beirut.' I see no way to reach him except by an appeal to his courage.

And it does work; he growls, 'Not that at all, and you damn well know it.' A pause, then his tone mellows. 'Don't you, Gran? Aren't some of your insults a testing to find out what I'm made of?' He decides to chuckle; we chuckle together. 'Two can play that game,' he says. 'Hell, I'm here now and we hadn't met before. May as well stick around a while and learn to find my way in my parents' city.' (With a dawning surprise, as if the family connection has only at this moment become real to him.)

'Tell me one more thing.' I'm tired but my curiosity is strong. 'The girl . . .'

'Oh yeah. Josie. Yeah, at first I figured she and I wanted the same things – simple life and all that. Then it turned out she had an itch toward the money, so my big renunciation-scene wasn't going to be allowed to happen. Quite an itch she had; it dissolved away all the things we'd had in common.' The Line begins one of its profound silences and his voice booms through it. 'Guess you could say I'd gotten so far involved with her, I got massively discouraged at the difference between us.'

'There's no chance of compromise?' The unexpected gentleness sweeps me again, because the boy is so naive, so sweetly and appallingly foolish.

'No indeed, she married a Seattle banker last week. Chehab's enforced plane ticket had its advantages for me.'

'Goodnight, Rick,' I say. He says goodnight and we assure each other that we'll sleep now; we leave our respective windows and the shutter of his bangs closed. I ease my shutter into place and go back to bed, but my head buzzes. I can't handle this charming young fool alone; must get Georges' help. The boy is so big, so male and yet uncertain, so brash and yet delicate. I don't know where to lay a finger on him and have it stick, let alone control him. But Georges will help me; he always does. Georges will know what to do.

A foggy morning, with the wind bringing the smell of petrol and wet ashes from the quays. After breakfast (at which Rick inspected the yoghurt and bulgur dubiously, but he'll learn) Seraphite under my instructions starts to brush up his French by a verbal tour of the kitchen. Half an hour after Brigitte has gone to work, the downstairs door opens and I gladly go to meet Georges (of course he has his own key).

I lead him into the living room and he shakes his head, as always, at this my cave which needs the lamp on all day because there's a false wall between it and the smashed front of the house. 'Sometime,' he says (throwing himself into a gilt-and-brocade chair too heavily, as always, and as always I shan't reproach him), 'you'll decide to get the house front repaired and this room opened up.'

He wears ragged civilian clothes – blue dungarees, lemon yellow socks and a green ROCK NOW! T-shirt – because I've told him never to come here in uniform at a time of day when Seraphite might be around. If she never sees him in uniform, with his rifle, she can't be sure he belongs to the Phalangist militia; if she *were* sure, she'd probably murder us all and then rush back permanently to her own people beyond the Line. Oddly enough my conscience still functions and forbids me to tell an outright lie, so whenever the subject of militias arises in talking with her, I've become expert at belligerent evasions. She's invaluable around here for practical reasons (I don't recognise any others).

His big stocky presence, in those outrageous rags and with the invariable tangle of gold chains swinging at his neck (a crucifix looped among them) makes my room perfect. I laugh, the deep relaxed mirth I keep for Georges alone. 'Get repairs done? No, I can recognise when I'm beaten. An old woman living in a cavern, waiting to reach her eighty years and die – why should she bother to get repairs done when the next round of shells will smash them?'

He bends forward to take figs and a peach from the bowl I keep filled for his visits; as always I savour the way in which my favourite hanging tapestry – a wan startled lady with prancing unicorn, birds and rabbits – outlines his head. He says, 'Seraphite's done you proud with these. A fine marketer.' He spits the peach-stone, leans back and grins hugely, a sign that he's about to say something important. 'I heard sales of sheet glass are up this week. Windows, shopfronts; somebody must guess something.' He squints at me past his thick lashes.

'You believe they're wrong?'

He slaps his knee and roars with laughter. 'Darling, I'm not infallible.' His cool eyes watch me; we two read much behind each other's obvious, laconic words. 'I wouldn't lie to you,' he says, and the shrewd eyes weigh me, 'there could be a renaissance. Of a kind.'

'But it'll be shortlived?'

'How could it be anything else?' He glances at the door. 'Where's Seraphite?'

'In the kitchen, coaching Rick in French. His father personally taught the boy his native language – an unexpected sentimentality in our dry Etienne – but since Etienne's death he's had no practice in it. Fortunately his accent's all right.'

Georges' face becomes tight, unsmiling. In childhood he was such a favourite of Seraphite's that we teased him and her about it all the time; really an absurd fondness. But now he's a grown man and she must have her suspicions about his sympathies, if not his activities. So she tolerates – barely – his occasional presence, but the old warm tenderness is gone. Till this moment I hadn't wondered if Georges minds too, if his affection for her persists and hurts him. And this boy, untainted by any political allegiance, may cut us all out. But Georges is brave; he'd never show unhappiness.

For a moment I think of calling Rick in from the kitchen to be introduced, but Georges has only a few minutes here and I'm selfish about those. He and Rick will meet soon enough. Moreover Georges shows not the slightest eagerness; why should he? He and Etienne hadn't a single thought in common, they bickered all the time and everyone was thankful when the bank sent Etienne overseas. Georges reinforces my selfish monopoly of his time now by saying, 'He's like his sainted father, no doubt?' in a tone completely devoid of interest.

I'll take Rick to Georges' shop one day when they can meet in a leisurely, peaceful way; no point in them getting off on the wrong foot here, now. 'Not so like Etienne. More relaxed and human, as far as I can judge.'

'Ah, it's early days yet, Madeleine. You'll find him out before long.' He stretches those muscular arms and gives me his special warm grin. 'He's got no Arabic?'

'Really, Georges! In this house?'

His gust of mirth sounds genuine; his body sprawls relaxed. 'When our militia discussions get fiery it comforts me to remember that one elderly woman is more extremist than any of us.'

'It's a matter of history,' I say, stiffly because he's deliberately annoying me; I taught him the facts myself in childhood. 'How could we Maronites ever give in to the Arabs? Our Phoenician ancestry and our close ties with France ever since—'

'Save your lecture for the boy.' He pulls a small package from his pocket and tosses it on the table. 'Foie gras for you from Rimmel's – their latest consignment.'

On my antique leather tabletop . . . but of course I'm ecstatic; he's memorised my little greeds. I quickly pick the package up. 'Seraphite will be delighted.'

'Seraphite be damned. I bought the stuff for you.'

'She'll get a nibble.' But I'm watching his face, his preoccupied eyes; suddenly he bursts out, as if he's wanted to say this for a long time.

'Madeleine, I should warn you – never take my guesses as certainties. You're much too prone to do that; you shouldn't rely so on the snatches of rumour I bring.

Don't you realise that this city's future is a barrel full of different options and I stick my hand in like everyone else?' He produces a cigar and lights it; he must be upset indeed – he knows I hate the smell of tobacco on my curtains and tapestries. He goes on, 'I pull out of the barrel rumours of an hour of peace or a bomb episode, and some day I may well pull out a live grenade which will blow off my arm or finish me off completely.' He puffs an explosion of smoke at the world beyond the false wall, and I so deeply understand his disgust with that world that the cigar doesn't bother me this time. 'Don't try to make me a know-all, Madeleine; that's a weight no one in the city dares carry.'

'Well.' Meaning, I hear you, but you're my well-placed and intelligent son, I trust your clever brain and your newsgathering sense.

He visibly remembers the smoking ban, stubs the cigar out against his calloused palm and grins shamefaced. 'Why didn't you stop me?' he says. But his gaze remains clouded with preoccupation. 'Ah, Maman, you'll never learn!'

Brigitte's 'Maman' jabs, every time, but Georges' is a caress. I say, 'You could have kept on smoking today,' and I hate myself because he's so loving and lovable – yet I deliberately didn't lift the ban till after his cigar was squashed. 'But you believe the next month will be quiet?' I say.

'You're worried about the boy's visit? But he'll only be a temporary problem. And anyway,' – he slaps those hardened hands and leans forward; his moustache and beard bristle and his aftershave reeks masculine – 'didn't he almost kill himself over there, according to what you've told me? And on more than one occasion too. He won't have much chance here of crashing an expensive car or falling in love with a blonde American, but he must take his chance on whatever difficulties crop up, along

with the rest of us. While he's h⌐
conventions of the place.'

'Georges, *conventions*!' What a wo⌐
mittent horrors. He laughs with me, then
dusts off his hands as if he's finished a job.

'Don't fret over him,' he says, 'nervousness doe⌐
you. I'll keep an eye on the boy myself during my ⌐ ⌐
time if that'll make you happier. A solid promise – how
about that?'

'It's good of you. But—'

He scowls tenderly at me; no one cares about me as
Georges does. 'The trouble with you, Maman,' – he takes
my hand and strokes it while he speaks – 'is that you so
rarely go out, you haven't realised how relatively normal
the city is most of the time. People eat and drink and
make love as they always have, and I lost a hundred
pounds in a bezique game last week – doesn't that prove
something?'

'Oh, Georges!' Smiling reproachfully, but he must be
right. Apart from the times of heaviest fighting there
have always been spaces between the gunbursts, the
bouts of shelling: spaces when ordinary things presumably did get done. 'Perhaps,' I say, meaning, You
know best.

He pats my hand with his big brown one. 'We must get
you out more,' he says, 'while the peace lasts. A more
normal life.' He pauses as if he's about to bestow a
luscious treat. 'I'm reopening my shop next week; will
you visit it and argue with me about the jewels?'

'Georges, are you insane? Trying to market top-quality
gems when the city's been destroyed?'

'You're a child in a closed room, crying into the dark. I
tell you businesses are reopening all across the city –
restaurants, nightclubs, chic clothes shops. I'm convinced
they've read the future wrong, they're fools, but the fact
is it's happening, and I might as well cash in on the mood

agance while it lasts. The city intends to live well again, Maman.' Inadvertently I glance toward the smashed house front beyond the false wall, and he says, 'I've even heard they're bringing in bulldozers—'

'To clear the Line? Don't make me laugh.' I start to count on my fingers how many times before, only his frown stops me. But there's a horror I must share with him. 'Georges, the other day I looked out through a crack in the boarding. You can see details closer from this floor than upstairs.'

'Well?' His fingers dance impatiently; he hates to be reminded of the devastation. Nevertheless . . .

'There's a tree growing out of the mosque wall, down by the corner. A sizeable tree, Georges, it must have been there six or seven years. Trees in the middle of the street too. Those earthen berms which your men and the others piled up must have given the roots a good start. Half-grown trees, blowing untidy where the Mercedes and the furs and crystal were.'

He says edgily, 'After we finally win, the whole place'll get cleaned up. Rome wasn't built in a day.'

'You were never one for platitudes,' I say sharply.

'Nor you for doubt.' He gets up and firmly kisses my forehead. 'I'm having some rather good rubies shipped in; will you come and put your valuation on them after I reopen? That'll give you something to think about beside imaginary horrors.'

'You're as expert with rubies as I am.' But it's true I've a passion for beautiful gems.

He says gravely (but his eyes sparkle), 'I value your advice.'

'And I yours.' I have no worries about the boy now except his clomping physical presence. 'Georges, the boy means well but he's all over the place, so large and robust. Crashing around the house. I'd forgotten how strong—'

'Poor Madeleine.' He chuckles. 'You'd like him taken off your hands for most of each day?'

'That would help a lot. He needs to be kept away from America for a while, and if he hangs around here doing nothing he'll get bored. A youth his age ought to keep occupied.'

'His high ideals won't prevent him from working?'

'Damn his ideals. I'll phrase the suggestion so that he can't refuse.'

'I bet you will. What work did you have in mind?'

I make myself look old-woman helpless. 'I hoped you'd suggest something.'

'Dear Maman, what are you plotting now?' He taps a finger against his teeth. 'Is the boy too proud to work for me?'

'For *you*?'

'I'll need someone in the shop to run errands and open the door to all the rich customers I'm going to have. A tiny wage, but he wouldn't need more.'

'Perfect.' Some movement behind his eyes makes me add, 'Georges, you will be careful with him?'

'Maman, haven't I explained—'

'Oh, not in that way. I accept that he'll be as safe on the streets as the rest of us. But – I assume you're not giving up the militia?'

'I'll keep my membership and serve part-time, if things get worse I'll switch back to full-time.' He whistles tunelessly and the finger taps his lips; his steady eyes regard me.

He won't expect to hear this from me, and I never expected to say it, but I've developed a sensitivity about this raw overseas boy, in these special circumstances we live in. So, 'The boy isn't necessarily the sort who . . . I wouldn't want him involved with the militia unless he freely chose to.'

Georges gets up and begins to pace. 'Is he too delicate-minded to accept his ancestry and to distinguish between right and wrong? Madeleine, shouldn't you let him make some decisions by himself?'

'Yes,' – I'm not putting this tactfully, and I hate to nag Georges about it – 'but I don't want him pressured.'

'He doesn't *have* to work for me.' Georges halts in front of me and thrusts back his shoulders, makes himself enormous, belligerent; in childhood he'd do this every time he meant to get his own way. 'Our terrifying bumblebee,' his nursemaid called him. And now that he's adult, this stance of his makes one realise that there's usually no strong reason for resisting him; he possesses a force, an intelligence . . . He goes on, 'You could probably find work for the boy elsewhere. Any of our friends would probably give him a job as a favour to you.'

'No, I'd trust you with him, whereas the others . . .' During my time overseas I lost touch with this local community, and I mistrust them.

He collapses amiably back into his chair; he knows he's won. And the boy and I haven't lost – at least I'm happy and relieved. He says, 'I'll need a person for the shop, and here he is. Dear Maman has arranged my life again.' We laugh, we laugh; there's no one like Georges. Manipulative but a delight. (And in serious matters I do trust him.) He adds, 'I promise not to say, "You must join my militia." But I can't say, "Our cause might be wrong," because it's the set of values I live by, and so do you, dear Maman. I won't push a rifle into his hands and order him to use it, but when he walks the streets and opens his eyes he'll be exposed to the constant presence of all the militias. It wouldn't be surprising if he came to a decision.'

That passive pacifist boy? No, I'm sure not, so with a smile I accept Georges' evasiveness. My problem with Rick is solved.

7

On that first morning he said, to test her, 'Didn't Brigitte forbid me to open my mouth in English on the streets?' and although she grunted sardonically he sensed that the current of her mind ran the same way. 'An exaggerator she, didn't I tell you?' But she and the maid bullied him with French all his waking hours for days on end. The first afternoon, while Madeleine was resting, he put his hand to that narrow back door which made the only exit from the house – and found it locked, the key gone.

The only exit . . . because the front door (a wide entrance between pillars) was barred with planks nailed together and reinforced by iron bars. 'Naturally,' Madeleine said when he asked her about it, 'this house was an observation post; they fired from here.' He said, 'But you weren't living here then?' and she said triumphantly, 'Although they moved me out during the worst fighting I came back very soon afterwards.' With the air of an innocent she added, 'You'd be surprised how fast one can get used to anything.'

Along with French, Madeleine began his political education; he, who years ago had decided to opt out of the whole Republican/Democrat mess and had made up his mind he'd never vote, was now forcefed new words like Maronite and Phalangist. These appeared like arbitrary morsels in front of him, and under Madeleine's insistence he gulped them down. He began dimly to see the big differences between parties, but they certainly didn't rouse in him any of the clamorous enthusiasm Madeleine showed. Once he said, 'But what does it matter? People are all people,' and her fury made clear that he'd better not say this again.

In that first week too he got to know the maid, who came daily. Buxom and tall, she wore brilliant dresses which gave her big curves the authority of pronouncements. She spoke French with a hurried fluency; sometimes when Madeleine rested the maid would croon to herself, a wailing cadence that made him say to Madeleine, 'Shouldn't I learn a bit of Arabic too?'

'Arabic?' she said briskly. 'Not necessary.'

'But your maid—'

'While she's in this house she's French-speaking.' Her tone made him tuck the anomaly away as one more problem he'd someday need to figure out for himself.

He was relieved to learn that Brigitte was rarely at home except to sleep, or to work in the boarded-up ground-floor front room. Madeleine explained that Brigitte worked for a photographic studio and in her spare time did freelance pictures, using this as her darkroom. Madeleine opened the door for him and a stink of chemicals and old dust caught his throat. 'As usual I must lament,' said Madeleine, closing the door, 'that nothing is as it was. Before the war this floor was my eldest cousin's jewellery shop. You've never seen such diamonds!'

The sour reek of chemicals lingered. 'Your cousin died?'

'Of fractured emotions. He was less tough than me. Georges took the trade over.'

'Selling jewels during the *war*?'

'You American-reared people take such a simplistic view. Even your father before he died was writing to me of peace and love and America-the-Beautiful and God-save-our-President. A tedious country.'

'Hey now,' he said, 'hold off. Didn't I tell you I wouldn't stand for—'

'So you did.' With that fiercely relishing gleam, which sat incongruously on her old face. 'So, there are renunciations I mustn't push you into – not yet.'

8

Several mornings later the priest arrived. I was thinking about how Rick and I would visit Georges' shop that afternoon, about jewels and how you could find or lose your soul in the glow of a ruby. So the priest arrives and I tie my lecture on covetousness to his presence. My 'tame priest', Georges calls him, but of course he's nobody's. Possibly he's not quite sane but that hardly matters; there'd be reasons enough either way. I watch his arrival from the kitchen window; he's young and briskly shambling. I told him once, 'There's no hurry,' (his church was long ago shelled into rubble and his congregation scattered) but he said, 'I shall be held accountable.' He carries, as usual, a bucket of eggs.

I fetch the key to the downstairs room from its nail beside the stove. 'Time for Mass,' I tell Seraphite.

She never converted, but many years ago she acquired the habit of attending with me on ceremonial occasions, and when Father Mesrop visits here she always plods downstairs behind me. But this morning she grumbles, 'Already? Wasn't the last time only two weeks ago?' Her gaze jumps away from mine like the spring lambs Michel and I used to watch beside our villa in the high Lebanon near Hermil.

'Holy people attend every day,' I tell her, and she, muttering, follows me. Perhaps priests do become, like him, a bit crazy as they mature? The true flavour of the vintage. And if their churches get gutted, stripped, that adds the final individuality of bouquet. 'A saint,' (I love this golden tossable label), 'mustn't he be?' She snorts.

Halfway down the stairs she says grouchily, 'How about the boy?' But he's busy rearranging his room and examining his scrupulous conscience, deciding that, Yes, he ought to work while he's here, therefore he'll go to Georges' shop with me this afternoon. Also, 'He told me he's "not much into religion".' As if it were an extra thickness of mould on blue cheese.

In the stone-flagged passage Father has set down the bucket of eggs and waits for us; like Georges he has a back-door key (I'd trust him with anything except perhaps the welfare of my soul). I keep this room locked although there's nothing in here except a clump of statues and a battered silver chalice and dish, which Father salvaged from elsewhere. Perhaps I lock it so that holiness, like a bad smell, shall keep its rightful place and not escape to bother the rest of our lives. This room is a windowless hole; before the fighting, Eli my eldest cousin had his necklace-and-ring shop in the front ground-floor room and this was his strongroom.

Father Mesrop tosses the white cloth along the altartop and begins the Mass. There should be a cosy satisfied feel to having the priest here, but there's no perceptible cosiness in him and there never was any between myself and religion. He's hooked his wandering self to this house; I've never asked why. Possibly because he was trained to serve – someone, anyone; if I seem to detect in his manner a note of personal service to myself, to my family, probably that's only my indestructible ego acting up.

The candle-flames stream, the room smells of faded incense and starch (the altarcloth). He speaks, I mutter the responses and I wonder where he goes, what he does, the rest of his time. Nothing clean or hopeful, by the looks of him. When he first showed up I offered him a bed, a bath, but he said he had friends throughout the city: a dangerous claim, but I'm sure he lied. Only why would he lie? And what does he still believe?

He lifts the wafer, bends over it, rings the little bell; Seraphite helps me get up and starts me toward the altar. I shuffle the usual route, thinking of nothing, or – today – of how Brigitte was home one morning when he visited. I asked her if she'd like to join us (I was curious how she'd answer). She spat, neatly and coolly, on the floor between her feet and mine; that's what Brigitte thinks of God.

I receive the fragment of wafer on my tongue and start the return journey – but Seraphite is *leaving*? I reach the door and clutch her arm, but obviously she's not ill; I hiss and she glares at me, at the priest; she walks out. I go back to my seat, swallow the hard dry wafer-fragment, and brood angrily on the nature of the soul. A petrol-stinking unquenchable flare, mustn't it be?

The priest says the closing words, he strips the altar and packs chalice and dish away. Useless to ask when we'll see him again. Sometimes I visualise him sleeping in ruined churches, curled on the floor while in the moon-light broken statues lean over him, with an altar nearby not only stripped but deliberately desecrated, while in his dream there moves . . . I'd rather not find out what. Once I dreamed he smiled and held a hand grenade, but that was only a dream and he never does smile. Now at the back door I dangle the iron key and thank him politely (for the eggs too) as I used to thank my hostess at parties. Did the other women in that fragile pre-war world feel, as I did, that we were mouthing stereotyped roles, some antique Parisian *grande dame*'s notion of etiquette? He accepts my thanks gravely with bowed head; a grey hair curls in his beard although he told me once that he hadn't been long ordained when the fighting broke out. He must be a year or two younger than Georges.

Georges pops into the priest's head too; the mouth within that wealth of moustache and beard opens and the lips say, 'News of your jeweller son?'

'He's well. He was here earlier today.' Georges' 'tame priest' gibe echoes, yet he does wear the little crucifix. Only as an ornament, I suppose.

'Ah.' This exhalation makes my casual answer seem significant.

'He visits me every day.'

'Really? Ah. Aha.' A reflective pause, then he says, 'That's convenient.' Another pause. 'Thank you, Madame, for your hospitality.'

'And I'm grateful for the eggs.'

He can smile, he can laugh; for an instant you never saw such gaiety. 'Those little fowls, Madame, I reflect on their lives – eh? The uselessness – because who needs eggs? We could always substitute other objects . . .' He shrugs his shoulders hugely (he's a big cavernous-bodied man, like Georges) and laughs, goes off across the yard laughing; his laugh travels amid the broken walls which magnify any echo, and past the dusty unused yards of the surrounding ruins. Is he insane? How sane ought a priest to be?

I go back into the house and upstairs to the kitchen where Seraphite is crashing plates around. As soon as she sees me she says, 'I couldn't stand the sight of him any longer – can hardly stand the lot of you.' She takes a deep breath and demands, 'Where does he get those eggs? Who does he steal them from?' Then she near-spits. 'Can't you imagine him with a rifle in his hand?'

'Seraphite,' – I'm pressed against the door like a skewered insect – 'how should I know?' The priest and his eggs mean nothing to her; why should she hate him so? Surely this violence of hers is for Georges whom she suspects of everything. 'You'd better take your wages and walk out.' I say, testing her.

She hesitates, she hovers, she says, 'If I had proof—'
But she hasn't; for the time being I've triumphed. Why
does triumph taste so dusty? 'A tough old woman,' she
says grudgingly, 'but you realise I do mean it?'

'Yes.' I daren't ask her whether something new and
terrible has happened in her life, nor what has been done,
these last years, by people on my side to people on hers.
And our moment of intimacy is over with (anger brings
the greatest closeness); she crashes chairs and platters
louder than ever but she turns away from me, she stays
here and works. I'm ashamed of my victory.

After lunch I'm in my bedroom getting ready for our
excursion; to check the weather I open the shutter and
look out. And there – as if it had waited for my gaze – a
collection of black smudges drifts upward in the western
sky beyond the Line, far beyond: might be near the
corniche beaches or the Pigeon Rocks where, when our
children were small, Michel and I would stroll with them
on hot summer evenings and he'd buy them smoky
butter-dripping corncobs from a street stall. This smoke
isn't a single series of cloudy puffs from some innocent bonfire, it's a bunch of disorganised chopped-off
smudges arising from several places at once. Acrid thick
smoke; even at this distance the smell of gunpowder
tinges the air. Hand grenades, then. Possibly also a car
bomb or two, but not shelling (we would hear that
clearly), so it's localised. Its presence certainly underlines
Georges' disclaimer, but Rick and I can safely make our
excursion.

Automatically I count how long since the last incident,
although there's no point; these happenings always start
suddenly like children testing a cache of fireworks. And I
don't, when I watch the smoke, wonder, How many
dead? Because catastrophe is the essence of our daily life.
Do you plan to rush over there and bury the corpses,

Grandma? Instead I finish dressing and pick out a garnet-and-pearl necklace to wear. Rick exits from his room and I from mine; we're ready.

9

Walking through the ruined cinema, Rick takes my arm to steady me and says unbelievingly, 'You lived in that house through the bulk of the fighting?' I've already told him, but obviously it didn't sink in.

'They made me move out briefly.' This is a deep grievance; the sore will always hurt. The house was – like the pre-fighting city – as much myself as I was, and I'd convinced myself that while I lived there the golden-brown stones, the curved roof tiles and arched windows and curlicue balconies, would stay intact. But Georges' militia ordered me to shift; his commander visited and lectured me, then Georges forcibly moved me out. I didn't speak to him for weeks after. He dutifully visited me in the country villa where he'd stuck me, but I was bored beyond endurance there and aching to get back to my house, my city. When all the buildings surrounding my house had been fought through and ruined, and the fighting shifted elsewhere, I hired a taxi to bring myself and luggage back and sent a message to Seraphite telling her I was home. Not asking her to work for me again – I was prepared to live scrappily, like a hermit – but next day she turned up; the two of us were brusquely polite to each other and took up life more or less where we'd left it off. But Georges was so angry I'd come back, *he* didn't speak to *me* for weeks after – the only time we've ever disagreed.

Beside the stalls crammed with scarlet and blue dresses and scraps of uniforms the taxi waits; Georges ordered it because my phone still isn't working and naturally he has taxi-driver friends. One day I said joking, 'You've got good connections,' and he made me promise never to use that phrase again; I hadn't realised that nowadays its only relevance is to killings.

The driver this time looks like a Palestinian. Along the way Rick stares fascinated at the streets and I stare too, but what can anyone decipher from the sight of the large new video shop amid the ruins (why *videos*? Haven't we enough comedy/drama/tears without?), the huge underwear billboard showing two elongated stockinged legs dissolving into a luscious pair of lips, the man in chequered *keffiyeh* headdress seemingly lost in his own private world while he strolls the street deliberately ripping down such directional signs as remain? At least the bookshops are familiar and doing business; can Georges possibly be right – despite those ominous smoke puffs I saw – about a temporary renaissance? We drive along Hamra Street and the boy beside me relaxes, as if these bookshops with their leather-and-gilt volumes and absorbed browsers are the first comprehensible thing he's seen. When I say, 'You won't mind this journey every day to Georges' shop?' he answers sturdily, 'Why should I mind?' He sits forward and his gaze at the street is interested, keen. No sign of violence in this part of West Beirut, but bustle and life. Perhaps a cut artery spurting . . . but anyway life.

In front of Georges' restored shopfront I pay the taxi (yes, the boy has polite instincts; he tenses because this old woman is paying and not he, a role-typed male). It's good to see the steel shutters cranked up and a handful of expensively dressed loiterers at the window, staring through the wire mesh. Dear God, there are some well-dressed women around! There's excitement in seeing the new dress styles, too.

The taxi drives off and we go toward the shop door;

startlingly Brigitte hurries out. Brigitte – that does surprise me. Rick holds the door open and I go in. Yes,
Georges has redone this rather well. The carpets are
thick, a discreetly glowing crimson, the metal-and-glass
showcases shimmer, and the gems (he, grinning abashed
like a proud child, comes forward to show them to
me) . . . yes. If we do have a period of relative peace, he
can make money here. I bend with him over a fine display
of cabochon-cut rubies (they shine like the eyes of wild
animals, red and hot with intelligence) and say, 'I've seen
worse.'

'Oh, Maman!' He leads me to a chair and we discuss
sapphires, diamonds, the ones he's taken delivery of . . .
Paris itself could hardly show finer. A rivière of diamonds
(theirs is a white intelligence so cold it scorches) reminds
me of Brigitte's visit.

'What was she doing here?' I say. 'She's never bought
a jewel in her life, claims not to like them.'

He looks embarrassed. 'Madeleine, she *is* my sister.'

'Well, yes, but I've always had the impression that you
two didn't have much time for each other.'

'Sometimes you're a bit simplistic.' He packs away the
rivière and hands me a diamond bracelet – pretty, but
cheaper gems. 'Perhaps,' he says, watching the decorative
twinkle of these inferior stones, 'for her I represent
security.'

'No one's forcing her to live so self-centredly and
promiscuously.'

'Ah,' he says, 'you don't approve of her evenings
either.'

I hesitate because I know nothing of his own leisure
hours; he has a flat but I've never enquired what he does,
who he entertains, there. With a full-grown man like him
I'd never probe, but with Brigitte . . . And beside me
Rick is flushing; does he think a woman my age should
have forgotten the facts of life?

Georges says, stumbling a little over the words, 'She's not happy. She flings one relationship off and takes another, but underneath . . .'

I realise that he's so old-fashioned he believes there should be love every time. A charming thought. I pat his hand and say, 'You dear.'

Into the silence a noise intrudes; it spreads like the coloured branches of a Christmas tree and takes infinite form and shape and colour. The door blows open like a shout, the street screams and hisses with fire. In this city we instantly catalogue all noises, so – a car bomb.

10

From outside the shop tyres shrieked, a woman screamed, a gulp of sound arrived, not like an explosion. But the new sound fired into his brain and he guessed it; his muscles tensed and he hurtled out, along the street toward the irregular wodge of smoke. He'd been pretty good at first aid and resuscitation in high school, so surely there was something he could do to help. Stop the bleeding till the ambulance arrived, or haul with the other dust-streaked men at jagged slabs of concrete which had been shopfronts and sidewalk. His lungs gladly sucked and spewed air while he ran, and his brain rehearsed old details of pressure points and bandaging; after his months of no initiative or an unpopular initiative, he was going to be useful for once; he was his own person. He reached the exploded car and circled its remnants.

Two ambulances had come and gone, and the third was loading when he straightened up from the sidewalk and remembered Madeleine, Georges, the shop. The ambulance attendants didn't need him any longer; he scrubbed some of the blood and dust from his hands with a rag they offered him. The filthy scrap of fabric made a warm bond with them, a fellowship. He murmured thanks and turned to leave, feeling oddly bereft. Then, while he picked his way along the rubble-strewn street back to the shop, the horrors he'd just seen sank in and he began to shake.

II

It's a shame the bombers always pack their explosives inside a Mercedes – those are such good-looking cars.

I stand in Georges' doorway meditating on this – and no, I'm not being the most callous person in the world. Each of us must find a way of coping with violence; mine is to notice the immediate details first, the effects on the car and on trees and paving stones; I'll get to the bodies later. They're statistics; there's no hurry. I ask Georges, who stands beside me, 'Whose was it?'

He moves a few feet away to chat with a bearded man who wears ammunition-clips like necklaces; a rocket-launcher sits natural as a toddler astride his shoulder. The man smiles, showing a mouthful of gold teeth like ransom money; fifty yards beyond him the car smoulders. Georges comes back to me and says (but with a business-like brusqueness, a reticence), 'It's all right, Maman.' The bearded man strolls away and I wonder how it would feel to speak face to face with someone you knew was a murderer. Direct combat – as in the militia – is different, but this surreptitious seeding of death some-how repels, however right the cause. Or have I often spoken with a killer and not known it? Georges seems more of a soldier giving or taking orders, a clean-hands raised-rifle type. But with the Father Mesrops you can never be sure.

I arrange my thoughts carefully, sending them step by step towards the sparse heap of bodies. How odd that the blast always strips the foliage from trees; it sends leaves flying and kebabs from a restaurant window, and pages of books and smashed fragments of wine bottles; it snatches at selected shopfronts like an irritable diner picking his teeth. How odd that – but someone bursts past me, running toward the heap of flesh. After a long moment I realise who ran: it's Rick.

At the heap he bends and tugs beside the newly arrived rescue workers. I say, 'What *is* the boy up to?' and Georges – sardonic, even amused – answers, 'Let him be.'

But can the boy really be useful? Won't he be a nuisance, poking around beside the rescue men whose job this is? Georges wants to take me back into the shop out of the harsh smoke, but no, I'll stay watching in case the boy gets into trouble. Beyond the burning car a traffic jam has as usual built up. I'd forgotten the pleasure of watching drivers hurtle backwards along the street at forty miles an hour, with engines screaming because like all the other inhabitants of our city they're in a hurry and the incident has delayed them. Something about their seemingly carefree backwards progress (between young trees that are bursting into flame with outstretched limbs like sun gods) reminds me of that insane television commercial – is it a perfume advertisement? – in which the militiaman and the girl he's propositioned at a barricade ride off together into the sunset, with his rifle sticking out of the car window. To my horror I find myself humming the theme tune. For once I've shocked Georges; he frowns and says, 'Tasteless, Maman.' But how can you deal with this sprawl of blood on the pavement, except tastelessly?

The ambulances pull away and Rick returns to us: smeared, breathless, filthy, but he looks *alive*. 'Kind of you,' I commend him, 'to want to comfort the injured.'

Will I never understand that superlatively clean and conscience-driven background of his? I catch glimpses of it in his eyes, but my brain can't grasp it. He says, 'There was more to it than comforting. We did first aid in high school, and resuscitation.' But his wide accusing eyes hold more than an academic pleasure at transmuting theory to proven fact. 'People were *dying*,' he says, 'goddam it, they needed help. You can't just stand by and watch people . . .' His voice tails off; perhaps he's realising that most of Beirut spends its time doing exactly that. '*Someone* had to help them – and quickly,' he says defiant. His first sticking point, his resolution. He sounds determined, furious.

We go back inside and Georges shows me other gems but they don't make much impression. I'm not in the mood any longer. Nor, obviously, is Rick, who roams the shop while casting incredulous glances at the pair of us. Georges tries hard to persuade me to buy a double string of freshwater pearls; he doesn't usually deal in anything so modestly priced but these pearls have an exceptional charm. Not classically beautiful – they're long and bumpy, each one insisting on its own shape – but full of character, and their creamy shimmering colour . . . yes, Georges knows I've a soft spot for them. But I make excuses, I put him off; a troubling shadow sits in front of them in my mind. A nameless shadow until, on our way home by taxi, Rick explodes, 'I'd have to do *something* – I can't just turn my back.' The words echo, as a single bullet or shell can send ghostly others like a full-scale battle throughout Beirut's ruins.

I say (and this is true), 'We've learned how to cope. If people get too emotional, the pain of it demolishes them. The sensible reaction is to take a deep breath and observe from a distance.' But I read in his face that he's given up expecting me to understand his viewpoint; this upsets my fingers so that they rush out to cover his (the warmth of his hand makes my skin-and-bone claw feel inhuman) and I say, 'I didn't intend that you should see scenes like today's. I'd decided that you would have a short, uneventful stay here and then fly home.' Idiotic, because no doubt that's what the boy will do.

My head is full of sanctimonious phrases he could have used but hasn't, about responsibility and solidarity with one's fellows and 'I thought you were a Christian and respected human life.' He could certainly have said that. I stare into his eyes, which are so clear as to be impenetrable, and I feel inside me not a warmth (surely there's no capacity for warmth left in me) but a shifting, a dissolving, an awareness of a problem. Because for fifteen years I've catalogued events and my responses to them so tidily – and now he tries to shift me . . . But there's nothing emotional about this internal tremble; it's more like the quiver that – as I would imagine – must accompany the approach of death. It resembles ice floes grinding on each other, and soon the whole world will be frozen solid again; only the ice floes will be differently arranged.

He says, 'You're tired, Gran?' and I answer, 'No, just thinking about the Arctic. An uncomfortable place.' He holds my skinny paw in his big hand as if he supposes I mean something different, an important bridge, but we're at cross-purposes: he'd like me to be compassionate and emotionally profound. That's impossible. I lean back in the taxi and say, 'I had such a good time, all those years ago – you wouldn't believe. Those years when I made decisions for all the family and travelled abroad, shaped my own life, I don't regret a moment of them.'

He lets go of my fingers and this makes me comfortable; that's how things should be between us. Coolly polite, separate. I can't endure being credited with good motives – a clutter of oozing sentiments and holy beliefs and general syrup, a nasty mess which attracts insects. Blowflies. I'll have no dealings with that.

The taxi stops beside the cluttered stalls. Rick and I

walk through the ruined cinema (sometimes I dream there are shows here still and the ghost-audience mock or applaud in their sleep. They enjoy the old cowboy movies best, as Georges does). Through the clutter of yards where Father Mesrop must one day have dropped an egg: its yellow smear, starred with insects, splays across a couple of paving stones. The back door. Seraphite has gone for the day but Brigitte is home; she holds the door open and for once her face, turned to me, is aflame with emotion. She says, 'I missed you,' and stoops to kiss my cheek; her perfume, after that stink of blood and smoke on the street, is the best in the world, and the touch of her lips is sweeter still. Brigitte never does this.

The three of us go upstairs and she's fussing gently at me, with malicious small glances at Rick. Out too long — tired — and some risk on the streets . . . Did I believe my heart couldn't be warmed? But there's a trickle of thaw now. She says to Rick, 'You kept her out too long, my dear,' and he who ran unafraid toward the explosion wilts before her.

I say, 'Leave the boy alone,' and she softly, with what seems like real affection, touches me and soothes. Does she really care, or is she plotting a devious route towards obtaining some massive concession? Can I trust her, rely on her? Because, as Georges' brusqueness and this disturbing boy and my own shifting self have shown, I can't wholly trust anyone else.

12

So he started working for Georges as a dogsbody, running errands here and there around the city. No more cars exploded, the days grew hot and the air rich with the smells of leather and fish and lemonade. Rick explored the technicalities of the jewellery repair and sales trade when Georges gave him a chance, but couldn't persuade himself that he was learning much about it. Couldn't care either, perhaps should have but couldn't; his true interest, his passion, was the city.

When he first went to the Corniche on the western side of Beirut, and saw the small waves lapping against the rocky coast, he felt − briefly but violently − homesick for the great marching breakers of the Pacific. But the pain of the memory faded; there was so much to do and see here. He turned eastward from the Corniche, and the city lay before him.

He walked its streets, and their scarring became as familiar − although still incredible − as the hot days, the dazzling sun on concrete. His errands − to deliver small paper-wrapped packages − took him (surprisingly) to all parts of the city centre.

On his way back to Georges' shop he passed the rubble-strewn harbour or the gutted Holiday Inn overlooking the sea (its windowless upper floors still used, in bad times, as a sniper's nest) or the northern Corniche and the fish restaurants at Raouche. These always made him remember the seafood eateries he'd taken Josie to along the Seattle waterfront: she'd had a restless and expensive taste in meals. How was she getting along with her sleek young banker husband? But there were some things Rick didn't want to try imagining. From her his mind travelled to the other people he'd shared that Seattle life with, the kids at school who were mostly planning to go on to college in the fall. He'd had good friends among them but no one close or special – there had in the past been several but their families moved out of town, even maybe went overseas. Not, though, to Lebanon.

From the grind of study, and books and colleges, his ears and eyes brought him back abruptly to the streets he walked through and to this city which, unlike faceless American campuses, couldn't be mistaken for anywhere else on earth. He drifted, anonymous, past women in headscarves and bright peasant skirts or black dresses, black stockings, or eccentrics in flowing garments of various eras (like Madeleine) or past some elegant crea-ture all sculpted cheekbones and simple moulded dresses and long legs, like Brigitte. Past men, too; he realised by osmosis that to ask anyone about details of appearance would be unwise, but with eyes and ears wide he ab-sorbed their variations, subtle or grotesque. The cripples – physical or mental – from the various shellings and fightings, who squatted on street corners begging or moaning or rocking their truncated bodies. The uniforms or half-uniforms or supposedly civilian clothes: khaki or olive-green or grey shirts and trousers, or the denims – mass-produced but with a suspicious bulge at a handy pocket. The berets or caps; once in a while a prudent tin hat. The flowing white Arab headdresses. He went unno-ticed and unspeaking past them all while their colours and diversity soaked into his mind, his heart. A falling in love, but not with any woman.

Sometimes Georges deputed him to take Madeleine out for a meal in some carefully chosen new restaurant. Rick knew from the accurate detailing of menus and interiors that Georges must have visited each one, and vetted it for her, shortly before. Madeleine loved these excursions; she would rhapsodise over the food till Rick jokingly accused her of greed.

'But,' she said, 'the stomach is important. I wonder how you can stay so indifferent to it.' She added low, 'That must be the result of your barbaric upbringing.' Her low voice and conspiratorial glance reminded Rick how alien this place still was to him, how he didn't in the least understand its dangers.

Yet when he lay in bed on quiet nights, the buzz of the day's events subsided and some casual remark by Madeleine or Georges would remind him that his parents were born and educated here, that they'd *belonged* here as perhaps they'd never wholly belonged in Seattle. The slight accent that always underlaid their Americanisms, the detachment they'd both shown from Seattle's culture . . . you couldn't say that either of them had exactly tried to mingle. They hadn't, perhaps, ever felt hundred-per-cent American as he most surely had. How would they feel about his walking the streets of their city, and had they never wanted to come back? Certainly his mother never had – her notion of a flight to happiness being that hippie commune – and his father was always busy at the bank; he didn't seem like a real person.

Rick had often in dreams said to his mother, Why didn't you take me to the commune with you, or wait till I was old enough to go along too? Now, on Beirut's starlit lampless nights, he listened to the small inhuman noises of the ruins and asked his mother, Did you hate leaving Beirut, and how did you spend your time when you lived here? And how did you get along with my tough grandma and Brigitte? But his mother's silent pensive face, in the photograph dimly visible by his bedside, told him nothing.

*

Sometimes he took Madeleine to the shop for an afternoon; she commented on the jewels with an interest and shrewdness that amazed him. After one of these visits he said to Georges, 'Your mother's really something. Although she's travelled, she's still so passionate about this city and everything in it. Even with the city in such a mess.'

Georges, repairing a delicate tracery of necklace, took the jeweller's glass from his eye and his mouth quirked. 'Too bad she never got devoted to Beirut till it had been killed; till then you couldn't hold her in this country except to beget and bear her kids. What kind of a woman prefers strangers and strange lands till her own land is a corpse, and then rushes home to howl over it? Ritual mourning, I suppose. Mother is good at that.' He screwed the eyeglass back in and bent over his work.

Brigitte too visited the shop, more often than Madeleine and never at the same time. She showed no interest in the jewellery and apparently only came to chat with her brother. Rick, returning from errands, would hear them as he entered; once in a while Brigitte would switch from French and Georges would shout, 'Not Arabic, damn you!' She'd give her gurgling laugh and return to French. On his travels around the streets Rick made efforts to pick up some Arabic; it seemed monstrous not to try learning the language that almost all the city and most of the country dwellers spoke. On a stall one day amid old magazines he found an Arabic–French primer, a crash course for learning Arabic in (supposedly) only ten weeks. He took it home and kept it in his pocket, because Madeleine might make a fuss if he left it lying around. She oughtn't, but she might.

Georges, before sealing each package for delivery, made a point of showing Rick what was in them and explaining why: this thin wire for an earring repair – a friend in a Damascus Road shop had expressed a need –

and that tiny hollow circle for a ring setting (a colleague in Ain-el-Roumaneh) and these loops of copper, as fine as filigree, to a friend in Raouche, on the coastal boulevard where above sandy beaches the luxury hotels had formerly stood. 'I tell you these things,' Georges said the first time, 'so that you won't suspect I'm using you, *hein*? What else could items like this be useful for except jewellery?' His fingers coiling the copper wire were precise, accurate as a gunsight. 'This shop of mine is legitimate and the luxury trade is starting to revive. These errands I send you on are legitimate too. Would I deceive my own nephew or send him into danger?'

Rick said, 'Hell, Georges, I never wondered—' and met the bright interrogative eyes and reflected that they were steel-backed. Play him loose, Rick thought (and disliked this new caginess in himself, yet he didn't dare drop it), don't trust him beyond what you can taste and smell and verify. A necessary wariness which made Rick sad.

He felt odd around Georges anyway because Georges was his uncle but never gave any sign that he felt like a relative of Rick's. More like a person transacting one aspect of business: I needed an errand-boy and Madeleine asked me to find work for you, so here are the errands. Rick tried to line up his father mentally alongside Georges, as brothers, a mortal effort which turned out unconvincing. And Brigitte as his cold, reserved father's sister? No, the relationships were a fact but unimaginable. Moreover, Georges was apparently enrolled in one of the militias. Rick laughed and said to himself, 'Goddam it, never in a million years!' at the notion of his supercautious father ever getting involved with anything like that.

He felt too that Georges had put him within a frame and kept him there to study; despite the outwardly exuberant friendliness, there'd be a laugh cut short, a prolonged stare across the shop in the long intervals between customers (how could you make a living out of these scrawny repairs? Because few customers came in to buy). And, most acutely felt of all by Rick, Georges hadn't made good his promise to take Rick around the city himself, to show him places a casual wanderer in daytime couldn't go. So, during those first weeks, Rick worked at the shop and ran errands and then, evening after evening, went back through half-ruined alleys and the gutted cinema to Madeleine's house. The city's hot dusty springtime blossomed, children played in the streets and lovers strolled while stray dogs or cats coupled on every corner; and Rick felt a pain like loss. Loss of the inner life of the city, which was being deliberately kept away from him. As if he were a danger to it, a contaminant.

He exploded to Georges one day, 'I don't intend any *harm*. And at this rate I'll never be able to identify closely with the place.' This seemed to clear the air; after it Georges talked more freely, asking a few touristy questions about the States but mostly chatting about Beirut. As if the city were a woman he loved, and his various activities were necessary to its happiness. Yet he didn't drop his guard very far; he only talked about those aspects of Beirut that anyone could see.

13

The season advances and each evening Rick bursts in big-footed and energetic after his day at the shop. During these weeks I watch the change in him too: he rushes nowadays – a man going to and from work – and with minimal prodding he'll talk about his day's events, he asks questions and begins to show enthusiasms. Not, alas, for fine jewels, but for some Rolls Royce or Porsche he's seen on the street, for a Wimpy bar which has reopened near Georges' shop, and for a band called Dead But Happy: the icons of all streetwise youth. I don't detect any sign that he misses the friends he had at home. He speaks French now almost like one of us; I suspect (and hate) that he's picking up some Arabic. His colouring and build are Lebanese but this imperiously developing self-confidence makes him seem, to me, typically American (our young people have more sense). And sometimes, instead of exploding his energy in other directions, he prods me. As, one evening, 'What's up with you tonight, Gran?'

'Up?'

'Yes, up. You look as if you'd just finished digging your grave.'

Too shrewd, young man. 'Perhaps I have.'

'Why, Gran?' He's too busy *living* to remember to call me Madeleine. If I were forty years younger I'd snatch that life-experience away from him and chew it raw.

Self-pity presents itself as a pretty flower; I accept and offer it. 'Because I'm sixty years older than you.' Put that way it sounds worse than ever; surely I've overstayed my time?

'Christ,' – he shoves his plate away and snarls – 'you should see some of the women in the States. *They* don't give up and start moaning because they've hit their seventies.' I insert, 'Nearer eighty,' but he goes on regardless. 'Like Josie's gran.' I'm glad he can pronounce his former girlfriend's name with barely a tremor. 'She's not that many years younger than you and she still surfs, entered a beauty contest for grandmas, too.' He casts a despising look at my face. 'Wears plenty make-up, colours her hair, the works.'

'A barbarous country.' This appalling picture he conjures up: ancient women riding the waves, gutting the cosmetics counters of stores, jiggling in dance halls – women like gargoyles . . . 'A person should have more dignity,' I say.

He pulls his plate back to him; he'll get used to Lebanese food eventually. 'I guess dignity affects folks pretty much like arthritis, doesn't it?'

I shake my head, reproving, and we chuckle. After our meal we watch television – detective serials, advertisements, American or French films, partisan news bulletins – then he plays bezique with this old woman; finally we go to bed. (But such quiet evenings aren't normal for a boy his age. How much longer will he put up with them? And what other amusements, safe or otherwise, will he then substitute?)

In my top-floor bedroom I sleep briefly, then wake. I get up, ease back my shutter and stare at the Line. It looks beautiful tonight, a backdrop for some as-yet-unmade film at the end of which all the couples will fall happily into each other's arms. Its shadows are carved, pristine, and the moonlit spaces between them virginal; in the sky the moon is a lean, efficient crescent which sorts the clouds like an impatient shopkeeper. So beautiful that I long to stroll down there in the stillness, in and out of the shadows. Of course I haven't walked the Line for years; even now, when it's nearly deserted, that's not an amusement one could recommend. But, leaning on the sill, I begin to calculate how long it is since I left this house by myself, how long since I went anywhere alone. Along the Line a rat runs in and out of moonlight like one of Rick's elderly surfers and I think with sudden excitement, Why not? I don't possess a torch that works (in one of our sudden mysterious shortages, batteries have become unobtainable) but you wouldn't need one tonight; you'd melt into the background better without. When I was young, one automatically did what one wanted to, without doubt or unhappiness; how can I have become so timid?

So I begin – hands happily chilled with excitement – to dress.

14

Absurdly, while dressing, I remember the daughter whose existence I'm reminded of only when her letters arrive – Helene. Carefully well-dressed, carefully coiffed and well-mannered, Helene who lives in Paris with her careful husband. Helene who from a sense (I suppose) of duty writes to me monthly and who seems to suspect that the intermittent lethargy of our postal service is directed personally at herself. 'A tidy life' – she and I quarrelled over that, her ideal, when last she visited here before the fighting. Once or twice in these later years she's suggested making the journey again, but she hasn't needed much dissuading. 'A tidy life' . . . not here, and anyway how could one endure such an existence?

I'm dressed and the Line lies tranquil, enticing; by which route shall I leave this house? If I take our usual back way there'll be a problem: Brigitte isn't home yet and when she does come in she'll bolt the door. I could leave her a note, but I'd rather keep my escapade private. So if possible, not the back.

The front door hasn't been opened for years and is reinforced with nailed planks and a couple of long iron bars; exit there is impossible. Rick's geriatric surfers may have made me feel ashamed, but I don't fancy my chances at abseiling down knotted sheets from this upper floor. So . . . Brigitte's darkroom window?

The air on the stairs sits as quiet as if the world were dead; briefly I fancy that it is and that I'm about to take a walk in a city inhabited only by ghosts, like one of those marble-tombed graveyards where on All Souls' Day families gather to feast and rejoice. But the stairs are solid under my feet; the chemical stink of the darkroom is real too; so are my fingers, which witter with a claw hammer at the protruding nails.

This shutter wasn't as securely fastened as it should be: half a dozen loosely holding nails removed, a couple of planks lifted out of place next to an existing gap, and I can easily get through. I stand on the Line.

Eight years since the door was nailed shut (Georges did that after he forced me to leave), nine years since I last stood on this street. The gunfire and shelling had begun years earlier, of course, and the damage; I took my last, brief, defiant walk past shops that had long been looted and gutted. A bruising walk – its bewildered stumbles are still a part of me.

One thing is certain (I begin to creep quietly along and that lean sorting moon paces beside me), some of Europe's best shops used to trade here. Saadi's, near this corner where the golden-brown shell of the Parliament building stands, and further along a chic *modiste*'s – a narrow shopfront behind its pink-and-white sunblinds, but her stock came straight from the Paris collections. I took Brigitte into that shop once and bought her a dress for some children's party, but mostly we shopped for the children's clothes at . . . no, it isn't there. Not even the ruin of it, only a seven-floors-high gap through which the moon sneers down. I stop to consider the gap and the scornful moon – and my footsteps don't stop.

I press back against broken masonry; I grimace and my heart bounds like a separate animal. The footsteps approach. A click of rifle trigger and an uneven-voiced challenge, 'Anyone there?'

He sounds young, as scared as me, and Lebanese. That's a slight relief; I'm prejudiced enough not to want dealings with Syrian troops even if they're supposed to be protecting us. 'Protection' with rifle and nailed boot is a violence. But I can't step forward, can't speak – from anger or fear; who are these various people who've raped my city? Did I believe I wasn't any longer capable of passion? But passion creases me into the dusty shards of wall. The sentry's repeated question hesitates and fades; go away, young man; no one's here but me and the rats.

His footsteps recede and vanish, and still I can't force myself to move. A bush taller than me grows out of Saadi's window and its leaves inevitably have a bitter odour. How have I crudely, blindly, lived a wall's thickness away with my leather-and-gold books and my velvets, silks, antique tapestries? Isn't our presence there an obscenity greater than any copulation of rats?

The moon has finished sorting stock; she slides downward and clouds and buildings (if you can call these shards that) replace her. If I keep on standing here, how long before the rats will start to gnaw my feet or the feral dogs investigate me? From the half-standing minaret of the mosque an ululation drifts which has no relationship to any doctrine the muezzin might have proclaimed. An inhuman noise, bestial. I sometimes used to stand at my window watching the congregation file in for Friday prayers and wondering caustically how many of them really believed. Wondering also, with the same ironic amusement, whether it was really worth their while to keep the hedges in front of the mosque in quite that state of topiary complicatedness. That question at least has answered itself: waist-high dead grasses, and bushes as bitter-smelling as the one next to me, have removed the hedges as completely as might detectives excavating a crime.

Out of those depths of shadow a deeper shadow – a human figure – crosses from the mosque corner and makes its way toward this part of the street, a figure strolling noisily, with what looks like absolute confidence, along the exposed and vulnerable middle of the street. Another sentry, who'll discover and shoot me? That would certainly be a solution. Yet in the starlight I can detect no rifle or army or militia cap. They say backs are unmistakable. He passes me, half the width of the street away, and when his noisily travelling feet catch on a clump of weeds I recognise him. 'Rick?'

He stops, turns around and stares; I'm as stony with fear and fury as the wall, but his young eyes spot me. '*Gran*?'

In the dark an insect – probably a cockroach – runs over my hand, which is pressed against the wall; I grab my hand away and shiver.

'Here,' says Rick – too loud, oblivious, doesn't he realise how it echoes? – 'let's take you back indoors. Unless you planned on strolling a few blocks further?'

'This is enough for tonight.' I still feel the track of the insect's bristly feet on my flesh. And I'm enraged at his loud voice, at the sentry who may hear us and return, at the need for concealing ourselves and talking low-voiced in this my city.

Rick leads me back, still talking cheerfully and impervious. At the window he chuckles and says, 'You beat me to this. I went out the back way, but I'd fixed these boards so that if the back door got bolted they'd yield at a little shove.'

Shame borders my rage; I was so proud of my strength, hauling those nails out. We stand in the darkroom and he fits the boards back into place, with the nails holding them loosely again in case – as he explains deadpan into my angry eyes – someone might want in or out. He dusts his hands off and turns to face me.

But I can't argue with him down here because Brigitte may arrive home at any moment, so I lead him up the two flights to my bedroom. (I can't stand the sight of my luxurious living room at present; my bedroom, for all its lace and satin, is spartan by comparison.) I shut the bedroom door, point him to a chair and say, 'What the devil were you doing out there? The truth, mind.'

He looks startled. 'Taking a walk, that's all. Any reason why not?'

'Every reason in the world. Do you make a habit of this?' And I begin, in the bluntest phrases possible, to explain how he – so visible in the middle of the street, so noisy – puts himself in the most appalling danger. For me, an old woman creeping silent and unseen a few yards this way and that along her familiar territory, it's a different matter altogether. 'If you'd met a sentry—' I say.

But his brows gather and his jaw sticks out mulishly; for the first time I glimpse his father in him. Etienne was mulish in his conformity; this boy mustn't be allowed to become dangerously mulish in the opposite. 'There's not that many sentries around, surely?' he says, and his eyes squint defiantly, his hands stiffen. 'The place seemed pretty much deserted. Anyway what's the worst they'd do to me?' And in his gaze I see that clear blue-green Sound he's told me of, that terrifyingly rule-bound society where murder – although they complain of its frequency – is still the exception not the overwhelmingly common occurence, the childish and lunatic simplicity of those half-baked dreams of his for the future. For the first time since his arrival I realise not only that Beirut could prove risky for him, but that he – by stubborn foolishness, by this damned simplicity which refuses to be warned and slides oblivious or uncaring into all risks – could endanger not only himself but could involve his household – us – his family too. Danger for Brigitte, for Seraphite, danger for and compromising of Georges – it mustn't be allowed.

'The worst that could happen?' I say. 'A sentry might

kill you.' Much worse is possible, but that bare statement will do for a beginning.

'I'm not going to play afraid,' he says. 'And anyway the recent bits of violence have all been way across the other side of the city. Surely there's not that many sentries around here.'

This is the dividing line and they patrol it regularly, you fool. 'One sentry is all it would need.' One nervous soldier, one bullet or, more likely, one skulking member of some Shi'ite or Sunni militia from beyond the Line. I can pad along as quietly outside my own front door as any wandering half-crazed Arab, but this stupid boy with his noisy mid-street saunter . . . 'One rifle-prod in the back, one set of wire handcuffs.' I'm explaining far beyond his understanding now; please God he never experiences the reality. 'It's not a question of running scared,' – I remember he threw this unlovely boastful phrase at me when he first arrived – 'but of taking sensible precautions. Don't you see the difference?'

His mulish look persists; I can only hope that behind it he's realising my good sense. Yet if he's one of those people who're obstinate because they suspect they're basically weak, that's the most dangerous status of all. He relieves my mind somewhat by saying in a more conciliatory tone, 'Besides, a person needs *space*.' His outflung hand expresses how circumscribed he's felt.

All my nervousness about our quiet evenings is rein-forced; the time has arrived when he'll separate himself from them. Then he'll be wandering alone in Beirut, getting into God knows what company, acquiring God knows what beliefs and habits (he's a natural victim, with his impressionable temperament, for all the extremist streaks that throng our streets); heaven alone knows where he'll finish up. Dead, certainly, but after what complicated entanglements, what tortures?

I can see only one possible solution. 'Our small country

with its constricting problems – of course you're bored; naturally you feel restless.' (That isn't exactly what he said, but we'll let it pass.) 'And your month of exile will soon be up; naturally you're anxious to get back to that big country of yours. I'd forgotten how much space you have there, how you must long for it.' The scars on his wrists are soundly healed; surely his mind is, too. 'You'll go back there and be happy,' I say, meaning it. 'I'll tell Brigitte tomorrow to phone the airport from her studio and book a flight for you.'

How can this not make him happy? But he frowns and twists his mouth. He seems – oddly enough – embarrassed. 'Well,' he says, 'of course I plan to go back before too long, yeah, but I'd like not to leave here quite yet. If you'll have me a while longer . . .'

No doubt he's developed a technical interest in our excruciating problems. I can imagine what traveller's tales he'll take back when he finally does go; I visualise his teenage friends at some pizza parlour or disco, suspended like our corpses on his words. 'And I walked their damn Green Line, didn't faze me at all, dared myself and went out one night and . . .' Yes, I can imagine. The unmeant cruelty of his and their foreign youth.

'This wasn't the first time I've walked there.' He's nervous towards me but resolute; he didn't show nerves so quivering on the Line. 'There's been other nights – for exercise or if I've got a problem.' Nervous as if I'm all the ogres of everyone's childhood.

I'll insist, I'll prevent him from doing this rash thing again, but for now I'll quietly sidetrack and distract him. So, indulgent, 'You've a problem?' A girlfriend in Beirut perhaps; there's been plenty of time and the young can always make opportunities.

'Uh,' – he shifts on his chair – 'a decision to make. Doesn't exactly concern you, only—'

These cautious words, and his sideways glance, call to

mind the person who's central to us both. 'To do with Georges?'

He sighs, relieved. 'I should have known you'd guess. Yeah, and maybe you can advise me.' An engaging youthful grin. 'I'm not sure that Georges is exactly impartial in what he says.'

Impartial . . . so not jewels or the shop. The way is signposted now, and a flare of anger at Georges rises. 'He's trying to involve you in—' Damn the man, he did promise.

'Very friendly and like I'm a kid being offered a treat – yes, he is.'

The next afternoon I enter Georges' shop and wait while he chats with a customer, a young woman looking at sapphire rings. She's acute; despite my preoccupation I enjoy listening to her attacks and Georges' parries. Not the best quality sapphires in the world but adequate; she and Georges finally arrive at this common ground. She leaves, promising to discuss with her husband and return next day. After the door closes behind her, Georges cocks an eyebrow at me across the glitter, the lush carpeting, and says, 'She'll buy.'

'At least about jewels you're honest.'

'Maman?' Both eyebrows up.

'The boy' – fortunately Rick isn't around – 'tells me you've been trying to involve him in the militia.'

'So he's run bleating to Grandma?' Georges' face is tight; he looks like not my loved son but any armed fighter.

'No, he was obviously brooding and I hooked the reason out of him. Georges, you *promised*.'

He turns to put away the sapphires, locking some in display cases and the finer ones in the safe, and I realise – ridiculously – that if I had a gun I could shoot him now, couldn't miss. But why am I speculating about killing my *son*?

No violence in the city today; beyond the meshed glass window-gazers swim, their mouths opening and shutting, like peaceful fish. The muffled beat of a portable radio briefly intrudes, and overhead a thrumming plane prepares to slither along the invisible mountain range of the Line. Georges pauses with a sapphire-and-diamond bracelet draped across his fingers and says, 'They've put on larger planes because there are more incoming bookings. Rumour says the 747s may start up again soon.'

'You *promised*, damn you.'

He locks the bracelet in the safe and brushes his hands together as if the jewels were dirt. 'You're getting soft-centred, Madeleine? I wouldn't have believed it.'

'Never soft,' – he grins maliciously at my quick retort – 'but this boy is only lent to us, he belongs elsewhere. I don't want him harmed.' The brash youth . . . he's a landscape that has never known attack, which lies trustingly open to sun and wind – and we with our car bombs and rocket launchers walk within him.

'I'm not bullying him into joining.' Then Georges becomes that infantile bumblebee again. 'Madeleine, don't you trust me? I merely asked if he'd like to attend our evening meetings. He's free to say no.'

I'm too old and tough to be intimidated by this noisy act. 'Did you make clear that you're a military force?'

'Of course, Maman.' He goes on hastily, 'And I explained the recreational side too – our football matches and the film shows we have.'

I jeer, 'You make it sound like the perfect youth programme.'

'Well, isn't it?' Then he thrusts at me, 'What'll you do with him otherwise?'

'Send him back.'

'He's a strong boy with a mind of his own. I'd like to see you try.' He starts to wheedle. 'The violence is low-key, not escalating; where's his danger? Let him play sports with us and watch our old comic films, do a bit of harmless target practice. He'll get fed up with those limited amusements in a few weeks and hanker for the luxuries he used to have, then you can easily ship him out.'

'Well . . .' The winking sapphires in the display case refuse to comment.

'He's young and energetic, Madeleine, he needs an outlet.'

Damn you, I know that. 'But I wouldn't want him persuaded to carry a rifle—'

Georges laughs richly. 'As if there were any chance of that!' He tries cunning. 'As a hanger-on of my militia, and as my nephew, he'll be safer on the streets than he is now. Don't you sometimes worry about him wandering around alone?'

Georges, you play my weaknesses. And the boy would get a whiff of the militia's discipline, which he sorely needs. They'd teach him to respect dangers. 'Very well. We'll let the boy decide.'

Georges kisses my hand (the acquisitive part of me); during this moment does he love me purely, as a son might? And I'm amused but devastated by the force of my love for him, my only satisfactory child. I nod to him over the display case. We've accepted that Rick shall be flung to the city's major outlet-for-emotions. The sapphires wink in agreement.

15

'Only a part of the meeting, for your first visit,' said Georges.

He and Rick didn't head for the busy areas of the city but after the ruined cinema took a different route, along empty alleys where the street lamps were blackened twists of metal and a faint glow from distant inhabited buildings showed up bullet-pocked walls and half-demolished barricades. On the dusty grass their feet made little noise, and in the ruins either side the silence was broken only by cat wails or by an occasional scurrying of which Georges said, 'Beirut has far more rats than people.' His whisper and chuckle were barely audible. 'I did hear that a truck made a garbage collection today – in Ashrafiyeh, the next district to this. A historic occasion.'

A six-foot sapling in the shadowed centre of the street made Rick stumble; he clutched its trunk and said, 'Where are we heading?'

The faint light patched his companion's bearded face and deep-set eyes, the sardonically curving lips, the flash of teeth when he said, 'To a cinema that is still functioning. Don't you enjoy going to the cinema?' He laughed – no louder than the scurry of the rats – and strode on.

Dimly a space opened before them, an area of scrubland surrounded by a bruised rectangle of buildings. 'There were twenty-foot palm trees here,' Georges murmured, 'and orange trees bordered the road on that side. A bad place to drive a car or catch buses; the traffic was always so heavy.' Nearby an owl hooted.

To the far end of the rectangle; Rick's feet were so accustomed by now to uneven lumps of concrete and metal that when suddenly the surface was flat he stumbled again. 'Careful,' whispered Georges, 'we'd rather not be noticed here. The cinema is pretty well soundproofed but we go cautiously in the surrounding streets. We don't want our meeting place to get popular.'

They padded along a side alley; to their right rose the cinema's dark bulk and Georges laid a caressing hand on its wall.

'I used to come here as a boy,' he said. 'They had such exciting films.'

Just inside a narrow doorway sat a man even more bulky and swarthily bearded than Georges, his stare on the entrance and a rifle slung across his shoulder.

'Look,' Rick said, 'I don't plan to get involved with violence. This whole thing isn't my quarrel – I got sent into it – and I'd reject using violence anyway.'

'Madeleine told me how you feel.' Smoothly, and Georges put a hand under Rick's elbow to move him smoothly along. 'A keep-fit class only,' Georges said. 'Most other facilities are wrecked, so where do you suppose we men go to relax after our day's work? Like the rats in the ruins, my friend, we enjoy our diversions where we can.' The hand tried to urge Rick onward. 'As for the rifle – if you'd lived these past fifteen years in Beirut you'd feel the need of personal protection too, especially if you're young and roam the city a lot, like most of my friends here. Try taking that man's rifle away from him and you'll deprive him of the only protection he's sure of. Shops and homes and cars can be blown up, but a man carrying a rifle, my friend, is a king in a world where there's no crowned rightful monarch.' His hand flickered at his jeans pocket. 'Try getting my revolver away from me.'

'Okay,' said Rick, 'but if it turns out there is violence

I'm having no more to do with it.' He sounded to himself prissy, priggish, yet the words came from very deep within him.

Beyond the first guard a short corridor, then another metal chair, another guard, at the entrance to the open interior of the cinema. Somewhere, cocooned within walls, a generator throbbed; bare bulbs lit the large space. A space seemingly undamaged – even the screen was intact – except that the front rows of seats had been ripped out and in this area youths and men were playing some game with a ball and goalposts.

'Holy cow,' said Rick, startled at the normality of the sight, and Georges said, 'Didn't I tell you? You like soccer? These boys play very well.'

'Never played it.'

'Easy to learn. You have good muscles, a fast mover, you'll make a good player. We have other sports too, sometimes evening keep-fit exercises – judo, karate – you like those?' The guard at the second table, unsmiling, waved them on.

'Judo – I used to fool around with that. Karate's more brutal, isn't it? But judo had a sort of . . . academic appeal.'

'How like you to find it academic!' A clap on the back, a belly-laugh. The game finished, the chatting, sweating men trooped up the gangways and flung themselves into the remaining seats. Georges said, 'Next time we'll get here earlier.'

'You wanted to test the waters with me?' And Georges grinned. Then to Rick's astonishment the lights went off, the familiar buzz of a movie projector sounded and the big dusty screen was bright. 'What the hell—' Rick said.

'You'll like this. Amusing. Our films are very good.'

It was an old Chaplin movie. Charlie – a waiter on skates – glided erratically between tables and distributed food down the backs or in the laps of various stately types, who all lost their tempers while the little man, apologetic, skated on. The movie seemed the crudest slapstick to Rick. Yet these tough-looking men laughed till they cried; they flung themselves about in their seats nearly ill with laughter, as if the movie industry had been newly invented and this were its first production. Georges laughed helpless as the rest of them, choked on tears and fumbled for his handkerchief and choked harder. When the movie ended and the lights came on he said like an apology, 'I used to enjoy cinema as a boy, but this – this is different.'

And Rick, studying the bare walls and harsh lighting, smelling the dust and that faint odour of garbage which seeped even into this enclosed place, had to admit that it was.

16

I've cursed Rick's foolhardiness, so I take my own advice and don't venture onto the Line again, but I do take other – daytime – excursions alone and acquire a taste for them. Especially I visit the new dress boutiques which are springing up, and sometimes I almost bring myself to the point of buying. The assistants obviously regard me as a 'character', an ancient formally clad relic of the previous city, and 'character' isn't far removed from 'caricature'. Which saddens me (I've no wish to be regarded as a gargoyle) but I act sprightly and sharp as a 'character' should, and they seem to relish me. New restaurants are opening too, but eating out alone is a bore. I must persuade Brigitte or Georges to visit one of the new places with me sometime. (Rick's tastes in food remain as primitive as those of the country he came from, and this new Beirut has snack bars, hamburger stands, enough to satisfy his wants.)

The violence is taking longer than usual to die down. It continues in the same sporadic way, not enough to disturb the current of life unduly unless you get too close to a car bomb or shell, but enough to be a reminder, an undercurrent. And Georges says the alleys seethe with rumours (he's not guessing this time, he's personally heard them). When I ask what the rumours say he gets his brusque businesslike look and says, 'Everything imaginable, Maman. All the tints of the rainbow. Soon we're planning to dynamite under them for the crock of gold.' He refuses to explain further.

When I go out I take taxis across the Line, but the high-quality shops have always been mostly in West Beirut, and I walk on the streets there; you never saw such a bunch of possible thugs. At least I never did. Where were all these people hiding, fifteen years ago, that they suddenly swarmed from the woodwork like beetles when Black Saturday arrived? During one of my visits to Georges' shop I ask him, 'Don't those men have jobs to go to? Such a bunch of idlers . . .'

He narrows his eyes as he does when I ask about his militia. 'Madeleine, some of those people are very busy, you've no idea—'

'Taking hostages?' Yes, I'm fast losing the remnants of my innocence. I've now seen a hostage captured. I went seething to Georges afterwards because the nature of the sight offended all my principles. 'Everyone on the street stared away,' I fumed, 'and let the men in black hoods pull him to a car.' Then Georges got really angry with me, which doesn't often happen.

'He may be one of our bitterest enemies – and you're making excuses for him?' His fingers tug and twist at his beard.

'Not excusing, only saying there could be two sides.'

He pounds the counter so hard that the jewels leap in their padded cases. 'You say that – you, Maman, with your principles? How could there be two right sides?' Yes, I shaped his views and I do still believe, but there was a ruthlessness in the sight greater than the sum of the pulling hands and the hooded heads and guns. Yet he says, 'I've seen hostage-taking several times, and it made no impression on me except of a job efficiently done.'

I say impulsively, 'Why have you never married?' and am thankful he sees no connection. Indeed he laughs, relaxed.

'Because I've never found a woman who impressed me enough.'

He must be capable of human feelings, of identifying with and forming close relationships, otherwise he'd be a monster. In my relief I joke, 'You're mean about giving me grandchildren.' This reminds me, 'Where's Rick? He's never in the shop when I visit.'

'Errands.' So smoothly that my mind stumbles on the slope of his preparedness. 'Here and there in the business district; I keep him busy fetching and carrying. He seems to enjoy it.'

'Carrying jewellery?'

'Of course, Madeleine, what else?' And he turns to me his graceful smiling face with the full moustache and beard and dark brown eyes, his brown strong neck where the gold chains and crucifix cluster, his big muscled body which doesn't fit the new businessman jacket and trousers; the militia uniform suits him better. 'Madeleine,' – he grips my shoulder – 'there's a lot of heat in the kitchen but some innocent flavours float around in there too and they survive, they don't get blended away or—' His analogy falters and we laugh together. His laugh and mine still chime almost exactly.

Father Mesrop shows up again and Seraphite in the kitchen stiffens, won't go downstairs, furiously ignores him, I daren't ask her whether she's heard something about him, or if something final has happened with some friend or relation of hers. After the Mass I cautiously ask him what living in West Beirut nowadays is like. He explains lucidly but in language of startling filth, then he blesses me as usual, hands me a sealed envelope which he asks me to give to Georges the next morning, and goes.

I duly pass the envelope on, so I've become an accessory, but that's logical. If I were younger there's no doubt I'd be carrying a rifle. And haven't I already had my suspicions about the priest? So I pass the envelope on and refuse to have qualms.

The main streets of East and West Beirut are bustling and lively at present; many customs and habits that I remember from years back have rushed into the city's mood of catch-while-you-can. Boys shout the sale of lottery tickets, the sun bleaches the tall apartment blocks with its familiar summer glare, and the sea, when I glimpse it between the broken buildings of the hotel district above Qantari, sways green-blue as if it has no problems in the world. Outside the harbour, boats wait for entry as they always have. A donkey-drawn cart, laden high with scrap metal and oddments of glass, clatters among the Mercedeses and Porsches, but when I remark to the driver, 'A rich harvest,' his stare confirms that I shouldn't say this. To comment on twisted lengths of iron or shards of glass is to make a partisan statement. Young Muslim boys play football on a cleared space; in two or three years they'll be old enough to join a militia.

The bookshops of Hamra Street are open, and the bookshops of Sassine Square. I browse as I used to, and enjoy it. There are rockets, there are shells and bullets, but they strike in the slums that fringe the city or in the narrowest alleys of West Beirut; they don't bother us. But those rumours . . . even I hear them. The city is a cauldron of boiling stew, and no one can guess what the stew's exact flavour will be till the lid blows off.

Rick in his travels browses in the bookshops also, for he comes in one evening with a pile of them and the topmost falls from under his arm. I pick it up and hand it back; he grins and says, 'I read that in high school. I picked it up today to see if it was as boring as I remembered.'

'*Lady Chatterley's Lover* . . . I've read it too.' In Madagascar with the man whose name I never knew. The novel had been published in Paris only a few years earlier, and the tattered copy which someone had donated to the out-station's library became an edgy joke between the two of us. We mocked its wrung characters in a vain attempt to distance ourselves from our own passion. I say to the startled boy, 'Damn you, I did love once.' I send him off to the militia that evening (yes, he regularly attends their meetings) and am glad to see him go.

I'm waiting hourly for him to get fed up with them, with us, to gather himself together and depart. I'd like him to be well away from here before the stewpot's lid blows off. But at present he seems happy with the rough comradeship of the militia and the other young hangers-on. He goes there most evenings and returns grinning reminiscently about some old Marx Brothers film or dirt-stained and baffled by the exotic rules of soccer. And Brigitte, startlingly, one evening when he's out, decides to stay at home in order to take photographs of me. I grunt, I try to refuse, but she insists, 'I've wanted to do this for a long time.'

So I yield and she fiddles passionately with lights and reflectors; obviously she warms toward my face as a subject. An odd notion, like a sculptor finding something other than rubbish in a block of stone.

'Too many bones,' I say.

'We can let bones speak for themselves.' She insists on draping a swathe of white muslin across me so that only the head pokes out. White, at my age? Yes, she says, it will sharpen the result. Do you always use white, Brigitte? No, she says crossly, we might use purple or black or chequered or striped, depending on the subject. But for you, Maman − white.

And the result . . . Brigitte spends a long session in her darkroom and looks uncharacteristically nervous when she hands me the prints. 'If,' she says, 'you don't like them, we can take others . . .'

Who is this woman? Scarcely sexed; she's been too busy for that. Scorched by decades of fires, a fair number of which she's started herself, she has a wild disregard for the results of tossing a lit match. 'I don't recognise her.'

'You haven't had a photo taken for so many years, you're older—'

'It's not that. And a camera can't lie—'

'It can distort. Any photographer will tell you so.'

'There isn't much chance of distortion here; the images are too stark for that.' And there's something else . . .

Brigitte says quietly, 'You're beautiful. Yes, I noticed that too.'

And I always assumed he was attracted by my mind, by the intellect of which I was so cursedly proud . . . A cruel elderly pain. But I'm grateful for Brigitte's whim, which has given me not the supposed beauty but a resolute image to hide behind.

Next morning I dig out a plain silver frame, put one of the photos in it and stand it on the side table next to my Pompeii cherub. Seraphite, dusting the living room, eyes it and says, 'A good likeness.' The muscles of her face shift like the hot wax Michel used to seal his most important letters with.

Something about her shifting face, and the glint of the silver edge, rushes me back in time and I say, 'Do you remember how you and I used to go shopping and buy fresh lemonade on the streets, packed in snow from Mount Lebanon?'

Her face stops shifting and she says, 'Those old wooden houses of ours in the slums looked picturesque, but you never set foot inside an insanitary one of them.' She runs her finger over the photo frame – not over my real face or the face in the photo, but over the frame – as if there were something under her finger that she had once cared about the feel of. Then she retreats to the kitchen and begins to scrub the floor as if she'll demolish it.

17

Those evenings with Georges and the militia became a ritual. After that first time Rick and Georges arrived earlier, for the start of the meeting, and stayed on after the movie finished. The route there – streets of ruins, then scrubland and the narrow doorway that led to the cavernous interior of the cinema – became familiar. Different men took it in turn to guard the entrance, but the acute scrutiny and ready rifle were the same each time.

Meetings started with an official roll-call. Sometimes after a name there would be a short silence, then a gruff voice would say in guttural French, 'Dead, yesterday.' Or maybe, 'In hospital. Caught in the gun battle.' Or, once in a while and always with a note of scorn, 'Fled to the countryside.' An excuse that brought raised eyebrows and tightening lips from Georges and the other grown men.

Rick tried to puzzle out their hierarchy. Georges was clearly among the most senior and respected members of the group but he wasn't in sole charge: while the younger members played soccer he and a huddle of other men would bend over a table in the corner of the big space and mutter there, leaf through what looked to be maps or city plans. Georges was different here from in his shop; he was not only more preoccupied here but also gritty, abrasive. You felt that if you crossed him he could lash out, furious and physical. Rick had never actually seen him use violence to anyone but the potential now seemed to be there: maybe you shouldn't be surprised at this in a militiaman but it disturbed Rick. And the secrecy of this elite bunch of older men was total. No one else could hear their low mutters and none of the junior members were called across that dusty space to join them, even briefly, to learn any of their plans.

So Rick played soccer with the other boys his age – this militia didn't admit pre-teen kids to the meetings – and in the hot, sweaty game he began to know some of them as closely as he knew anyone in Beirut except Madeleine. He learned their names and that, because this was a Maronite militia, they were all French-speaking like himself. But they were streetwise kids; they knew Arabic too. And they knew the city intimately, as if it were a part of their family. Indeed, he gathered from their casual remarks that some of them hadn't much family left, after almost fifteen years of civil war and the bombing and shelling which had destroyed entire apartment blocks and whole families. This gave him a sort of fellow-feeling with them and he felt ashamed of his own loneliness. His mother's death had hit him extra hard because it was caused by an act of random violence and so unexpected – but it was, after all, the only violent death in the family. These boys had lost five or six family members at a time, sometimes as many as fifteen.

He said something of this one evening to Pierre, who loved to play goalkeeper and dreamed of someday playing international games in Beirut's now-wrecked stadium. (Something flickered in Pierre's eyes when he mentioned the stadium: Rick discovered much later that the various groups of fighters often kept their prisoners there.) While Pierre and Rick rested, sweaty and breathless after a game, Rick said tentatively, 'But how do you manage? Where do you live since your apartment house and family are gone?'

Pierre's lively grin vanished and he shrugged. 'It is

hard perhaps,' he said, 'but many others have the same problem. I know no different life; for me the war has always been happening.' He lived, Rick gathered, with other refugees in a gutted hotel on the seafront. No electricity, and only a trickle of water from the hotel's ancient private well, but at least he had a roof and four charred walls. Rick remembered Madeleine's luxurious house and felt deeper ashamed. Did Madeleine ever think about these contrasts, and did she ever feel ashamed too? And did Georges and Brigitte, who also lived in luxury?

But then Pierre's face lit up and he began speaking again. 'At least,' he said, 'I belong to the militia. One day soon we shall drive out the rabble who don't belong in Beirut; we'll fight and defeat them and they'll run away screaming. Then Beirut will be our own city again. We Maronites shall give the orders and everyone must obey us if they want to stay.' His eyes flashed. 'Come!' he said, jumping from the table he'd propped himself against, 'tonight there is no movie. Tonight we have rifle practice and your uncle will let you stay, won't he?'

Rick liked the liveliness and sudden enthusiasms of these boys but he felt awkward around them, and not only because he hadn't shared their harsh experiences and instinctively shrank from the idea of further blood-shed as an answer to their problems. The truth was that Georges, on the first evening, had introduced him almost contemptuously to the group. 'My little nephew, who's been living in a sheltered mountain place until he came to join us –' That sort of thing. One of the older boys had said sharply, 'What mountain?' as if only the right name could establish Rick's credentials.

But Georges with an easy smile and his arm lying casually along Rick's shoulder said, 'If I tell you it was east of here . . .' with a meaningful head-jerk, and his smile's abrupt disappearance meant, You impudent young fool, don't you dare ask *me* any questions. So the questions had dried up and no one else said anything about Rick's background, but he felt uneasy. None of this made for straightforward happy relationships.

He was allowed to stay till the end of each meeting now. Instead of the movie, or after it, there was a sort of military drill; Rick had seen those in action movies and this, by comparison, looked less organised but fiercely energetic. Was it just another way for the members to let off steam, like those exuberant games of soccer? But after the drill, each time, came rifle practice, and their skill at this was so accurate it made Rick shiver. They never seemed to miss; you could imagine any of them as a deadly rooftop sniper. The meeting lost its cheerful casual aspect then. Even Pierre, who at sports time laughed and joked with Rick as few of the others did, squinted at the target and hit it without fail, his face suddenly twenty years older. Rick brooded over this; he put it together with what he'd learned about their lives, and he could understand their eagerness to get back at whoever had killed their families. They'd use sniping – or would they use some less exact method? Like those older men who came to the meetings with rocket-launchers perched on their shoulders like some bizarre decoration: would these men, or Pierre and others his own age, also use savagely indiscriminate methods such as car bombs, killing or maiming everyone within reach? Rick knew he couldn't safely ask the question of anyone at this meeting, and he couldn't ask it of Georges, either. The bearded face would stiffen, the eyes flash, and Rick would be told brusquely that it was none of his business, that he didn't understand the special conditions of this country, this city. An outsider again, though in a way he longed to belong.

The break, when it came, was shocking and its cause unbelievable; it bruised him and the mark didn't fade. The day began like many others, a July morning of dust and noise and bustle, while Rick walked to the shop under an already hot sun. In the afternoon: Georges teaching him to restring pearls, a few nearby errands. When the shop had closed, Georges said, casual as a throw of the dice, 'We have a special addition to the meeting tonight. Very interesting; you'll enjoy it.' His voice seemed to hold an extra resonance.

He pushed home the iron bar that reinforced the front door, then checked the safe, switched off the lights. They always left by the back door. 'Precautions,' he said with a general wave of the hand, 'you see no harm in those? Or are you so puritanical that you object to those also?'

'Of course not, if they're reasonable.'

Georges unlocked the back door, swung it open; they stepped out into the alley. The stink of explosives and burnt wood and dust grew strong; there'd been an incident somewhere. Rick reflected that talking with people like Georges was like skating on a frozen pond: you could never be sure of the surface thickness, nor of the depth and quality of water, the currents, underneath. And no one travelling the pond except himself . . . you missed the usual landmarks on the banks which would tell you your whereabouts. And the chance of a thaw, which here wouldn't be good but would develop into a white heat of anger . . . At the first sign of trouble, Rick resolved, I'll quit him and his goddam group. A firm decision this, tearing through the complex strands that tried to tangle themselves around it.

They arrived at the cinema in time for the start of the meeting. The movie this time was a Marx Brothers; in this setting Harpo's eldritch charm seemed more beguiling and convincing than Chaplin's slapstick. The militiamen laughed and applauded wholeheartedly, as before. Then a quick drill and target practice, after which some of the young members gathered up their jackets and guns, said goodnight and left. Rick glanced at Georges, who gave him a reassuring nod.

Introduction, of new recruits: apparently they'd an elaborate system of stages, testings, and for some of these recruits this was the first stage: a series of rapid questions and answers about defending the homeland and fighting for the righteous cause. Rick had seen this kind of thing in movies about guerrillas too. One youth stood aside, waiting, and Georges explained in a whisper that for him this would be the last test before full membership. The other recruits gave their answers and filed out; apparently they didn't have the privilege of watching the full proceedings. Rick's presence must be an exception, due to his relationship with Georges. The youth went to stand in the middle of the cleared area and his ordeal began.

The questions and answers this time, and the humiliations they put Alexandre through – like blindfolding him, then tying him up and screaming at him – could, in the States, have been belligerent kids' stuff. Alexandre was around Rick's age but very thin, and his lean body stayed wary, tense, silent, through whatever they did to him. Rick flinched for him, especially when they yanked him around hard and yelled right in his face. But Georges merely smiled a little and sat interested, absorbed.

After a while the physical violence stopped and, still blindfolded, Alexandre had to repeat various promises after the leading interrogator. The sort of promises which, back in the States, could be the macabre drunken boasts of those college fraternities Rick had heard about from the elder brothers of his high-school friends. But here, in this city which was so different, the words took on a mortal significance. Hey, Rick told himself, these are only wordy questions and a few damn fool tests. Surely no one could do major damage with them.

The questions and insults finished and he thought

Alexandre's ordeal was surely over. But one of the older men disappeared into a side-room and came back carrying a bucket. Rick strained between the heads of the others to see what was in it. Ice; he couldn't imagine what they meant to do with it, but wasn't ice mostly harmless too? The youth, still blindfolded from the last stunt, waited patiently like a cow at a slaughterhouse. Rick tried to catch Georges' eye but his uncle's gaze was fixed on Alexandre.

The older man lifted a chunk of ice from the bucket and approached the boy. For an instant Rick couldn't see what was going on, but there was no mistaking how the youth fell limply, the soft thud as his unconscious body hit the floor – a rag doll without stuffing. 'Christ,' Rick said, 'he isn't breathing.' He shoved aside Georges and the others, reached the lad, flipped him over and began the automatic checks. Pulse at the neck artery: none. Movement of the chest: none. Air movement through the nose or mouth: Rick bent his face to the boy's but no emerging air was detectable. Clear the airway: he tilted Alexandre's head back but there was still no sign of life. So begin resuscitation: Rick concentrated on performing the chest compressions and ventilation perfectly and ignored the silence, the occasional mutters, behind him.

After the second round of compressions and forced breaths, Alexandre's chest began to rise and fall shallowly. Rick, sweating, sat back on his heels, pushed the hair out of his eyes, and checked the pulse at the youth's neck again. Unsteady and weak, but at least it was there. Moment by moment it grew stronger, until the lad's eyes opened; even in his half-conscious state he looked mortally afraid still. Colour began to return to his face, he glanced nervously around and tried to struggle up. Rick helped him to his feet and yelled at the silent circle of men and youths watching, 'Why the hell did you do that to him?' Then, arm around Alexandre's shaky shoulders,

Rick led him through the crowd and out of the building, with Georges' furious condemnations ringing in his ears. 'You're making a fool of yourself over nothing,' Georges had said, 'this boy has been proved to be a coward by our simple test. He believed that the ice was a knifeblade, and he collapsed from fear. So what does it matter if he lives or dies? We can pick a hundred more from the streets any day to take his place.'

'Expendable,' said Rick, 'then so am I — expendable out of your family.'

He led the boy out to the dusty dark. There were of course no streetlights but he could feel Alexandre trembling and hear the gasping breaths. Rick said, 'After what happened in there you can't just walk off into the darkness and — are you okay?'

The youth said in an uneven voice, 'Everything is useless now. Because I failed.'

Rick choked back his stock of American swearwords, remembering just in time that he mustn't speak English. 'They nearly killed you. How could you want to be part of their group any more?'

'You don't understand,' said the shaky undertone. 'If I don't go with them, how shall I learn to kill?'

Oh Christ, said Rick's mind. While he fumbled for words, the low voice started to mutter again and an icy hand came out to touch his.

'You aren't a Beiruti, it is different for you. People say —' with a rising intonation as if there must be hope somewhere, 'life is quiet usually in the mountains? They had a little trouble up there last month, but on the whole didn't you find it peaceful and pleasant? Didn't you find it very different from this city now, here?'

So these boys Rick played soccer with had already invented a history of their own making for him, and no doubt a detailed one. This gave Rick a creepier feeling than anything else, as if he were a zombie. The cold hand squeezed his and retreated, and the quivery voice spoke again.

'You are kind and well-meaning. Your uncle will explain to you our problems here; he is an excellent militiaman. Now I must go, please.' His feet shifted on the gritty surface of the road and air moved past Rick's face.

Alexandre was already some yards away when Rick found his voice again and spoke. 'But are you sure you're okay? That was a nasty experience, it could have . . .' His words dried into the dark silence and Alexandre's incomprehension.

'Oh yes, I feel well.' At least he sounded less shaky and his breath had quietened. 'Now, please, I must go.'

'But you won't go back to them?' None of Rick's business this, and the boy's curt answer made it clear.

'Yes, I shall go back. I hope they will forgive me for being so weak tonight; sometimes forgiveness is possible. My elder brother is a very good forger – I shall ask him to make a medical certificate saying I had the grippe this evening and that next time I shall not fail them. Oh yes, of course I shall go back, what other choices are there?'

'But—' No, arguing with him was useless. 'At least take it easy first. Go home, try to sleep.' Wherever 'home' might be. After Pierre's revelation Rick didn't dare ask anyone else where or how they lived. He stood motionless, listening to Alexandre's footsteps fading in the distance.

18

This is the decision of his I've been waiting for, the decision that will send him safely away from us – but his tone and eyes are wrong.

For the rest of my life I shall remember how a large brown moth burst into the house with him; Rick leaps the stairs to his bedroom and starts hurling clothes around, I pant upstairs after him and the moth flings itself against me as if it too has made up its mind, as if it's supped full of horrors. I strike it away and say, '—at least a valid *reason*.'

'I've gotten you out of breath. Sorry.' He continues throwing clothes into a suitcase. His tone is totally ex-patriate.

'—must have been Georges.' I'll kill Georges and all his militia if they've harmed the boy.

'Not him directly. His buddies.' The suitcase is full, the drawers and cupboards almost empty; he's rooting among the last oddments.

My breath has returned; the moth bangs despairing at Rick's open door, then stumbles away and cascades down the stairwell. The boy's hands pause and he says, 'You want to hear?'

'I must.' So he stops packing, he turns around.

He says, 'Some kind of initiation ceremony.'

They meet in what was an expensive cinema, once owned by a rich Sunni Moslem who's fled to Iran; Georges and I often joke about that. Off the Place des Martyrs, not far from here.

Rick didn't, he says, take much notice of their military stuff — 'Kids playing soldier' — and he'd no intention of joining them, so he let the formal drills and such pass him by. And their periodic initiations . . . 'Like a fraternity,' he says, 'at college. Weird rituals, but if you're lit with a few drinks or a smoke or just high on excitement, you could go for it.' Suddenly his face dives behind their bizarre routines and pulls out horror.

'There was a kid — my age at most — standing waiting after the other new types, all blindfolded, and an older guy brought in a bucket of ice. I swear I'd no notion what he planned on doing with it.'

'*Ice*?'

'Yeah, ice.' He pauses; for a moment he sounds almost tender. 'You're sure you want to hear this, Gran?'

'I've lived here through the fighting, how about you?' Then I say, 'Ice is a horror?' and force myself to laugh.

Cold on the back of the neck, he says, to test for fear. 'They told this kid it was a knife, that it'd cut him if he flinched.'

'Well?' Our risks here are harsh, and you can't take the chance of a disabling cowardice.

'If I'd had any notion what they planned, I'd have objected and risked whatever they'd—' His mouth twitches. 'I never guessed. But that youth, he . . .' his fingers beat a tattoo on each other — 'he passed out. Not fainted but quit breathing. I've heard of that before. It's the result of—'

'Spare me the anatomy lesson. So what did the leaders do?'

'Held a fast consultation among themselves and then started the next item.' His mouth twitches stronger. 'I realised and jumped down to him and got him going again, but he was on the edge for a while. And — guess what Georges said to me afterwards?'

No, I don't want to. But he's telling me.

'Said why hadn't I left the kid be. Said cowards were no use alive or dead, said I'd made myself look silly and embarrassed him. *Embarrassed* – can you imagine?'

My standards are stripped away. If Georges really said – of course his remark would be strictly . . . no, I can't defend that either. 'You're inventing this.' Yet his shaking hands and the pressure lines around his mouth convince me otherwise.

He turns back to his packing. 'Thanks a lot. I should have guessed you'd stand up for your precious son. Just as well I'm getting out; I've had my doubts about him for a while. Things he'd say . . . Those packages he had me deliver – he showed me, each time, what was in them, that it was harmless jewellery metals and suchlike. So he couldn't pull any tricky stuff on me there. But if he'd tried, there wouldn't be much use me running to you to complain, would there?' His searching hands become frantic; they break out into speech of their own. 'Where's my fucking passport?'

Downstairs Brigitte arrives. Her feet scuffle as if she's kicking that damaged moth aside, then she climbs the stairs and stands at the door. I go to her, she puts her arm round me and her face, when she sees his full suitcase, shines joyfully. 'He's leaving,' she says.

His hands keep busy. 'Sure am. Tonight. I'm getting the next flight out, away from all of you.' He flicks a scornful glance at me. 'No disrespect, Gran. I realise you won't say a word against him. Misguided, that's what you are.'

So we're corrupted, we occupants of this city? And so would he be if he'd spent the last fifteen years here. Our lives have been shaped by necessities he couldn't imagine. And perhaps (I tell myself) we're not as totally corrupted as he believes. The arrogant woman of the photograph starts forward in automatic fury, but Brigitte gleefully restrains her. 'Let him go!' Then Brigitte taunts him, 'You've missed the evening's last flight, but since you're so virtuous no doubt you'll sprout wings?'

'I'll grab a taxi to the airport and wait there.' Anywhere rather than this house.

Brigitte steers me to a chair. 'What are you *waiting* for?' she says to him.

'My passport.' Hair flops over his face. He should be standing under some efficient American shower already, cleansing his body from the filth of us. 'I can't find my passport.'

She picks up his Lebanese passport from a chair and throws it at him.

'Not that one – I had an American one too, damn it! Old Chehab insisted I enter this country with a Lebanese one – was that your blasted pride of race, Gran? – but I've got pride of country too, and it isn't for this dump. So I got a US passport and carried that along. How'll I get back into the States else?'

We spend the next hour searching the room; no, his American passport isn't here. (But by the end of the hour I've *possibly* persuaded him that Brigitte and I didn't steal it.) Halfway through, a question occurs to me. 'What happened to that other boy?'

Rick says, 'As if you'd care.'

'Look,' I say, furious because he's assuming too much, 'I don't waste my breath.'

'He left the meeting,' Rick mumbles, 'he and I left together. I'd meant to see him home, make sure he was okay, but he said not. Didn't trust me, I guess.'

'But according to you, you'd saved his life.'

'Would that make any difference? Haven't all you Lebanese been taught from your cradles up not to trust anyone except within your own little clique, and maybe not even there?' He scrabbles through a pile of T-shirts.

I'm unhappy about the manner of his going; the only way I can reach him is by causing him pain, so I'll do that. 'What will you do when you get back to the States? Pick up those pretty ideals of yours again and cultivate them?'

'Christ!' he says. 'You lot sure do hate me. Are you after some of the money I plan to reject? Haven't you got enough for yourselves?'

'We have plenty. And we've never claimed to possess any major pieties, but you expounded your high ideals to me when you first arrived. What happened to them?'

The T-shirts slew in a patterned stream across bed and floor. 'I've worked here, haven't I? Not earned much but worked anyway, not sat on my backside eating food I'd no way earned. And the bank – I didn't draw much since I've been here.'

'So the money's piling up nicely.' Brigitte starts to speak but my raised hand stops her. 'And you'll pay your fare home out of it, buy your select little Eden and furnish it, stock it. Whose money will you be using for that, my high-principled grandson?'

'Damn you,' he says quietly across the patterned T-shirts, 'goddam you, oh damn.'

Into the silence Brigitte says, 'Is this passport so necessary?' Meaning, Get out of this house, don't hang around here insulting us.

'Sure it's necessary.' He looks bewildered and terribly young. 'The States might not let me in without. A foreign passport's no dice without a visa, and I've not got that.'

'Neither my mother nor I have stolen your passport, and Seraphite—'

'She couldn't.' How eagerly he rushes to clear her; how slow he was to accept that Brigitte and I weren't involved. 'I kept it with my travel documents and the other passport, locked in my suitcase in this cupboard ever since I arrived—'

He stops abruptly and Brigitte voices the obvious question. 'Are you sure it was there when you locked the suitcase?'

'Christ,' he says again, younger and more vulnerable than ever, 'I didn't exactly check. The other travel stuff was in this big brown envelope and I assumed the American passport was too. Because—'

'When was the last time you saw it?' Brigitte would make a superb inquisitor.

'At the airport, I guess,' he stammers, 'when that minder—'

'Which airport?'

He sits down suddenly on the bed. 'Yeah,' he says, 'you're right. Being the same nationality as him, you'd know how these things operate. I last saw the passport at Seattle airport when we left, that's where. He said I'd better give him charge of all the documents till we arrived here – Chehab's orders, I assumed, so I wouldn't be tempted to light out along the way. Least, that's what I supposed, so I handed them over and thought what a poor obedient sod he was, how biddable. Now the laugh's on me.'

Brigitte's face flickers with delight. 'No wonder he disappeared so fast when you arrived at Beirut airport. You silly boy, can't you guess how much a foreign passport is worth on the second-hand market?'

He pushes himself up from the bed. 'Details like that,' he says, 'of course you'd be as expert in them as he is.' He hauls the open suitcase to him. 'Pardon me for existing. A hell of a big mistake this whole trip was.' He rapidly throws shirts, underwear, trousers, back into the suitcase, and briefly when his wrists turn those healed scars flash before us.

I daren't say, Not quite a mistake; he would grasp my meaning. He slams the suitcase and locks it against us, picks it up. I say, 'Will you fly over and try with the Lebanese passport?'

'And risk my own country deporting me? God, no. I'll hang around out there —' his head-jerk indicates Beirut the bombed, the ruined, the rat- and cockroach-infested city where sentries and other men with guns still walk at night — 'till morning, then I'll go to the embassy and get a new passport, catch the morning plane.'

Already in my imagination he's a corpse. 'Go to bed,' I tell Brigitte; she's furious and mistrusts me, but my will is the stronger. She sets the door angrily wide and goes.

He stayed the night; I bullied him into that. In the small hours a ragged collection of distant pops sounded. I ought to be glad he's going back to relative safety. At first light I heard his step on the stairs and the back door closed; when Seraphite arrived I told her he'd left.

She grunts, pouring sugar on my yoghurt and fruit. The coffee's thick strength gives me courage that there might be a possible day ahead.

Brigitte enters and grabs her usual slab of bread, her coffee. In her white broderie robe she looks haggard. The brusqueness with which she says, 'He's gone?' makes clear that she's sure of me again. Her affection, like deep shadow, is present only under a near threat. She gulps her breakfast, rushes upstairs to dress, then down; the back door slams.

Seraphite says, 'So what will you do now?'

I remember those aged surfers of Rick's. If nothing else, he left one indelible image to shame me. 'Don't bother me,' I say into my coffee cup, 'I've given up trying to arrange people's lives.'

'*You?*'

I get up, cross the hall and living room and unlock the door to that shattered half-room which borders the Line. I scrabble at a plank till its edge gives way and allows me a centimetre-square view of my city. From the harbour area a thin trail of smoke rises; the air is silent, so perhaps they're merely burning rubbish. Can anything so normal be going on in this teeth-bared place?

At my elbow Seraphite says, 'Will you tell his guardian that the boy's left here?'

'Chehab? Of course not. You know what our phone and postal services are like: Rick would arrive in Seattle long before my news. And he's old enough to decide what he wants to do; he's much saner than when he came here. He and Chehab can argue the future out between them.'

Seraphite squints out through a crack in the planking, then turns and coolly regards me.

I tell her, 'Go away.'

She says, 'Because you've got money and been educated, you claim the right to—'

'The Congo,' I say, 'was easier. Madagascar,' – no, not Madagascar – 'Guadeloupe was too. Devil-dances and headhunting tribes and spirit-possessed trees were simple to understand and accept. But this country—'

'I doubt,' she says, 'if you've ever loved a person in your whole life.' She narrows her eyes at the crack. 'That boy – you only cared about what you could get out of him. Suck him like a rind, chew him into your beliefs, and if his flavour didn't blend you'd spit him out. Well, he spat himself.'

So he did. Overhead a plane sears the blue sky along the length of the Line; will this plane take him away, or has he already gone?

She says, 'Aren't you going to take your after-breakfast rest and read the newspaper, then listen to music on the radio or a chat programme, then eat lunch and after another rest take a taxi to Georges' or the bank or do some pleasant shopping, and return here to complain, with your belly full and your purse bulging, how there's no happiness in life?'

She leaves the crack and goes back to the kitchen, then begins one of those wailing Arab songs which she's aware

I detest. The faint scent of patchouli that stays behind her mingles with the dusty, bitter tang of the Line's air to produce an essence-of-Beirut which twists my heart.

I too leave the cracks. I go upstairs and dress for outdoors. By some miracle our phone works and I call a taxi. I go out and pick my way through the ruined cinema, the alley.

I stand across the road from the American embassy (or as much of it as is visible behind its barbed wire entanglements and tank traps). I came for one wistful glance at the place that freed him to leave us.

Above the harbour, smoke continues to blossom purple-clouded like the irises that grew in the garden of our mountain villa. It's smoke without noise, but further west the alleys above the seafront rattle like an invalid's coughing: the irregular staccato of rifle fire. Father Mesrop told me on his last visit that he'd heard the city was getting some new rubbish lorries (the old ones were burned long ago for barricades), and he smiled, telling me. The notion of rubbish being picked up from the streets and taken away for disposal is a fit subject for mirth.

And there are other mirths too. Beside me on the street two Shia militiamen pick over a stall full of spare bits of uniforms. One of the two crams an Israeli cap on his head. Under its Star of David he mock-levels his rifle at the other man, says, 'Bang-bang,' and the two of them explode in laughter while the stream of tolerant half-smiling passers-by parts round them – yet these militiamen are standing next to the posters of their and everyone else's *martyrs*? And a travel agency has re-opened. The owner with bald head and thin moustache proudly dusts his window, placing posters with that twenty-year-old message 'Snow and Surfing' between a fake decorative rug, 'Roman' coins fresh from some basement mint and an 'ancient Greek statue', which wouldn't deceive a baby. They want visitors *here*? Despite the coughing alleys they *expect* visitors? This isn't the city I've brooded over in wakeful nights; this is a sprightly harridan who hasn't looked in the mirror for so long that she doesn't realise how grotesque she is. A scarred harridan, busy painting her face.

A bunch of gunboys pass: shaven heads, the eldest perhaps twelve, they kick a football between them but their rifles – nearly as tall as them – lie snugly on their backs; every once in a while the hand of one of them reaches around to make sure his weapon is intact. And from the embassy a limousine issues with elaborate springing-to-attention of guards and levelling of guns. Rick must long ago have left Lebanese airspace.

Obviously I didn't understand him, never understood a particle of him, and he's gone. So I do the only possible thing: I hail a taxi and go home to start trying to forget him.

19

He came out of the embassy dazed and breathless; everything was so much more complicated than he'd expected.

At the first guardpost on his way in they'd confiscated his baggage, then a grim-faced Marine escorted him to the next guardpost and another took his Lebanese passport and disappeared to consult someone else. It felt odd to stand in the roasting sun without baggage or any passport, as if he were now stateless and would be shunted from the outside of one embassy to another for ever – no formal allegiance, no home.

After a long while an American in civilian clothes emerged from the embassy compound. He spoke to the guards and one of them pushed Rick up against a wall, searched him thoroughly, then let him go with the civilian. Through the guarded door, where the civilian showed his pass even though he'd exited only minutes earlier. Into the embassy, with a uniformed Marine bringing up the rear.

Along a corridor. The civilian was replaced by another and the Marine by a big fattish guy with Internal Security flashes. Doors, all shut. Then into a room where typewriters buzzed, a fax clicked and a computer flickered in the corner; the young male operators eyed Rick sternly as he was escorted through. A smaller room beyond, empty except for chairs lined round the walls. The guard motioned Rick to a seat and himself stood beside the door. The civilian turned and left. An interminable wait, then another entered.

Crewcut, red-faced, bulky, tropical-suited. He sat down across the room and subjected Rick, under the guard's watchful gaze, to a grilling such as he'd never experienced. 'Weren't you aware,' – in the little window-less room his voice boomed and the thick cords on his neck stood out – 'that as an American you mustn't travel on the passport of another country?'

'But I'm Lebanese too. Because of my parents' nation-ality. That's the only—'

'You've broken Federal law by travelling as a Leban-ese. Therefore your primary nationality—'

'I've done *what*?' The States were receding, further away and more desirable all the time. They'd never let him in again and he'd be an agonised exile for ever . . . Finally through the other's formal explainings he burst out, 'But those other guys made the arrangements and I never – as far as I'm concerned I'd always travel on an American passport. How the hell can I convince you?'

Silence. What were the penalties for shouting at a consular officer? Most likely enormous.

The man began talking again, explaining slow and clear as to a noisy child that dual nationals owed their primary allegiance to the States; they couldn't dither between the two nationalities and grab the most con-venient aspects of both. So Rick must decide which country he regarded as home, which nationality he chose – and so on. Finally the officer decided he could be forgiven, for this one time only. Rick had to hold up his right hand in front of the consular officer and an eagle-and-shield facsimile of the Great Seal, and solemnly swear that he hadn't intended any disloyalty to the United States of America, then he had to part with a fairish number of dollars (apparently various degrees of dis-loyalty had their differing prices) and finally he got to fill out the regular passport application under the officer's unwavering gaze, and to stand in front of a picture machine for his mug shot. Finally the stern official left and a lesser minion (a smiling one, now that Rick had been officially forgiven) picked up a blank passport, stuck and stamped the various bits of Rick into it, handed it to him and said, 'You're leaving right away? Sensible guy, but go careful till you're off Lebanese territory, son. It's a jungle out there.' The security man escorted Rick along the corridor. At the door Marines again took over and guided him past the truck defences and various guardposts to the wall and wire; at the last checkpoint they handed him his suitcase and he walked out to the street.

After the shady air-conditioned rooms the heat and light dazzled him. For an instant he seemed to glimpse Madeleine hailing a taxi, but that was ridiculous: there was no reason for her to be around here. He'd simply got her on the brain.

He supposed he'd better get moving, grab a taxi and head for the airport, get the hell out of this country as the embassy man had advised. Smoke drifted lazily above – no, not the harbour area now (he'd heard those pops in the night, too) but further west near the seafront, behind the Avenue de Paris. Of course smoke in Beirut could be harmless, but you automatically checked the various options . . . He hailed a taxi but it was busy. In mid-wave to another he remembered that phantom sighting of Madeleine, his hand dropped and his mind split into two. On one side yelled the dangers he was running every minute that he hung around: an American in Beirut, of a wealthy family, loitering outside the embassy itself – could you put yourself at higher risk than that? On the other side niggled Madeleine's jibe of the previous night: 'What are you going home to – those fine ideals of yours? Will you pick them up again and put them into practice with your father's money? But how comfortably you'll play at living simply, how you'll manage to amuse yourself, how soft a life you'll have compared to us, how little risk you'll run!'

A taxi stopped beside him and he said, 'No, sorry – I'm not ready yet. I've got to think.' The driver cursed him and drove off. Rick picked up his baggage and began to walk at random, not noticing his surroundings. After a while, more of those surreal poppings broke into his reverie and at the noise his mind was suddenly made up; his body followed without question. He hailed another taxi, and this time he knew exactly where he needed to go.

20

In the basement cafeteria of the ambulance station the other new guys were ribbing each other in fluent Arabic; he blended into a corner with his thyme bread and mug of hot tea and silently interrogated the two faces, two bodies, of himself. Part of him was still astonished, couldn't grasp that this was happening; that sensible part of him had already in imagination run the dangers of the airport road and the terminal where anonymous gunmen always lounged, and was midway across the Atlantic, eating plastic food off a plastic tray and planning where he'd head for after he landed in Seattle, how he'd skirt the city centre so as to avoid any sighting of Chehab or Josie, how he'd grab a car and aim for some remote skyswept spot, get work in the woods, rent a derelict homestead up there and start chopping fenceposts and brambles, planting beans, how before too many more years he'd meet a girl with similar tastes and life would have neatly arranged itself. That part of him was . . . not running scared but prudent, knew where it belonged, couldn't understand or accept that the impulsive other part had taken control and was forcing the body to sit in this underground dump amid the reek of disinfectant and sweat, nibbling on bread and black olives and wearing a uniform.

The standard-issue blue shirt and jeans, the red-and-white shoulder-flash, were unfamiliar and didn't reassure him. A man clattered down the stairs and shouted, again in Arabic, 'Class time!' Rick thought briefly, and without amusement, of Madeleine.

How could you live barred and fanatical for ever, cutting off most of a city's population because you'd got a hang-up about their language – which was nevertheless one of the country's two official tongues?

The other guys got up and headed in an untidy throng toward the stairs, and he joined them. His surreptitious language primer and the streetside chatter he'd listened to, the attempts he'd made at speaking Arabic with food vendors on the Corniche or the owners of bookshops, all these helped him to catch phrases and sometimes more, but there was so much he didn't know. He grasped at familiar words and followed the other guys' actions: some of them spoke French as their main language too and had an imperfect command of Arabic. The instructor allowed for this, repeating his orders in both languages. Some of the guys were Rick's age, some older, some maybe mid-teens, but in this official work they apparently didn't accept anyone younger. Rick had already noticed that some of the militias had no such scruples, and the city was full of nine- or ten-year-old gunboys roaming the streets. You couldn't equate age in Beirut with age any-where else. Rick remembered the young brothers and sisters of some of his high-school friends, but their behaviour and interests bore no relation to those here.

There would, the man in charge said, be classes every afternoon for a month, mornings driving the streets with an experienced partner; after the month, ambulance work would be their regular job and they'd all spend twelve hours a day dealing with whatever Beirut decided to chuck at them. Why the devil (Rick's rational sensible self asked) are you doing this?

End of classes for the afternoon; the others – joshing or silent – poured out onto the street. The basement cafe-teria had closed, but in a battered cloakroom a trickle of water allowed him a cold shower, then he couldn't post-pone leaving the building. The clear evening sky mocked the reasons his mind had invented for staying in Beirut; the ordinary city noises laughed at words like 'useful' and 'justify my being alive'. They underlined how *smeary* honest-to-God feelings could get. And if the violence didn't hot up again, would there be any point in hanging around here, routinely ferrying people with minor ailments?

He walked out and the babble, the summer heat, of the streets hit him. Hell, he told himself, I'll face whatever does – or doesn't – happen a day at a time, as it comes. Can't be anything wrong with wanting to help, damn it. He shifted hands on the suitcase he was still hauling, and began to speculate about getting a meal, and a bed for this and the coming nights.

Shame burned him because he had money and because most likely he'd need to use it. He'd no notion how to go about sleeping rough; stories of people taken hostage – foreigners of all kinds, or Lebanese, and for some visible reason or none – popped into his head and wouldn't leave, and the alleys, even the main streets, looked murkier as the evening passed. It struck him that he with his suitcase and decent shoes and watch might be attracting attention. At night he'd several times gone sloping out from Madeleine's, when he felt restless, to roam the near-deserted Line in battered jeans and T-shirt and worn-out sneakers, but this, now, was different. Danger gathered itself up and walked alongside him; he'd never realised before how danger could feel like a flesh-and-blood person standing at your shoulder. Danger might be this man who was staring from a doorway, or that woman who might have simple prostitution or worse in mind; danger was a person and the streets were full of them. So finally, ashamed and weary, he walked in past the portals of an expensive hotel.

He grew to know that hotel well, yet, every time he went

inside it, the place struck him as being a collection of Beirut's oddest people and events. You could get anything there if you had money, via fixers you could contact anyone, and any friend or foe would eventually show up there to drink at the bar or, eyes glittering with a fanatical rage, to shoot its bottles to bits or to help replace them. The shag rugs in jewel colours, the huge dim restaurant, and the clientele of journalists and hurrying businessmen and curvy multilingual whores and uncataloguable types who communicated by nods and quick pocketings rather than by speech, all these became as familiar to him as his own face – shaving each morning and astonished at being there, doing the work he was – in his bathroom mirror. Two days after he reached the hotel, major violence flared up across the city, as suddenly as Madeleine and Georges had always warned him it would, and spectacular in its black-and-rose explosions, its drowning of every district, every street, in noise and grief and blood. This was the big one, this wouldn't – the chattering foreign voices in the bar said – fold up soon; it was here to stay. And the locals in the restaurant and bar didn't speak about it; their silence felt more unsafe, more scary, than the gloomy chatter of the overseas types. His life took a tight routine, necessary for survival; but in street or ambulance or hotel, at any hour of the day or night, he discovered in himself a shaming capacity for terror.

The more he travelled in the city during its new incarnation of violence, the more deeply he realised that his body could be wrecked at any time, in a single moment, by the whine of an incoming bullet or the whistle of a rocket or shell fired from any angle, any building, by a militiaman who thought he had good reason to fire, or who was high on excitement and simply had no reason to fire at all. Even celebrations of a ceasefire could lead to deaths: men fired supposedly into the air, but in fact the bullets could go anywhere and everyone in his ambulance crew had a horror story to tell.

Afternoons of study and tuition at the ambulance station (they'd shifted classes to the basement for safety), mornings on frightening work-rides with an experienced worker, then a return in early evening to the hotel by whichever sideways route seemed least unsafe that day. He didn't worry any more about sticking out in a crowd; in the blue uniform and with his hair mussed, his skin sweaty and grimed, he was indistinguishable from plenty of other young men. But the danger that walked the streets now wasn't an imaginary enemy, which might seek him personally, it was random death, without logic or argument; it leaned from any apartment building and sat in any parked car. He learned, from the casual chat of the others at work, some details of the previous years, and when his feet weren't treading on real blood they were plodding through the ghostly stickiness of the people killed in every month at every corner, in every shop or apartment building.

Back at the hotel he'd shower and eat, then study in his room (with its crimson carpet and assortment of service buttons which you could play like piano keys to produce either no answer or the same tirelessly smiling youth each time) till the question 'Why am I hanging around in this country?' became intolerable, then he'd quit study for the evening and make his way to the bar – downstairs or in whichever hidden room of the hotel the extremists had temporarily forced it to.

In the States he'd been underage for drinking. That hadn't stopped him doing some, but he liked the lazy way of nursing a single drink while he watched things happen in front of him. So now, at the hotel he'd sit with a beer, brooding on the day's events (amid all the horrors he still had a genuine interest in the work; first aid classes had been the one bright spot in his high school career –

you could see the point of them) and watching the various exotic types, male and female, who were knocking back their cocktails or straight whisky or the sweet nutty-smelling 'araq. While he'd lived at Madeleine's and worked for Georges, he'd gotten partly used to the city, but his leaving both of them, and the events since, had smashed those props away. Nowadays the only solid centre was himself. So he hung onto that, stayed as silent in the hotel as one of its mystery visitors, didn't mix. He saved his chatting for the other guys in his class and for whoever was his driver. Plenty of those guys didn't want to talk about their personal histories either; he wasn't the only one. But they'd all discuss anything else under the sun, and would get excited too. A fiery passionate bunch, these Lebanese . . . which led him, after he'd been in the hotel a couple of weeks, to think of Madeleine.

He'd not gotten in touch with her to say he was still around. He sipped his beer (that evening the bar was open next to the lobby as usual – the militiamen hadn't visited for a while) and thought, Hell, why should I contact her? Didn't she take Georges' side about that damn meeting? She could have said straight out, That's terrible. But no, not Madeleine.

The lively small face and cascading dark hair of a girl drinking with two men at the bar caught his attention. She broke away from the two and did a snatch of wiggling dance in the middle of the room, laughing and singing some French song in a breathy little voice while the taller man raised his glass to her and grinned and the other glared. Rick thought, I'll bet Madeleine was a charmer like that when she was young. Lively and all. But she'd gone to university and worked and travelled; must have been a person with a lot of layers. But this dancing girl . . . her face and body didn't connect with anything like studying or tough work. That mass of dark hair tumbling down her back, and the tight black dress, the slim arms and legs, and the body curved in all the right places . . . she certainly was loaded with the equipment for one sort of life.

She ran back to the men, climbed up on her stool and leaned her elbow on the counter. The taller man bought her another drink and his broad shoulders bent over her. She shivered – prettily, exaggeratedly – and he, grinning, draped his jacket (Phalangist olive-green) around her. Rick drained his glass and got ready to go back upstairs. The girl attracted him because of her lively good looks and because, unlike most of the local women, she was small-built, but obviously she wasn't available for him; she'd got two escorts already hanging over her (she kept the shorter of them in play by a word or touch every once in a while). Then the main door crashed open and a man in a ragged black uniform walked in. Everyone stopped talking and watched him.

Rick thought, This can't be happening. But it was. The gun had no silencer and in that confined space the single shot echoed like an army. The tall man at the bar closed his eyes and slid quietly to the floor. One small spurt of blood from his forehead fell across the sleeve of his jacket where it hung loose on the girl's shoulders. She shrugged the jacket off and dropped it neatly across his prostrate face; the man who'd fired the shot turned and walked out. Chattering began again – nervous, disjointed, energetic – while the barman strolled around to the front of the bar and examined the fallen man. He let the dead hand, the head, fall and strolled back, but Rick had glimpsed the back of the head where the bullet exited. No point in trying to resuscitate this one. The hotel manager appeared (white bow tie, dazzling white shirt-front, calm expression) with a couple of waiters who under his instructions pulled out a stretcher from a corner behind the bar. In no time the body was gone, the floor mopped, and another round of drinks issued.

The girl and the second man had moved several stools along; now the man put down his brimming drink and stealthily eyed the girl, who was scanning the line of occupied stools as if searching for a replacement. Stealthily he eased off his stool. The girl glanced round and he said a few words to her, gave her a firmed-up smile. He headed for the men's room.

The girl opened her handbag and with elaborate care redid her face. She finished her drink; several of the men at the bar eyed her but their glances slid away as the corpse had slid from the stool. The guy who'd gone to the men's room was taking a long time.

The bar was full, mostly with stranded business types discussing broken-off deals and foreign destinations and the safest places to eat meantime, the best place for a quick lay. No one mentioned, even by a momentary silence, the dead man or the intruder who'd neatly, swiftly, shot him. The girl folded her arms across her breasts and stared at the men's room door as if her gaze could pull it open. Rick had ordered another beer. He was about to leave it and offer to go hunt up the guy (there was no other exit, and it shouldn't take anything like this long to do the necessary, wash your hands and drop a coin in the ancient female attendant's saucer) when the man, as furtively as he'd gone, reappeared.

But he didn't return to the girl; instead he went fast, almost shyly, along the far side of the room, out through the main door to the street. As he went he cast one look at the girl – a discreet nervous glance as if he wished she weren't watching him – then he stared straight ahead. After the door banged behind him, talk ebbed. The girl tightened her mouth and stared around. Rick thought, She's putting up the palisades. Then her gaze met his.

His legs got him up and took him across to her without his conscious thought. She watched him blankly but when he stopped beside her he saw the flash of disbelief on her face. 'If,' he said in French 'you'd like to join me for a drink—'

He made the offer from pity for her nearness to danger, from the squirm of remorse you'd feel for a trapped creature. If she'd not been beautiful he would have planned to offer her one drink and stop at that. Only she was so spectacular-looking, and her husky voice fascinated him, and her aura of being caught in some catastrophic situation. She nodded briefly and went with him to his corner table. When the general conversation had started up again, he said in an undertone, 'That man who died . . .' and she, ruthless as a hunting beast said, 'I never saw him before. He dragged me in here and insisted on a drink – I was on my way home. I don't pick men up.' Her small fingers twirled her wine glass. 'Must have been a crazy man. I've no idea who shot him or why. Probably he deserved it. And I shan't ask any questions. I'm glad to be rid of him.' Rick longed to ask, How about your other escort? But you'd never get in past the steel of her eyes. 'Good riddance to them all,' she said, and smiled brilliantly and lifted her wine glass.

Her gaze commanded him not to probe . . . but it suggested something else too. He'd not slept with a girl since Josie, although in the States he'd had some casual relationships before her. A lot of Lebanese females were good-looking but so far he'd admired them from a distance, telling himself that his eye wasn't tuned to them yet. When he was being honest he found a few other reasons too: the break-up with Josie had damaged deeper than his pride, and also he felt diffident because he knew he didn't understand the Beirutis' partisan line-ups. Yet this girl . . . no, it wasn't exactly pity. He felt he was already involved with her, and he firmly wanted – even if a future with her held disappointment or risk – to get deeper involved.

She was wonderful in bed. Josie's brusquely dissatisfied ghost faded away at last, and the hotel bedroom, which had been so cheerless, bubbled and spun around with happiness. Afterwards neither of them suggested her leaving; they slept in each other's arms. In the pre-dawn half-light he woke to find her bending over him and tracing the outline of his eyebrows with her small spatulate thumb. 'A good hotel this,' she said, 'you must be rich.'

Her frank calculation, so unlike Josie's careful reticence, amused and touched him. He caught her travelling fingers and kissed them.

'Your name.' She took the hand away from him. Hugging herself within his white towelling robe she was tinier than ever, an absorbed child. 'You must tell me your name.'

'Rick. What's yours?'

She shook her head disapprovingly. '*All* your names, otherwise how can I place you?'

He rubbed sleep from his eyes and gave her the family name he hated because it meant so much in this city. Sure enough her eyes gleamed.

'Of that big bank? Your – no, it couldn't be your mother – your grandmother then? Living all by herself next to the Line? Brrh – I don't understand how she can!' But the eyes, gleaming coolly, measured him. 'And you – where did you live, all these wartime years? Not in Beirut; I'd have heard about you sooner.' Her gaze narrowed. 'Some expensive hotel in Cyprus, yes? Isn't that where many rich Lebanese fled to when the bombs here became interesting?' She laughed. 'I don't condemn you, I only try to understand. So now you've returned, ready for the rich life to start again. And you meet this hotel, the things which can happen in it. You meet me. She turned away so that he couldn't see her face. 'A pickup,' she pronounced the phrase with contempt, 'that's what you believe I am, isn't it?'

'Not a bit.' He sat upright. 'Takes two,' he muttered while her glinting eyes surveyed him again. The details of the previous evening flooded back and he longed to ask, How well did you really know that man? And the other man, and the killer, what was your relationship with them? But a new caution, bred in Beirut's peculiar circumstances, told him, When – if – she's ever ready, she'll tell you.

'I was never a whore. Whether you believe or not, I never was.' She flung back the dark hair, the robe slipped from her young shoulders and breasts, and she said, 'Once I almost married your uncle.'

'*Georges*?' He'd already noticed how she would make the most extraordinary statements in so quiet and matter-of-fact a tone that they sounded more incredible than ever. She tossed them like her hair and let them lie where they fell, visible but beyond belief. Yet he hadn't figured out how to respond. At his silence she slapped the bed hard, as if she wished it were him.

'Didn't I say already that I'd met your grandmother? Not introduced to exactly, but if you tell her you've met me she'll realise who; she and my grandmother were close friends.' She pulled the robe around her and pursed her sulky mouth at him. 'Next time you go to visit her I shall go with you. A charming elderly lady – she'll enjoy meeting me.' She slid off the bed and began to dress.

His brain was spinning at how many leaps ahead of him she was. 'Truly you almost married Georges?'

She looped a black bra around her small pointed breasts. 'Don't ever disbelieve me, Ricki. He is so handsome, and that money . . . I had our courtship all arranged.' The bra hooks clicked into place. 'He would have been a good catch. A dangerous man, of course, but who isn't?' She pulled the skimpy black dress over her head and from its muffling folds her voice reached him. 'When I said that, you remembered last night, hein? But last night was special; I am not often so near to gunfire.' Her head emerged like the centre of a flower within ruffled black petals and she smiled at him – a neatly arranged smile. 'Don't waste time disbelieving me,' she said. 'We could be friends.' She picked up her handbag – gilt, with tiny black flowers – and, hurrying now, made for the door.

'You'll come back here tonight?' he said.

'Where else?' She poised at the door, one hand on the handle ready to open it, and the way she'd arranged her body was careful, controlled, too. Within this controlled arrangement she gave what sounded like a genuine gurgle of mirth. 'Better than using a gun encampment on the beach, isn't it?' And when he stared she went on, 'Of course one bribes the guards and on warm nights it's pleasant enough, when there's no fighting, but it doesn't give much privacy.' She flung both hands out toward the ivory drapes, the many service buttons, in a clutching gesture of frank greed. 'I prefer this. You see I'm keeping nothing from you; I believe in truth. And, darling – your grandmother. She'll enjoy meeting me; tell her Solange wants to. She and I have much in common: we both love beautiful possessions and expensive surroundings.' Her hands caressed the door handle and she laughed. 'You see how honest I am?' Under his gaze a shadow passed across the transparent joy of her face. 'As for last evening . . . there's no point in my going into details about that. It was unimportant, truly I hardly knew the man, had only just met both of them. Sometimes one feels generous . . .' she gave him a bright smile, 'and I paid for my generosity to them last evening, didn't I? What a price for a drink and chat – to see the man shot! And the man who did the shooting . . . truly I'd never seen him before.' She was talking fast, her voice high. 'I would have remembered him,' she said, and pursed her lips tight.

Suddenly Rick didn't care who she was, what her

relationship with the dead man had been or what other secrets her past held; he wanted to protect her and convince her that in the extraordinary conditions of this city she had no responsibility, no blood-guilt. He got out of bed and crossed the room to her. 'It must have been hell,' he said, his lips against her shoulder where the perfume she'd worn the night before lingered, 'all these years – you must have been tiny when the fighting started—'

She detached herself and said, matter-of-fact as if they were making a business appointment, 'Your grandmother, darling, I'd love to meet her. One hears so much about . . . and your whole family has an aura, you know?'

She teasingly pushed him to arm's-length. He said, 'The aura of wealth?'

Again that frank gurgle. 'I truly believe I care for nothing in the world except money.'

'At least you're honest about it.' Better this open laughing covetousness than the snide, poking approach of so many people in his own income bracket in the States, or of many who longed to be that rich. Surely it was better to say simply, 'I want,' than to measure folks' income silently by their possessions, their clothes and cars and boats, the stock market reports, and to covet their wealth secretly, like a wound festering under the skin, as Josie had? He wouldn't soon forget that evening when he'd told Josie – stumbling and hesitant because he hadn't spoken of this before – how he planned to renounce his father's money, deed it to charity and live frugally from some blue-collar job. Her eyes had opened wide and her face – not, like this girl's, a delicate unknown landscape but healthy, tanned, exuberant, not a face where you'd expect secrets – had fallen apart abruptly like some overblown bloom, an unsubtle and stridently coloured rose. 'You'll do *what*?' she'd said, and in that moment, past his stumbling explanations, their closeness had fallen apart too.

He said now to this unknown girl, 'The family money's not important,' and wondered why explaining to her was so easy when it had been so hard with Josie. 'I intend to make my own way. As soon as I'm twenty-five and inherit my father's capital I'll—' Her smooth face gave no clue to whether she was listening.

'Tonight, here,' she said, opening the door, 'and your grandmother quite soon, hein?' She paused, then sounded shy. 'She's a sort of . . . legend, you understand? Nearly alone in that big house by the Line – brrh!' She swung her handbag, and the little silver-rimmed black flowers on it danced while she assured him, 'She and I would like each other very much; we must meet.'

'I haven't seen her for a while, but—' Hadn't his conscience been prodding when Solange first appeared? So, Madeleine was as prejudiced as they come, but she was old and pretty much alone, and anyway . . . mightn't there be reasons, even if wrong ones, for her attitude? He saw her past as a series of dim caverns that stretched away into shadows he couldn't visualise; what beasts or beauties lurked in them he'd no idea. And whatever moved in those shadows had shaped her. 'Yes,' he said, 'I should see her anyway. Tell her I'm okay and still here.'

'Tonight then,' she said, 'or very soon. Lucky you work a nice ordinary job – regular work, and paid. You're a lucky man, one way and another.' She looked at him soberly, as if she were memorising his face, then she left. The door closed quietly behind her.

He went over to the window; from this height her figure was tiny, a doll hurrying along the grey dawn street. He found himself smiling down at her, grinning like an infatuated fool at this girl he'd only just met.

When she disappeared past the street corner he made his usual morning survey of the sky: into its pallid blue one smoky imperfection lifted, then another. Then the sky flowered across its western length in a score of smoky blossoms. Beirut was waking up.

21

Bodies and parts of bodies. Streets that literally did stream blood. The soldiers and police who arrived ineffectively after each incident: the soldiers searching the streets absent-mindedly – like men looking for dropped coins of little value – for live ammunition and unexploded shells, the police shouting to each other (almost as loud as the militiamen, who had the biggest yells of all) and waving their white truncheons and sometimes, if their audience got extra noisy, chucking at random a canister or two of tear gas. Militiamen with rifles and rocket-launchers climbing and fighting from balcony to balcony, from street corner to corner amid sandy barricades and earthen berms and cocoons of rusty barbed wire. One man (Phalangist, from his olive uniform and high black boots) running through the smoke along a street deserted except for the uselessly busy ambulances; he stopped to curse, wipe the sweat from his face and call to another Phalangist who appeared at an intersection, 'Where's the war gone?'

Some incidents, some bodies, kept Rick awake at night. Especially wounded or dead children and babies; he never got used to those. Also the way in which this random violence could alter for ever the lives of the survivors. Like the young woman in a sleek black dress and white jacket whom he rushed to help after one car bombing. 'My leg,' she cried, 'how is my leg?' But her right leg below the knee didn't exist any more, and her left leg was badly mauled. Rick glanced up from his bandaging to see if Jameel was bringing a stretcher, and he met the gaze of a militiaman strolling by. The dark eyes, the mouth hidden behind a beard, showed not the slightest emotion, and Rick felt a spurt of anger such as he'd never known before. The militiaman was, from his uniform, a Phalangist like Georges; had he been one of the group that met in the old cinema? Could be. This man could have been one of the older men there who stuck together, weren't friendly to newcomers, and whom Rick hadn't really gotten to know even by sight. He might or might not have had some responsibility for this car bomb. Rick would never be able to prove anything and often, after such an incident, no militia bothered to claim responsibility.

The city bristled with checkpoints like the ugly blisters of some uncatalogued disease; Rick never got used to approaching these. Surely the risk of encountering an explosive temper beyond the barrel of a rifle ought to be greater with some militias, some tribes, than others. Oughtn't the whole city to be tenser and more dangerous at those times when the violence had escalated? But Jameel, his usual driver, approached each checkpoint, each day, with the same string of ribald jokes, the same seemingly relaxed sprawl in his seat, the same steady gaze from his swarthy face, and when Rick said, 'Don't you ever get nervous?' Jameel said surprised, 'How could I guess which place is safe? Every checkpoint and every gunman is like I descend into a tunnel carrying a lit lamp – a tunnel where there is much inflammable gas. You take things too serious, little boy. We might as well joke. We are no closer to death when we laugh than when we weep.' But even Jameel, at the end of every morning, would grip Rick by the shoulders and say unfailingly, 'We're alive still, little boy.' Said this every morning, with a wide white-toothed smile, as if he and Rick were talismans for each other and could depend on no other help.

The violence fell and rose again like the Mediterranean waves, like the gust and fall of hot summer breezes. After hours or days the shooting and shelling would become sporadic, then the shops and nightclubs and restaurants would reopen, people would queue for bread and, if the peace lasted, would visit the gourmet shops for caviare or pâté, and hotel bars or nightclubs for Martinis or Beirut Specials and entertainment. The newspapers still carried ads for perfumes and sexy lingerie new from Paris, fresh billboards appeared along the highways with posters advertising lipstick or movies. The sun, rising each day, commented with its hot glare on whatever might be happening along the streets, and each evening when it fell it turned the mountains rose-coloured and the sea silver-green in its daily beautiful inexorable way.

Rick went to and from work because he'd promised to do this job. There were relaxed, happy moments at the ambulance station in between calls, snatched minutes of pleasure when the crews compared and argued over pop music they'd heard on the radio, and other times when Jameel, laughing, taught Rick Arab curses. Some, Jameel explained, sounded trivial or silly but had a sting to them: 'May your moustache wither' expressed real anger. And some – the four-letter insults to the anatomy of the recipient's sister or mother – meant a fury that you'd do well to stay clear of if you could.

But always, sooner or later, these amusements would be interrupted by the siren's wail, the rush to their vehicles. The streets full of dust and blood and bits of bodies again. Rick tried to persuade Solange to stay holed up in the hotel till the city quieted, but she refused. 'Ridiculous!' she said, laughing, when on her second morning he suggested it, and when he persisted she got angry. 'Listen, little boy,' – the humiliating nickname for him which Jameel also used – 'I've lived in this city all my life, right? Through all the fighting. Whereas you – I don't ask what cave you came from, but it wasn't a Beirut cave. I can tell that by the way your eyes jump.'

'I'm not scared.' Honesty made him amend this. 'Not more than any sensible person would be.'

'That is why I say you're not a Beiruti. No,' she held up her hand, 'I don't want to learn where from. But you don't understand this city and how we forbid ourselves to be the least bit scared of these happenings. Let them roll past you, Ricki, like a line of lorries thundering into the distance. And if one lorry should happen to swerve and hit you – well, you've made love to women, you've eaten and drunk and had a good time, maybe you've tried a little hashish like many of the militiamen, you've enjoyed being alive. What's so special about you or me? We certainly wouldn't be the first to die here. Or the last. Also I must go to my job today. Your silly worryings mustn't make me lose that.'

And he had no rights over her. 'Where d'you work? I'll meet you and bring you safe here.' But he couldn't guarantee his own quitting time if the streets got wild, and anyway her frown was thunderous.

'No, I move around at my own pace, my own timing.' You trespasser, said the glare of her eyes. Then they softened, as if deliberately. 'I work as a singer. Some night you shall hear me, but not tonight. We go to see your grandmother tonight, don't we?' Briefly he hoped this haste was concern for an elderly woman who lived almost alone near the fighting, but her next words made clear it wasn't. 'She has beautiful jewels, they say, and many clothes – the real Paris couture fashions. Old, some of them, but classic. I shall enjoy to see those.' Her smile ignored the smoke staining the sky, the intermittent explosions, the scream of sirens and car tyres.

'I won't let you go out again tonight,' he said strongly, not caring if she did get angry, 'if there's still fighting. Someone should check on her, of course; I've been feeling unhappy about that already,' (belated yet true) 'but if the streets aren't safe I'll go alone.'

She was already dressed to leave, in a pale green dress that darkened her hair and eyes. She swung the door gaily, like a toy on a string, while she argued. 'Listen, little one. Didn't I say I work late, as a singer? I shall arrange to leave early tonight for this visit,' – she spoke as if there could never be any problem about her getting whatever time off she demanded – 'but will be much later than when you finish work. I know these ambulance crews, they work long shifts sometimes but so many hours only. There is an enforced limit. So when you finish you will please go and make your apologies to your grandmother, then wait for me there. I shall arrive—'

He suspected she'd been about to say, 'When I'm fully ready.' He wouldn't put it past her. 'Go through the fighting and the Line by yourself? Absolutely not.' He stood naked in the bathroom doorway, not the best-clad for arguing, but her casualness made him furiously afraid for her. 'When you finish work, come back to the hotel, you hear me? And I'll be waiting; we'll go to Madeleine's together. I'll phone her beforehand so she'll be expecting us.'

To his amazement she broke down in giggles. 'I do enjoy you at times, so very crazy. "I'll phone" you say, as if this were any ordinary city. Where have you been living that you don't know our phones are often out of action for months at a time?' She came across the room and laid her small, thin fingers against his cheek. 'Sometimes I do enjoy you,' she said softly, 'not only laughing at you but when you insist at me I like that. We make a pair that fits together, don't we?' Swiftly she moved away, the door clicked; she was gone. His cheek where her fingers had touched it shivered like a separate afraid person.

By evening the violence had subsided to intermittent mutters (what Jameel called 'the-militias-have-gone-to-eat time') and Rick got back to his hotel not very late. Solange had been right about the phones. The telex machines in the lobby swarmed with foreign journalists thick as cockroaches, busy filing the day's disasters, but the private phone lines were out and his enquiry to the reception clerk when they'd likely be working again was met by a fatalistic shrug. Solange arrived at about ten. She wore a floaty yellow dress, yellow shoes, and it crossed his mind that he knew nothing about her life except for the nights. Where did she live regularly? And alone or with whom? And had she bought all these expensive-looking clothes on her singer's pay? Someday he planned to ask all these questions if she didn't tell him before that; if she stayed around he'd have the right.

The two of them made their way on foot through streets full of people shopping and stuffy air and the reek of cordite (all the taxis were busy, now that the violence had eased) to the museum checkpoint where a handful of militiamen stood around smoking or toying with their binoculars or gold chains.

Beyond the checkpoint, in East Beirut, people scurried to and from the shops too but there was more tension, as if the western half of the city were a sleeping monster which might at any time reach out toward the east with open jaws. Rick remembered his night-time walks along the Line in the previous months when there was no fighting. He didn't count himself imaginative but, although no one was firing or shelling there at present, the area had a hollow, apprehensive feel now. He led Solange (who was wide-eyed, excited and apparently completely fearless) through the ruined cinema and across the dusty rubble-strewn yards. 'Gran shouldn't stay here,' he said, 'it's insane. I'll have to persuade her . . .' The back door;

to his embarrassment he'd discovered he still had a key. He'd left in such a self-righteous rush that he'd forgotten to hand it back. Up the stairs, and so that she wouldn't be afraid he called, 'Gran? It's me.'

He'd forgotten how little and squinched she was, and yet in a way majestic. She stood on the landing looking down at him and said, 'Well. An unexpected honour.' Those few words were enough to make you uneasily aware who was boss and whose territory this house was. She wore a purple robe with some sort of gold scrollwork at neck and wrists, and she looked imperial. 'You fool,' she said with an odd roughness in her tone, 'I'd written you out of my life. I thought you were back in that safe stupid country where you belong.' But she stood aside and pushed open the living room door. Solange's hand squeezed his, not timid but excited, and the two of them went up the remaining stairs.

He let Madeleine's apparent fit of temper go past him; what was it to her whether he went or stayed? 'Sorry I didn't get in touch with you sooner,' he said. Solange's fingers gripped his imperatively and he added, 'A friend of mine. I hope you don't mind her visiting.'

In the living room, with its faint spicy smell which he'd never identified, Madeleine motioned them to a couple of the brown-and-yellow cut velvet chairs and settled herself in her big leather armchair. Beside her the table full of silver ornaments jangled when her irritable fingers touched it. 'What do you want?' she said. 'Won't they give you a passport to get out? But I've no influence with them.'

She could readily find his sore spots. 'I got fixed up,' he said, cautious because he'd not explained all that to Solange, nor where he'd been reared. She had concocted for herself a fantasy that he'd spent the war years safely holed up in some Cypriot or Turkish mountain villa as a result of his family's money and pull, and if she wanted to believe that fantasy it was okay by him. Safer for both of them than her knowing the truth. And (he told himself) no lying was involved; she'd constructed this story with no help from him, and he merely hadn't contradicted it. (On wakeful nights, while she slept peaceful beside him, he saw his silence on the subject as itself a sort of corruption, the beginning of an insidious slide in him who'd always been so prissily fussy for the truth, but in the daytime he didn't doubt that his omission was right and necessary.) 'No problem with the documents,' he said, 'only I, uh . . .'

'A new interest.' She gave Solange a swift examining look and Solange gave her one. He'd have liked to make clear to Madeleine that his feeling of a bond with the country, a stake in it and a wish to do something useful for it, had preceded his involvement with Solange, but he couldn't say so with Solange listening. So he let the ambiguity pass and added it to the other. Anyway, was truth so absolute? Rather it presented itself to him nowadays as a bunch of shifting brightly coloured facets, and if some of them wore the garish colours of Beirut's explosions – wasn't that what you must expect if you lived around here?

Solange leaned forward, her yellow dress swishing arrogant across the muted browns and golds of the velvet. She said boldly, 'You're just as I heard about you from my family. My grandmother – it's almost as if you and I had lived closely together all my life.'

'Ah. No doubt. There are friendships it's convenient to claim.' But Solange didn't flinch; instead she sparkled and her face, her tone, became wheedling or manipulative or defiant by turns. You couldn't, Rick told himself, blame a girl like her for posturing, you really couldn't, when you considered the conflicts, the hatred that she'd grown up among. He couldn't forget the effect the civil war had had on Pierre and Alexandre and others in the militia, and in a way the situation must be harder for girls because mostly they weren't allowed to take part in the fighting.

Solange spoke now with more animation than he'd ever heard in her, and Madeleine's answering voice thawed to enjoyment. They compared family trees, acquaintances from Madeleine's generation, houses and famous shops in the pre-war city. At last Madeleine said with a sigh, 'There's no definite tie of blood . . .' She sounded regretful.

'But,' said Solange, 'such a *close* friendship.' She flopped back in her chair and laughed, and Madeleine's lips twitched into a smile. His ignorance, his foreignness, had shut him out from their conversation. He put his arm around Solange to reassure himself that the physical bond between them still held, and Madeleine turned her attention to him.

'So you stayed on. And you've been slightly bloodied, no doubt – are you less shockable and self-righteous than you were? – but this bout of fighting has been minor, nothing like in previous years. I've watched; I have a wide overview from my window.'

He choked back the retort that if she'd been on the streets amid the blood and rubble her scale of measurement might rearrange itself. 'I've got a job,' he said. He hoped to God she wouldn't ask where he was living; he felt so ashamed of his monied comfort. Something had got to be done about that to salve his conscience, but he hadn't figured what, and Solange's presence complicated matters. For the first time he wondered how long she'd stay with him. The cool detachment of the question alarmed him, but you couldn't handle Solange's impulsive fluctuations any other way. Would she stay only while he offered her a luxurious lifestyle?

'A job,' Madeleine said, 'well. So that's what he's come rushing to tell us – he's so proud to have escaped the family's clutches. And what's the nature of this wonder-ful job?'

'Ambulance crew.' Then he thought she'd hit him.

But she controlled herself; only her voice was harsh with fury. 'You mad boy! Why the devil didn't you fly away and leave us to carve each other up? You had a chance of safety; why didn't you take it?' With a visible effort she sat back in her chair, her spine rigid but her fingers shaking. 'Did you have to come and boast to me about your idiocy? God knows Georges is rash enough and in enough danger, but at least he's got convictions. A strong commitment to one party and a sense of loyalty – he'd cheerfully die for those – but *you*? If I mentioned partisan loyalty or political convictions you'd spit in my face, wouldn't you?'

'Things aren't that simple.' He tried not to see the engrossed radiance of Solange's face. For her this quarrel must be an absorbing spectacle – how could you hope she'd respect family feelings when her own family had most likely been torn apart? – but he cared about staying on good terms with Madeleine; affection and respect struggled in him alongside frustration. He didn't want to alienate her for always. 'I can't explain,' he said. 'I could never find words that'd join you and me on this, Gran, and anyway I haven't made future plans. But for the time being that's the work I'm doing.' He tried to recapture the intimacy of the months when he'd lived in this house. 'Georges and Brigitte okay? And Seraphite?'

'Brigitte goes her own way – perhaps exaggeratedly so since you left, because she's sure of me.' (He let that one go past him: too deep, he couldn't figure it.) 'And Seraphite – at present she's still working here. With a face like all the funeral processions of the city, but if I asked her about that she'd be mortally insulted. Father Mesrop visited us a couple of days ago, more distracted and unholy than ever.' Then for the first time the fierce

certainty of her tone faltered. 'He and Georges . . . I don't
know what business they transact together. I don't ask
them.' Her chin nestled defiantly in the cup of the gold-
bordered collar. 'One hopes that a priest wouldn't . . .
but of course there's danger for all of them and . . .' Her
hooded old eyes, full of a guarded darkness, stared at
him.

'So you've seen Georges since the fighting restarted?'

'Of course, he's very faithful. Every day he visits me,
in or out of uniform.'

So he was fighting in the militia. Of course he would
be. Solange broke the tension by saying, while she gazed
with open covetousness at the hanging tapestry of a pale
lady in blue with unicorn and shrubbery, 'So beautiful –
I've heard for a long time about your treasures.'

'Ah.' Madeleine eyed her as a pirate guarding buried
treasure might eye an approaching boatload of muscled
types with shovels, then the two women burst out laughing. 'Where did you find her?' Madeleine asked him.
'She's an amusement.'

Fortunately she didn't wait for an answer. He'd have
politely fudged, of course, but he was beginning to
believe Solange had found him. There had certainly been
a moment when he'd taken the initiative and made a
decision, but the before and after now seemed equally
wrapped in her gaze, inevitable. Instead Solange said,
quickly following the compliment, 'Madame, you and I
have met before.'

'I'd have remembered.' Brusquely, as if Solange must
be lying. But to his surprise and Madeleine's obvious
pleasure, there was proof.

'My grandmother told me—'

'Yes, I did visit their country house once. The year
before the fighting started, they had a party – a delayed
christening perhaps, there was some infant around –
and in the summer weather their garden fluttered full of

butterflies. Then a stupid servant let the budgerigars loose from their cages in the salon. I remember this pretty infant was toddling along the garden path. One of the men had in fun dropped his hat over its head – much too large, of course, it covered the whole head – and a couple of metal studs on the hatband glittered in place of the child's eyes. The infant toddled shrieking in delight, and the butterflies and birds fluttered like coloured dress-maker scraps around it.' She looked suddenly ancient and shrunken. 'Soon afterwards God gave up making days like that. None of us were appreciating them.'

'Madame,' – Solange's fingers wound around each other in a rare gesture of confusion – 'I was that child. One person at least appreciated.'

After that the two women talked oblivious through the renewed poppings and explosions from outside; they recreated a world of palm trees and twisted old fig trunks and of cicadas that said Tssk-tssk in the luxuriant corners of the garden. Apparently for them that was the reality and these noises of violence, this wrecked city, were a scarcely noticeable interruption. The two of them were passionately travelling a path he couldn't follow.

22

Next day Solange said, 'That villa might still be empty.'

'What villa?' She had the evening off. They were spending it sprawled naked in the heat across his bed because his room wasn't more likely to get blown up than anywhere else, and the bar downstairs felt unsafe when the various militias wandered through it as they were that evening. He couldn't forget the circumstances of gunfire and death and desertion in which he'd met her.

He rubbed a hand across his eyes, which smarted from the day's smoke, and she said, 'You're tired.'

This was the first personal comment she'd ever made. Usually her own body, her wants and the immediate circumstances in which she moved, marked the limits of her attention. There was no point in wondering how much of this might be due to the war; you just accepted her as she was. When he'd asked whether she possessed close family, she'd said, 'None of your business,' with such raw sharpness that he suspected not mourning but a tangle of live relationships, brambles which she'd broken free of. So when she commented on his tiredness he had to guess that there might be more to the remark than simple concern. He reached across to put an arm round her and said, exploratory, 'It's dull for you up here. I'm sorry.' 'Dull' might seem an odd description of the sky which streamed with smoke and an occasional jet of tracer fire, but she would understand what he meant. Beirut-dull.

'Not dull,' – she sat up crisp and unreadable within the circle of his arm – 'but I was wondering about the villa.

Clean and . . . of course we'd need to travel in daily to work; that might be complicated.' He frowned, baffled – the day's bloodshed and sweat and grime had already overlaid the idyllic conversation between her and Madeleine – and she said with quick impatience, 'You must remember! The villa where your grandmother and I once met.'

'Oh, that villa.' The shine of happy anticipation on her face puzzled him. 'You mean if it's empty we might go and live there?' Beneath the layers of bodies and splintered beams and charred reinforcing-rods in his mind, something moved, something he hadn't thought about in quite a while. A notion of peacefulness and quiet living in a beautiful rural place, that was it. An old dream, dusty now like everything in Beirut, and its appeal had gotten entombed under the pressure of real hurting flesh and real stinks and each day's unending practical dilemmas. 'Fine for you,' he said, 'just right. You could give up your job and be safe there, and even Madeleine might—' But Solange was already scowling, they were on different wavelengths again.

'You stupid, of course she won't. She'll never leave her fancy hole beside the Line. And anyway . . .' She snuggled up to him and murmured, 'Just the two of us?' She gently bit his earlobe, then went on, 'My second cousin Jules owns the villa now, and if it's habitable I'm sure he'd rent it to us cheaply. A rich man's villa on the coast in Lebanon – who'd want that nowadays?' She eased herself from his arms, got up and strolled over to the window. 'No foreigners around any longer,' she said with satisfaction, 'they've scurried away to their burrows.' She turned, outlined like a pale stone monument against the smoky night sky. 'But of course I shall keep my job. In the country all the time I'd be bored to silliness.' She added casually, 'Except for necessary times, of course.'

'Necessary?' Did she consider lovemaking sessions

with him 'necessary', to be timed like boiling an egg? His mind slipped away from the pain of her casualness to chivvy at the problem of Madeleine. The previous evening, after their villa talk finished, he'd argued stormily with her about shifting her somewhere safer till the fighting eased, but no, she insisted on staying in that half-wrecked house, and virtually alone too. She would stay, visited briefly by Georges, waited on with something near to hatred by Seraphite, and mostly ignored by Brigitte. She'd stay and some day a bomb or shell would get her. And he'd feel partly responsible because he hadn't argued toughly enough, and very bereft.

The sky beyond Solange's head muttered into stillness, the columns of smoke died down and the pure night flowed back. As usual the street lights weren't working and battalions of stars invaded the jagged skyline. Solange laughed freely like a child and came back to him. 'See?' she said, cross-legged on the bed and running her silver-painted nail along his bare shoulder, 'the war cooperates, it always slows down when we have something important to discuss.'

'We have?' Again it surprised him – brief and cool and troubling – that this hummingbird creature hadn't yet flown away from him. He feinted past her scratching nail and twiddled one of her dark curls. 'If you'd really like to live in that villa—'

'Really I do – you've no idea how important, Ricki. When your grandmother spoke of it I thought, "Ah, the perfect place!" A lovely villa, a dream house. The furnishings all satins and silks and the garden a colourful jungle. It must be completely overgrown by now. Jules can't ask much money because no one would pay. Won't you easily afford his rent?'

He set aside his buried dream and the inconvenience of daily travel, and tried to consider the matter dispassionately. There'd be danger to the commuting and mightn't she be safer here? He could easily afford either the hotel or villa – or rather his inherited income could. And that was something else too: he still hankered after a simple life cut loose from the wealthy past, but circumstances and this city had snarled those ideals into complicated webs which caught at his feet; he couldn't any longer trace the single thread of them.

'What are you thinking?' Solange asked in astonishment. 'Such a busy face!'

He pulled her to him. 'That in another incarnation I might have been a friar happy to possess nothing and beg for my bread.'

'A *friar*?' She giggled under his hands. 'Ricki, you forget they must promise chastity.' But he'd already seen his wish as wholly pride. Whichever way he handled the giving away of wealth, he'd enjoy renouncing because that would make a big splash, a dramatic gesture, or at least make him feel good.

He gave up on the ethics temporarily and dropped into the simplicity of her happiness. 'Of course we'll ask about the villa if you'd like.'

'Ah,' she said (but she was remote now, a million miles away and no direction-posts up), 'what fun you and I are going to have!'

He insisted on conducting the negotiations with her second cousin Jules (a thinner version of Georges in appearance, and he insisted on meeting them in an unfurnished room in the basement of a half-ruined block of flats; it certainly wasn't wise to ask questions about people) but there would apparently be no formal lease, no contract signed. Jules said, 'You are family, Solange is my dearest little cousin,' and gave him a friendly clout on the shoulder. Yes, the villa had escaped damage and he would be delighted for them to use it. 'My great-uncle who owned it died two years ago—' and Solange, giggling, interrupted, 'Ricki, not that sympathetic griev-ing face of yours this time! He was eighty and died peaceful in his bed of a neglected hernia. You are so *funny*.' Rick got the scanty negotiations tied up as fast as possible and took her out of the basement before she could say anything else to draw attention to him.

With the men at work he rubbed along and felt pretty much at home. Their blood-and-guts days made a common interest and the talk mostly didn't extend far beyond that, especially when they were busy. But all his spare time was spent with her and during it he made mistakes constantly, tiny ones which he noticed too late and which her darting mind mostly hurtled past unnoticing. But some mistakes were bigger; they made him catch his breath as soon as he realised, and his heart thump. As when, after they left Jules and were walking back to the hotel along the cluttered alleys, she said, 'We'll need a little car to commute into the city. You drive, of course?'

Automatically he answered, 'Yes, but I haven't a local licence.'

She stopped abruptly, there on the street, and stared at him. 'Really, Ricki, where *have* you been living?' Then to his vast relief the irrepressible giggle took her again, as if she realised that this further idiocy fitted in with what she already knew of him. 'You and your Turkish mountain simplicities!' she said. 'How many drivers in Beirut do you suppose bother with a *licence*? My dear, surely you know that the issuing office only opens once in three months, to pay its staff? You'll be telling me next that you expect to pay taxes!'

Next day after he finished work they drove east and north, he at the wheel of a battered Volkswagen. The sky was for once undisturbed blue and quiet, but the traffic was, as always at this time of day, atrocious. He'd noticed already how in Beirut drivers ignored parking restrictions and such traffic lights as were still working, and they drove with one hand continually on the horn. But the honkings and screeches were bliss after some of the previous month's noises. At least this was a city going about its relatively lawful business.

Beyond the tower blocks of the city centre stretched acres of shantytowns with among them wide flat areas of rock and scrubby bushes. The low sun picked out the irregular stripes of yellowish-white dust which streaked the red rock. 'More war damage?' Rick said.

She trailed a hand from the car window in the cooling air. 'A slum area and so-called refugee camps. Every time I drink champagne I think of this place.'

'Champagne?'

'After the isolationists came in and shot everyone, they opened bottles of champagne to celebrate.'

'Dear God!'

'No,' she said absently, trailing her fingers in the cool air, 'that doesn't arise.'

'Madeleine still prays occasionally.' The rocks and scrubby bushes were behind them now, and more shantytowns ahead.

'No doubt your grandmother can order God around. That explains why her dear son has had good luck so far. Georges the isolationist, the militiaman Phalangist, is protected from above.'

'Were you really his girlfriend once?'

'Pfft!' She brought her hand in and examined the silver-tipped nails as if she'd never seen them before. Her eyes slid sideways at him and she said, 'One must amuse oneself somehow.' Her gaze stayed on him as if she were producing possible phrases like new clothes for his approval. 'I was a hanger-on, perhaps. The films, the sports, a dance once in a while . . . that was fine. I know nothing of the militia's other activities.'

With all her contacts across the city, naturally she would have heard the reason for his explosive opting-out. 'News travels,' he said.

'Darling, that's Beirut.'

He stopped for a red light and instantly beggars hopped or crawled toward the car. A man sawing wood in front of a house looked up and shook his head in wonder.

'Really,' she said, 'don't stop, it makes you look absurd. Do you see anyone else stopping?'

'No, but—' A gaggle of children pointed at him and jeered. He drove on.

He lost count of the number of slum areas and stretches of broken cement before the countryside began. Beirut lay bleeding for miles. Then suddenly the highway became a narrower road with less traffic; olive groves and citrus plantations lined it and his mind fell gratefully into their silver-green depths. He'd almost forgotten his question about Georges when she spoke again. 'Why not Georges?' she said. 'A girl must find pleasures.'

Palm trees and little flat-roofed houses and a white minaret sped past. He couldn't say, 'Georges is a killer,' because she would inevitably retort with some stock jargon about him being a soldier who was fighting in a good cause.

After a while she went on, 'I'm not just a good-time girl.' She pronounced the silly phrase carefully, in English, like handling a saint's bones in a reliquary. She smiled at him – a smile that seemed like total purity. The little town had gone. To the left of the road waves splashed on amber sand and the sun fell like an exhausted fireball. She began to talk about the villa – its beauties, its possible shortcomings – and kept on in a high voice, not letting him get a word in, till they arrived.

Dusk showed only a white curving stone entrance, then a

white mass with balconies, ironwork, a flat roof, the whole surrounded by a thicket of intertwined branches and weeds. He went from room to room flinging windows open and the mustiness of years sifted out, the salt air in. The scent of roses drifted up from the garden, and rank weedy smells. Far to the east the mountain tops lay scarlet in the sun's last rays.

The next three weeks stayed in his mind as a dream, scented like the expensive perfumes of which Solange had an unending supply, a dream brilliantly and variously coloured like the birds that had flown around her infant head. From the first day the two of them developed a routine: drive to the city after breakfast so he could start work – she'd spend the morning with some girl-friend – then when his duty ended in the evening he'd shop for the next day's food and go along to her night-club. At a secluded table he'd nurse a glass of the wine or brandy which he, like Madeleine, preferred to 'araq, while Solange sang from the stage or worked the other tables. As soon as her act finished they drove back to the villa, she drowsy against his shoulder and he happy, at ease. And even the war cooperated, because their commuting really wouldn't have been practical if the level of violence had stayed high. Instead relative peace now engulfed the city.

The villa with its silver surround of olive trees was enclosed like an iridescent bubble, and Solange's body fitted perfectly with his every night. True, the villa was large, a massive pile of whitened stone, but its flaking paintwork and general dilapidation, the simplicity of their makeshift kitchen and bathroom arrangements, and the well still usable in the back yard, made it oddly unpretentious and touching. In the late evenings they sat on the terrace in the sun's afterglow with a flight of outside steps swirling down from the floor above. On his free days he worked in the garden, attacking the clawing vines and branches with hacksaw and spade and sensing behind them his old dream of a Washington State holding, and the dry heat of summer helped by shrivelling whatever he cut off. So that soon there were places where through a gap between ilex and struggling roses, or lemon tree and almond, you could glimpse the olive groves like tossed mercury and beyond them the highway with its coloured specks of traffic, the amber beach, the Mediterranean. Love for the house and garden grew in his heart like a tropical seed, as if he'd turned away and when he glanced again the plant had overflowed the pot; he was engulfed.

His happiness persisted until, at the end of the third week . . . 'Impossible,' said Solange in the sharp, dismissive tone she had used several times lately, and which puzzled and perturbed him, 'to get your attention when you're here. You're worse than any dull old peasant.' Her empty glass clinked on the table – was it for the third or fourth time that evening? (He'd discovered that she often took largeish doses of tranquillisers too, bought over-the-counter without limit, but she'd retorted, 'Darling, so does all Beirut.')

He said apologetically, 'I'm listening,' and turned his back on the octopus-fishing boats which were travelling along the shoreline in the dusk. She picked up the 'araq bottle, poured herself another sloshing glassful and glared at him.

'So I drink plenty,' she said. 'So I'm taking happy pills. But obviously I take them because I'm nervous, and what if I've good reason to be?' The 'araq in her glass caught the last of the light as she gulped it. 'More reason than you with your petty worries and pleasures could ever imagine. What if I'm pregnant?'

23

Into his blank mind clichés arrived and were spoken, but she spiked them one by one; none of the scenarios that emerged was likely or predictable. 'No,' she said, 'you're not the father. Yes, I'm sure of that; how could you have fertilised me two months before we met?'

'You already *knew*?' In the darkness of the terrace, inside his mind, a blaze began, as if her admission were a torch which charred to death all their past happiness and lit this raging anger in him. His sudden capacity for fury astounded and terrified him, but he had to let it run free. 'You already *knew*, when we first slept together?'

'Darling,' less assured, faintly uneasy, 'I never claimed to be celibate.'

But she'd already known about the pregnancy in those early days when they looked forward exuberantly to each hour they'd spend together? 'When we visited Jules and arranged to rent this place – so peaceful here and we'd be alone and could enjoy the time ahead – you *knew* already?'

'Jealous of a baby?' Uneasiness was palpable in her fingers which sought his across the darkened table, and when they found his hand played on it lightly like a musical instrument, as if she believed she still had the power to play on his emotions.

'Not jealous,' – how could you be jealous of an unborn child, and especially one carried by this most casual mother and fathered by God knows who? – 'but you talked – you acted as if—' As if he'd been the only real one in years, that was how. As if she cared about him the way he'd cared about Josie. Solange had talked as if she looked forward to a future they'd share, and she'd certainly given no hint that she was pregnant by another man. Josie and he had discussed their future together and there'd been no sign of any problem until suddenly the issue of his wealth broke his hopes and their plans apart. Had Solange taken up with him only because of his money, too? Did she think he'd be her protector temporarily until she sorted out the problem of the baby, and until then only? How soon was she, like Josie, planning to move on to somebody else, and had she never cared about Rick at all?

'Why shouldn't I go with you?' she shouted. They were leaning at one another across the table in the dark. 'Why shouldn't I take whatever you're ready to give me? You can afford to spend plenty on me. Did I promise to bear no one's kids except yours?'

No, in fairness she never had. Rick tried, not very successfully, to get his mind around the idea that some man she'd relied on had gotten her into this position and then ratted out on her. She always gave the impression of being so competently in charge of her life; but could that be a cover for her real problems? He tried to put himself in her position: pregnancy, when you had no one to help or support the baby, was an unhappy state to be in. Especially when you lived in Beirut.

She cut these thoughts away from their anchor with her next words, and he decided he'd never understood her at all. 'No abortion,' she said, 'not this time.' She sat down and her voice now was as coolly resolute as the cold well water. 'This time I'll at least bear the child and find out what it looks like.' Her handbag clicked open and Rick smelled the fragrance of her lipstick. In the dark she made up her mouth, and her murmur, 'And then . . .' came from between pursed lips. 'I do apologise,' she said, abstracted, putting the lipstick away, 'if you feel you've been used. Truly I like you, Ricki – and haven't we had fun together?'

Yes, they had. That helped to fuel his anger. He said, hopeless, meaningless, 'If you'd told me at the beginning—'

She let fall a trickle of genuine-sounding laughter. 'What a start to a relationship!'

True, with the first words they'd exchanged, that evening in the hotel, he'd noticed her steely gaze and warned himself not to ask questions of her because she would tell him nothing until she was ready to. Hadn't he told himself that he didn't care what secrets her past might hold (that past which she would never talk to him about), and that he overwhelmingly wanted to protect her in the future? Her honesty about her longing for money had amused and delighted him, but hadn't he tacitly agreed to let her secrets stay hidden? So the two of them had planned their daily life together, and the villa, but her past had stayed hidden from him – until now. 'And this villa—' he said, but she broke in to answer; in some ways their thoughts did chime together.

'I didn't make plans that first night; they came to me bit by bit. And the visit to your grandmother suggested . . . I decided this would be a pleasant place to wait.' She added – in the same calm tone, which made it sound as calculating as all the rest – 'And I supposed you would be kind.'

He had to take her into his arms then, from an impulse of pity, because there was after all a possibility that she had genuinely looked to him for help. He gazed over her bent head into the dark and remembered the tiny brothers or sisters of his high-school friends, how they'd had every advantage of birth and upbringing. What would the child of this drifting and secretive mother, in this ruined city, be like? She moved in his arms and again answered the practical question he'd not asked.

'The father? Darling, I can guarantee he won't take any interest or make a claim. How could he?'

'Because you won't tell him?'

'Because I don't know who he is. Really, you can take your pick.' She gently bit his earlobe, then assured him – in that voice so coolly self-confident that he couldn't at all read what lay behind it – that she didn't intend to keep the child.

'But if you'd like to—'

The lights of the octopus fishermen had disappeared behind a rocky outcrop. In the dark she was shaking her head. 'No question. A girlfriend of mine wants children and can't have, so I shall give to her. That's all arranged.'

And perhaps, he thought, she was wise to do this. Anyway, a generous impulse.

Yet, in the weeks that followed, their quiet life fissured into a million cracks, all on account of her restlessness. She spent an increasing amount of time in the city, staying at night with one or another of her nameless girlfriends, and when he suggested she leave a note of the address in case he needed to contact her, she said, 'Darling, not your affair. You don't need to know.' When the pregnancy started to show, she wore her usual tight dresses over a barbaric corset such as some old peasant crone might wear. She shouted at him that she didn't intend to show till the damn kid spilled out of her, and she'd work till then too; she'd go crazy without the people at work.

He said, 'You'll never keep it secret till the last minute,' and she turned on him with stories of various girlfriends – those unnamed laughing creatures like herself, in their pale expensive dresses – who'd done that very thing. He got the impression from her brisk chatter that her girl-friends, married or single, arranged the world to suit themselves with an adroitness he'd never encountered before. Josie and he, when they'd argued and made up and clumsily hurt each other in the Seattle era, had been childish by comparison. When she was away the villa life became hollow, a series of chores and necessities which were pointless because she wasn't there. The peasant simplicity of the life became an irritant, not a pleasure, because it was empty of people other than himself. After the baby was born Solange might be happy to live there, but he doubted it; most likely there'd need to be a major rearranging.

On evenings when she worked or stayed with friends, he occasionally visited Madeleine. He'd go there once or twice a week, not more often; so when a note from her was brought to him at the end of his shift, the day before he'd planned to visit, he hurried to change his clothes and go; Madeleine had never asked him for anything before. 'Is she ill?' he asked the taxi driver who'd brought the message, but the man shook his head and gave the happy, careless laugh of so many Lebanese.

'A sprightly old woman, eh?' The gold-filled teeth flashed, the brown neck was thrown back in mirth. 'No, lively as ever, only she say you come quick as soon as you finish work. She say there is a job she need you to do.'

24

But when he arrived I had trouble getting to the point. I'd forgotten how young he is, how open-faced; the errand I have for him made me nervous. But I told myself not to be silly; there could be no real danger to him. He's no longer the dangerously naive innocent who arrived early this year: since then he's travelled the city and seen plenty of the men of at least one militia, while in his recent ambulance work he must have mingled with all types of people. Not perhaps a true Beiruti yet, but he's had experience. No, there can be no danger – and what I'm asking of him is no more than many others have needed to do.

First I poked around, asking about the details of his life with the girl, and he answered politely, managed not to tell me to mind my own business.

She's pregnant (he says, after my poking), been so for months. Well, that's the news you'd expect of her. She and I connected in friendship that evening like the two halves of one fruit; we recognised our likeness, but that doesn't mean I approve of her for him, any more than I'd approve of myself when young, or of Brigitte.

'You're the father or not?' He shifts in his chair at my brutality, but we might as well be honest. No, he says, according to the date the girl gives there's no chance. 'You've no idea who is?' None of his business, he says with an unconvincing shrug. Clearly this stings and yet he won't back out. 'You're a fool.' Yet probably he realises that too. And there's something else connected with the pregnancy, some defensiveness in his eyes . . . 'She's played around?' But of course she would have.

He says firmly, 'None of your business, Gran, any more than it's mine. And the father could be dead. Or maybe not, I'm only guessing, but . . .' He picks a handful of cardamom seeds from a dish and nibbles them (we'll make him Lebanese yet). 'While she's happy to stay with me,' he says, 'I'll let things ride.'

Yes, a fool emotionally, but a kindly one, and not as shapeless-dispositioned as he was. This ambulance work – which I hate for him because it puts him among all the perils – has toughened his jaw and put new lines at the corners of his mouth. 'You could find quieter work,' I say, 'out there in the countryside.'

'Oh no, I plan to keep my job in the city. That's important to me.' And his jawline tightens more; he looks a bit like Georges in his mildest mood. No doubt the boy feels *needed* in this work – a cruel and massive delusion; muscles are cheap in Beirut and one set of muscles, one mind, can push and tug and plan as well as another. Fodder, all of them. 'She'll go on working too,' he says, 'she claims she'd go stir-crazy out there at the villa all day.'

'Yes.' That lithe body and smooth skin and mass of dark hair were created, by a fine-tuned evolution from generations of beautiful women, toward one purpose only, and it wasn't to cook and clean in a country villa or even to sing *chanteuse* lyrics in that tiny breathless voice. Doesn't he realise this? But he flushes duskier; he's not as stupid as I guessed and I suddenly am sorry for him.

He says, 'I can read what you're thinking. But this is my choice and I've made it. If I said "Forget it" she'd move back into the city. She grinned when she told me that, like having no home and no guy is fun and she wouldn't mind starting over. But at times she enjoys the villa, wants to be there. And I'm willing.'

His attempt at a scowl makes him resemble Georges more than ever. Georges in a good mood, with the flaming anger and passion calmed down and only firmness left, Georges as he might have been if the fanatical thread which runs through our family had missed him as it missed placid Helene. Georges my dear child, my wrecker. The boy stares at me; he gets up, hurries across the living room and puts an arm around my shoulders. 'What's the matter?' he says. 'Gran, what's wrong?'

The spurt of relief at his question is the lancing of an abscess, so I tell him my news. 'Georges is missing.'

Georges hasn't – perhaps I'm foolish to worry, but he hasn't been here for eight days. 'And even when there's hard fighting he rarely misses. Every other day at least. So I went to his shop and he wasn't there—'

He hugs me like relief. 'Is that all? He'll have closed up shop temporarily because he's busy with the militia. What else would you expect, Gran? You know how Georges—'

'Listen to me. Not there, and no jewellery but another man, turning it into a different sort of shop altogether. Pharmacy with chic sex articles. I said, Where's my son? Where's Georges? And the man looked sly, greedy, not afraid. He claimed he'd taken over. A change in the lease. But that lease had four more years to run and the landlord is a stepbrother of my late husband's. He would never make trouble for Georges or try to throw him out prematurely. Moreover he couldn't; I made sure they had a written contract drawn up, and I went with Georges to witness his signing it. No one else could take over except in case of . . . That man made me so angry. There must be some redress. And he wouldn't tell me anything about Georges.' No tears, not even for the possible 'except': I've never been an easily weeping type, I burn rather. That lit fanatical thread again. No tears, but I'll smash the world apart to find my son.

Rick holds me at arm's length and stares into my face. 'You're afraid he – oh, but surely that's crazy, Gran. Maybe Georges just decided to give up the shop. I'm sure you don't need worry about some guy busting the lease.'

'But he hasn't visited me. I know my son through and through. You think we're obsessed with our ancestry? Georges has a love for me as obsessional as any of his political or military ties. All the years since he left home he's visited me almost every day. I've teased him about it but I could feel how his affection pushed him to visit, and that made me proud. And now *eight days?*'

'Okay, we'll assume he might have been slightly wounded – in a minor skirmish, because there hasn't been any serious fighting lately – and holed up somewhere to recover. The phones aren't the most reliable; maybe he couldn't let you know. Surely it couldn't be any worse than that? With all these damn contacts of yours and his, you'd have heard. I can't believe you wouldn't.'

'I've asked.' Illogically that necklace of contorted freshwater pearls jumps into my head, and my mind calmly asks, what happened to all his stock? They wouldn't throw it in the grave with his body. 'All the militiamen I've been able to contact claim to know nothing. But there's a silence among them. When I asked to speak with the man who's been Georges' immediate commander, he couldn't be produced either. And not hiding, I'm sure of that from the parallel enquiries Brigitte has made. Not hiding but disappeared.'

'Brigitte's worried, too?' He frowns; his clear young foreign face isn't suited to messy problems like this.

'She's frantic. Hysterical. I've never seen her so upset.'

He's startled by all this but not, I think, afraid; thank God he isn't. He leans forward, chin propped on fist and face earnest. 'So you want me to look around for him? I cover quite a bit of the city in my job, and of course I know guys in the other crews too. You want me to ask around, Gran?'

For an instant my reluctance to involve him recurs, but surely that's ridiculous. He has no major responsibility for the girl at present. I can read between his words and she's obviously spending more time elsewhere than with him. And the streets are quiet; moreover he now looks and sounds like a Lebanese. He no doubt – damn him – speaks fluent Arabic too. Surely this errand can't involve danger for him. And I *must* find out, can't live without doing so, yet there are so many people I can't personally make enquiries of and places I can't reach. For these he'll be invaluable. Surely there'll be no risk to him. So, 'Yes, that's what I want.'

He scrunches his chair close. He's sober about this but eager, ready to start. He asks me who I've enquired of and notes down their names; no point in duplicating. 'And,' I say, 'I've searched along this part of the Line without result, but of course there are other areas—'

'You've – are you crazy?'

'What would a sentry's bullet aimed at me matter?' I say, and mean it.

'Hell,' he says, 'no way you'll keep on doing that. At night too?' I nod. 'I'll make all the enquiries for both of us in future. So listen, Gran—'

Thus we sort our arrangements. Certainly he's eager to take responsibility but it's difficult to estimate his strength. I assure myself again that I wouldn't ask this of him if it meant putting him into danger. (The girl would undoubtedly manage very well without him but, although life runs cheap in Beirut, he's different, special. I have no intention of putting his life at risk.) He'll ask around discreetly in the course of his duties and perhaps in his spare time too. Some ambulance crew is as likely as anyone to have hard information about what's happened to a missing man and where the incidents – even minor ones – have been. I lend him a photo of Georges to show around. On the doorstep we listen to the city's brooding silence and I say, 'Go carefully.' I don't say, Go with God, because Father Mesrop hasn't visited for a while either and what with one spurt of hatred and another I'm feeling distinctly unshriven. I detain Rick with a hand on his arm and ask the final question, 'These colleagues of yours – your driver and the other ambulance crews – they're mostly Arabs, aren't they?'

'I'll use good sense,' he says, but his face holds a defiance too, addressed to whatever else I might mean.

'Human blood is blood,' I say, 'and no doubt those men do noble work in picking up the fragments. But if I find someone has killed Georges, I shall do a personal assassination of my own.' He looks disbelieving but I mean it. I walk with a stick lately but still travel on my own feet, and my hands may be elderly claws but they've strength enough to hold a knife or gun . . . and who would suspect an old woman? If he finds out something definite, I've a vendetta to pursue.

25

The army sentries, and stragglers from various militias who at present wander the Line know me well by now. They've obviously decided I'm insane, an old woman who hobbles among the ruins muttering, and I'm happy they should believe that; it's a safe status, almost cosy. Despite Rick's orders I don't stop my systematic combing of the Line – one night I dreamed Georges was lying dead in one of those buildings, but of course he's not, he must be alive – though I do take certain precautions. As I have done from the beginning, only Rick didn't give me time to say so.

And the precautions might sound hollow to him. I don't go out if I hear any shots fired nearby. I search mostly at night, when a lone human is almost as hard to spot as the rats and padding wild dogs, and I keep to one segment of the Line at a time, so that I come to know its risks and possibilities. In this way, by sections sliced like the rind of a rotted fruit, I'm gradually covering all the Line within walking distance. (My dream about Georges wasn't specific as to area, and I wouldn't believe its limits if it were.)

Those roofless half-walled buildings have a quality I couldn't share with clean and hygienic Rick, no matter how wide his experience of picking up discarded bits of bodies and mopping blood. Sometimes when he and the girl visit (that tough little creature who is so unsuited to him and so amusing, so comradely, for myself) I long to ask his tired eyes and bruised hands, You believe your work is the messiest part of life in this city? Take a tour with me along the fourteen-year-old ruins and you'll learn different. Those ruins have, these past days, been a revelation to me. At least the blood he handles is freshly spurting, the breath if it's absent has only just gone, there haven't been many minutes since the flesh lived. But this . . . fourteen years of on-and-off fighting have left grimed-in blood and other fluids long since unclassifiable – but, dear God! The slime, the stink! Mostly I don't enter the buildings but call through some opening. I'd dare anything to find Georges alive and needing me, but if I found him and the ruin collapsed on both of us, then I'd have failed him. If he's alive somewhere, if he's not dead or in irreparable coma, he'll hear my voice and answer. Then I'll plan in detail how to rescue him. So, night after night, I call softly amid the unlit silence and the occasional mid-distance crackles of rifle fire. The dogs and cats of those buildings are permanently tense too, so we're all feral together. And, night after night, Georges doesn't reply.

During the next weeks Rick visits me often in the midst of his own quiet search; like myself he's having no success. Not a whisper, he says, but there are areas he hasn't covered yet, crews he hasn't yet spoken with . . . So he plods on.

And when he brings the girl we talk about other matters. He asks kind questions and makes gentle comments and she chimes in, and I automatically make suitable answers. Unimportant, useless chatter, but he means well. Only with *her* – this wildly unsuitable and non-caring girl toward whom I feel such kinship – do I find moments of honesty and grim humour and a sense that both she and I are vividly, vigorously, terribly alive. For example: Rick gives an idyllic description of the villa (he doesn't mention the daily journey which must be a dusty nuisance even in these relatively calm times) and she beside him says quietly, with a devil that I understand and love in her face, 'Scorpions.' Well, he says, yes, but if you leave them be, stay away from their haunts. Etcetera. The cicadas, she says, take chainsaws to our ears at night. Cicadas are harmless, he says hastily (grinning yet bemused; he's catching the drift of our game but it's not one native to him). Spiders, she says with a wide ferocious smile I could take her in my arms for, the size of them! Yeeaaghh! He says, Wait a minute, I thought you liked the place once in a while too? ('Mostly not poisonous,' he dismisses the spiders as an afterthought.)

'You should try nights with tropical birds,' I tell her, 'much more restful.' The cicadas bothered me too whenever Michel and I slept at the country villa; they never kept him awake but myself . . . Whereas tropical night noises, in whatever part of the world, lulled me and never disturbed. Come to think of it, that divergence probably means something that I didn't at the time want to face, about marriage and Michel. We were happy most of the time, but it was so calm a pleasure that in retrospect it feels more like unhappiness. This, or some other vagrant thought, makes me brutally direct with Solange when on one unique night she comes alone to visit me (there's a local disturbance further down the Line, in Chiah, and Rick is working late). I'm glad of this opportunity for frankness and at once attack her. 'Haven't you any consideration for him? We all know by now that I'll be fine here. Too old and tough to get killed. But you – didn't he tell you not to wander the city alone tonight?'

She leans forward and picks an apricot from my fruit dish, bites into it and lets the juice run down her chin like an infant. She chews and her sly eyes regard me. 'Yes, he forbade me,' she says, 'said if I didn't stay safely at the Instant Chicken till he's finished work, he'll never speak to me again.'

'You're worrying him by doing this; doesn't that

bother you?' Of course she shrugs, she laughs at me from behind her part-apricot. (The Instant Chicken, outlandish name of that restaurant-cum-nightclub where she sings.) 'This baby,' I say briskly, because I came in halfway through the situation and there are questions I've longed to ask, 'surely you have some idea who's the father?'

She shrugs again, a generous expansive movement whose meaning is clear.

'Rick isn't that sort of person,' I say, 'you shouldn't have let him involve himself.'

She takes the messy apricot stone from her mouth and deliberately drops it to the middle of my pale grey Chinese silk rug; Georges' masculine spitting on a rug that could easily be cleaned was another matter entirely. But I've deserved this; never offer such advice, old woman, especially to such as her. 'He insisted,' she says, and the wide, undefeated smile, the triumphant stare . . . Can there be anything this one's afraid of, anything she wants and doubts whether she'll ever get? I think not.

'But afterwards?' I say, and she shrugs stronger. The future is a realm we have no business peeping into. Meddlers, all of us.

'There'll be opportunities,' she says, and I visualise her drifting, picking at whatever − whoever − she casually chooses. In a way she almost reminds me of Brigitte except that this one has vastly more stamina, needs no props; whereas poor Brigitte has apparently always been searching for attention. Plucking at a succession of men and, when I've been available, at myself, and − it seems deeply − at Georges.

'You're fortunate,' I say, 'but other people may not be able to cut their affections loose as easily.'

'You don't understand, old woman.' From her I can accept the adjective as simple truth.

My other question (because no female has ever

sounded as unmaternal as she): 'Didn't you consider abortion?'

'Not this time. I was curious to see who this one looks like.' She picks out a purple fig, almost overripe, considers it, puts it back. She eyes me sideways and giggles like a schoolgirl. 'Blast you, you're not shocked,' she says.

No, it would take much more than that. 'Your reason seems adequate.'

She reaches for the fig again, deliberately scores her thumbnail through the purple flesh and sets the scarred fruit back on top of the pile. 'And there's another reason,' she says slowly, staring at the apricot stone she'd dropped on the rug. 'I can tell you, because you're not sentimental.' She pulls a cigarette case from her handbag and makes an elaborate performance of lighting one. She's aware I detest the smoke, but her action now seems absent-minded.

'Surely there's not a sentimental cell in your body either.'

She snaps her lighter shut on the tiny wavering flame. 'No,' she says, 'I didn't think there was.' I wait; she fidgets with the cigarette, then with the gilt chain of her handbag. Finally she begins.

A dream, she says, a few nights after the pregnancy had been confirmed. About a kitten ('I don't even like cats,' she says, bewildered) which was crouching on the hood of a car when she walked to work one afternoon. An afternoon, in her dream, of spring sun and showers and prickling half-distant noises of violence. She felt an urge to remove the animal from the car, to carry it along the street and put it down some distance away, but she did nothing, she left the kitten crouching there. Not a tiny kitten but half-grown, vixenish, tricky, skittishly attacking green leaves which were still falling on the car from some hours-earlier incident. If she'd touched the animal it might have clawed her. Definitely not a beautiful or appealing kitten.

At this moment I'm old and slow; her jittery voice and hands baffle me. 'But why—' Why did the dream make such an impression? All at once her face loses its careful, sophisticated control; it opens up and becomes the lovely peaceable meditative face it was born to be. 'Safe on a *car hood*,' she says, 'in *Beirut*?'

Then she bends down, picks up the fruit-stone and silk rug together, carries them away and next day brings the rug back, exquisitely cleaned. The scarred fig I eat myself and smile over it.

The summer heat starts to moderate, to shade into November, and the violence trickles along – only at a low level, but it persists. This time we can't, even temporarily, get rid of it. The girl looks radiantly healthy, and Rick . . . he's no boy any longer; it becomes apparent that these past months have toughened something in him. His face is thin and he's a brusque tone no matter who he's talking with, a quick superficial grin at jokes. A necessary toughening, no doubt, the approach to adulthood, but its hardening effect makes me sad. I ask myself, Have we – has Beirut – done this to him? And of course the answer is yes.

He continues his surreptitious enquiries about Georges (the process has taken a month so far but seems interminable) and visits me often, with or without the girl. He worries about me, he'd like to reassure me. In order to avoid voicing my permanent torment about Georges we talk about generalities – the generalities of Beirut, naturally. A certainty has seared itself into my brain during these fourteen years that what is happening to us Beirutis, and to this our city, is so frightful that it demolishes any prospect of a co-existent normal life. 'Normal' in the sense of the ordinary events he's talking about.

'Look, Gran.' He leans forward earnestly but I still plan to disbelieve him. How could it be any other way? This thing has gone on so many years, and lots of people have gotten killed and others moved away, but aren't there still folks around, buying food and clothes and going to and from work in between the bouts of shelling? Have you never seen a kid with a Kalashnikov slung on his shoulder and he's got a bunch of checkers in his hand, and is frowning over them like any other kid? Hell, he *is* any other kid.' He pauses, breathless. 'In the inhabited parts of the city there's living as well as dying,' he says, 'like weeds from under paving stones there's games and energies and births pushing themselves up.'

And I remember from months ago how Georges told me the same, how he urged me to get out more and see for myself. Well, I got out more, and the result is that I'm sitting in this room again listening to the intermittent crackle of rifle fire and sputter of grenades. And Georges – so much more optimistic than me, so much more involved with the city's life as well as with its death – is missing.

On their next visit, a week later, Rick tells me tersely while Solange is in the bathroom that he's explored every channel he can to find news of Georges, with no result. 'I'm truly sorry,' he says, 'Gran, but I guess we have to assume—'

I'll assume no such thing, and I tell him so. No one can convince me of what might have happened unless they bring proof.

'But,' he says as Solange's steps return, 'there's no one else I've got contact with that I can ask, nowhere else I can look.' He chews his lip; at least he feels for me. 'In a battle—'

I stop those words on his tongue. I'll act and look like a crazy woman perhaps, but I'll search the battlefields of

26

'You'll kill yourself brooding,' says Seraphite, while she grills eggplant slices for our salad. She sets the eggplant aside to cool and resumes her pounding of chickpeas for a hummus; the chickpeas she hasn't yet crushed have tiny pallid faces like fragments of flesh. (Yes, that's morbid, but in Beirut we've a right.) 'What's the use?' she says, and again I wonder what procession of mournings she's suffered which she'll never mention to me, what special bitterness perhaps, comparable with mine over Georges. Or is she lucky in knowing that all her casualties are dead – no missing torments?

'You needn't keep working in this house,' I say, 'no one's forcing you.'

The chickpeas are all crushed, their faces disintegrated; she's pounding garlic into them and chopping mint. At my remark she pounds harder.

I say, 'You can walk out right now. I'm ordering you to.' Self-pity isn't a luxury here; at times it's bread and water. I saw refugees struggling from those camps that had been massacred, and I *know*.

'Oh, Madame . . .' Meaning, 'You useless . . .' This formal title, to which my mother like a religion trained all her maids and I trained Seraphite, reminds me of another disappeared person.

'Father Mesrop,' I say, 'how long since—'

'A couple of days before your son's shop changed hands, Madame.' An answer of such startling precision, from her who's so constantly evasive, that it sends my fingers out to grip the collar of her dress.

'You would tell me,' I say, 'if—'

But a *something* in her face terribly like pity, like a painful comradeship, loosens my fingers. She resumes her pounding. 'Yes,' she says, 'I hate everything your son stood for, but if I'd heard anything definite about him I would tell you. As for the priest, he used to wander the city. I picked that item of news up in the bazaar.'

I brush the priest aside and fiercely correct, '*Stands* for – unless you really have heard something.'

She lays aside her pestle and says, 'You trust no one, do you? Not even that boy who's been searching the city on your behalf. Madame, did you never consider the danger to him in doing this? He may dress and sound like a Beiruti, but how much does he understand of our tribes, our politics? Is he smart enough to know who he can safely question about Georges and who he should stay away from?'

Yes, the struggling voice of my own conscience has pleaded this point too, but I've already argued at it that surely the boy must have acquired street sense along with all the externals. Argued and won the argument. So now I say without heat, 'You always exaggerate.' I lean across the table to steal a mint sprig and chew on it.

Her implacable face, as resolute as is my determination to find Georges, confronts me.

'You needn't worry,' I say bitterly, 'his enquiries have finished; he's still safe and he's found out nothing.' The mint sprig tastes harsh. I throw it into the sink and say, 'If you put any more sesame into that hummus it'll be too much. Haven't you any sense of taste?'

She answers calmly, mixing and pounding, 'I've been tempted to throw this basin in your face many times, Madame.' For all her 'Madame', I probably couldn't endure any maid who was totally respectful. Into our fragile intimacy I probe, trying not to sound desperate.

'Did the priest really disappear about the same time?'

'So I've heard, Madame.' Lemon juice and olive oil follow each other drop by drop into the hummus. She really is an excellent cook but it wouldn't do to tell her so. Keep them in their place, my mother always said, though I doubt whether that 'place' would be the same for my mother as for me.

'Disappeared to where?'

She covers the bowl of hummus with a cloth and stands it on the windowsill to cool. 'Disappeared is disappeared, Madame. Gone, vanished.'

'Gone . . . you mean gone out of the city for safety perhaps, not dead?'

Despite myself I can't keep the tremor out of my voice. The rough brushing of her warm, bare arm against mine, as she returns from the windowsill, might in another existence have been meant as a caress. She answers my unanswerable question, 'How should I know, Madame?'

When the hummus is cool we eat lunch, and the eggplant salad is good, although to me it tastes slightly over-grilled – a smoky tang which perhaps is merely from its surroundings. A series of rocket-bursts during the previous night, and various bangs and poppings during the morning, persuade us that the level of violence is rising again.

After lunch Seraphite piles dishes and I go up to my room, officially to rest; lately this is immutable also because I've had no heart for making casual shopping excursions along West Beirut's glitzed-up streets. I'd see the ghost of Georges' jewels everywhere. So I lie on my bed in the warm half-light; on the other side of the shutter some bird almost as attached to the Line as myself screeches, and the words form in my head, 'Georges can't be dead.' Not because I couldn't face his death – I can bully myself into facing whatever I must if there's no alternative – but because a possible alternative, so far an unexplored one, presents itself: Seraphite blindly suggested it when she said Gone, disappeared, vanished. As, not a corpse, but a removing by the person himself. A running away to hide.

That hummus has left a difficult, unblended aftertaste – essence of bitterness, as if the lemon juice rises up and shrieks at me – and I can't rest. I get up, ease back the shutter and regard the charred but currently empty Line.

So Georges disappeared, and Father Mesrop at the same time. My knowledge of a connection between them gathers itself up and streams away from me like a pack of wild dogs through the ruined buildings. But if they were in serious trouble, the sort that would require a long hiding period, the city itself wouldn't be safe enough; they'd need to go further. Then where . . . ?

The obvious possibility arrives and at once I dismiss it: no, he wouldn't go as far as the mountains without getting word to me. The umbilical cord may be under stress but it still tugs for both of us and I'm certain that for a long absence, a long way off, he'd let me know. Would tell me first or as soon as he arrived there and got settled. The mountains are full of Phalangists and he's had plenty of time. So I don't believe it's the mountains.

Then where? The blue sky, with puffs of dark smoke rising absurdly into it like signs of a stalled antique train, gives me no help. Nor do the blackened half-buildings, nor the clear warm sun. The sun . . . yes, we used to follow the sun and enjoy days of pleasure outside the city. Not the beaches – too obvious, and anyway full of all the militias. Not probably a rural villa like Rick's – too much chance of whispering by the locals. Somewhere Georges could be safe, unnoticed, if in a crowd then a busy self-absorbed crowd, busy or too glutted with other satisfactions to notice or care. A safe place . . . but where could he safely hide from the assassins who populate all our Beirut tribes?

Suddenly I remember: Summerland.

27

Yes, I'll visit Summerland as soon as possible. Rick can drive me there in the car he bought when he and the girl moved into that villa. The various checkpoints along the road won't pose any problem for him: when he started working for Georges a very good fixer made him a beautiful set of identity papers. Beirut would have problems indeed without its submerged population of expert fixers.

So the next time Rick visits I tell the girl I've an errand for him, its details to be discussed in private. I take him up to my bedroom and there, in the slits of yellow evening light that pass the shutters, I explain. Yes, he says readily (*he* isn't nervous like Seraphite), sure I'll take you there, how soon? The sooner the better (fingernails clutching my palms so that my impatience won't show) because Georges may be deciding even now that he should move on. If he went there as soon as he disappeared he's been there a while. Although Summerland is the sort of place where you could laze around privately for weeks and if you paid your bills promptly no one would care how long you stayed. And the security there has always had the reputation of being excellent. Ever since the complex was built, three years after the fighting started, they routinely run their own militia and search all visitors at the gates. It's a refuge whether you need to hide or simply want a break; all it requires is a lot of money, and mercifully Georges wouldn't be short of that. But the priest – would he be there too? I don't know.

We can go there on Tuesday, says the boy, three days

from now – his first free day. Very well. It's a quick journey there and back, not far beyond the airport. I try to explain to him about Summerland, what sort of place it is, but that's impossible and I soon give up. He'll have to see for himself. Then I ask about his other slight entanglement: Seraphite can't claim I'm inconsiderate. I say, 'The girl – how soon is she due? Because you won't want to be away around that date. And when she slips out of that ridiculous corset of hers, to be comfortable, she's getting quite big.'

He says, 'Another six weeks.'

Really? I'd have guessed sooner. But no, according to what she told him she's sure of the date. Then he looks confused, embarrassed; I can't imagine why till he says like a confession, 'She doesn't exactly, uh, spend every night at the villa. I mean . . . apparently there's other folks she stays with and can turn to, besides me.' Does he think I hadn't already guessed this? Other men, very likely. But he says she has women friends in various parts of the city, girls she's worked with, or former schoolmates and so forth. I try to picture her demurely in school, conscientiously keeping up with her studies, but although my imagination is usually adequate it fails at this.

'She's an opportunist,' I say; from the living room below us floats the husky timbre of her singing.

His skin gets that angry glow. 'Maybe so, maybe not; that's no one's business but mine.' I've opened my shutter and he hits the window-frame with the side of his open hand to emphasise his words. Fragments of the rotted wood drift down past the wistful half-entreaty of her song.

I let his answer ride; the situation obviously won't last. Her voice drifts up like one of the Line's ghosts and I say, 'She sings like Piaf.' That weary, wishing, enchanting little voice . . . Not exactly like Piaf either; there's a genuine something of her own.

He frowns, baffled – my (and her) sudden turns of mind puzzle him – but he's tenacious; he stumbles after our meaning. 'Oh,' he says, 'yeah. The manager of her nightclub is always mentioning some French singer.'

The song ends and the girl calls up to us from the smashed wall, through the dead air of the Line. 'Still talking secrets?' She sounds bored, sulky, jealous, ready to walk out. He calls back to tell her we've finished – it's a matter of family business – and he'll be down in a moment. Tuesday will be (I assure him) a quick, routine journey. The fighting remains at its simmering but not impossible level, and the rival militias always leave Summerland strictly alone. All of them do; the place is sacrosanct.

28

Madeleine said, 'It's months since we drove this road.'

'Yes.' The day he'd arrived at the airport, that was when. Plenty of new scars since then: former embassy buildings smoking like giant cigar-holders, areas of broken tarmac stretching across the wide boulevard, trees split lengthways or knocked askew. What an innocent he'd been that first day; how he'd grown accustomed to the city since! Yet the barricades along this road gave him more than his usual tremor of nervous excitement. He wasn't driving the ambulance now – a vehicle which, if no one made way for it, at least wasn't considered a primary target. But a private car, even if fourth-hand and shabby . . . that could be suspected or wanted for any reason or none.

The militiamen at these barricades weren't brisk, impatiently waving you on like the ones in the city centre. Out here, though there was little traffic, the men would argue among themselves or turn from the car and chat in low voices. They acted as if they'd gladly delay all the vehicles on the road for ever. And this period of a few months had taught him that they never needed an excuse. So each time he was profoundly nervous when he handed over his papers and Madeleine's for inspection, but each time the papers were eventually returned and the car waved on. Madeleine's papers – tattered from fourteen years of use – could hardly fail to convince, and his had already been grimed and smeared when Georges handed them to him during that first week. Which had seemed odd at the time, but details like that fitted into the general picture perfectly now.

Past the airport turnoff the traffic thinned; Madeleine in the seat beside him said suddenly, 'White-hot needles,' and he knew better than to associate this phrase with the usual damaged suburbs which limped past. He tried to find words to reassure her that Georges was almost certainly okay (yet was he? When a person disappeared, anything became possible, only you couldn't somehow imagine big hearty Georges at a disadvantage. Surely if he'd gotten into a tight spot he would wriggle out of it). But Madeleine said, 'Don't bother.' She said it kindly, but Rick felt trivial, useless, small. And every bit as uncomprehending of this city, this country, as he'd been that first day.

Madeleine, her gaze on the road, said, 'Do you believe in an afterlife?' Not as if he were a person, rather a trash can into which she was dumping this useless question; but she waited for his answer.

He steered carefully around heaps of rubble, which sprawled half across the road. 'I guess not. The truth is, I've never really thought hard about it.' Which sounded strange to him, but it was honest. His mother's death had left an enormous hole, his father's left respect tinged with bafflement because Rick and he had understood each other so little. But both parents were gone, and Rick had never supposed that any part of them could still exist somewhere. Unlike Madeleine, they hadn't practised any religion or brought him up to believe in one. Nor had the question raised itself for him in Beirut, although he dealt with bodies and bits of bodies and the general presence of death every working day.

A trail of possibly live ammunition spewed onto the tarmac. He eased the car well away from it and she, reading his mind again with her uncanny ability, said, 'But one wouldn't want a belief in immortality to be the result of a hopeless situation. That would insult, wouldn't it?'

'Truth is,' he said slowly, trying to be honest, 'we're always so busy – it's a matter of practical needs, urgent ones, all the time.' There were so many problems in Beirut for the living, he hadn't gotten around to brooding on the dead. Nor usually, he suspected, did she.

He started those useless reassurances again but Madeleine interrupted, saying briskly, 'Two hundred more yards, then we turn off for Summerland,' and he was glad. They swung from the wide, battered road to the side road, the big guarded gates of Summerland, and while they waited to have their papers and the car checked one more time, Madeleine began to tell him details about the place. But nothing anyone could have said would have prepared him for the reality.

'Beirut corrupts,' she'd said, 'and Summerland is the extreme example of that.' As he drove along the winding private road, past landscaped shrubs and glitteringly maintained *cabañas*, he glanced at her wide-eyed and she said, 'I know. Obscene, isn't it? That wealth can insulate so totally from the crude happenings of the city and the world. But here it does.' She shrugged her skinny old shoulders. 'That's Lebanon.'

She told him how, in the early years of fighting, Georges had often taken her and Brigitte there at a week-end; how they'd arrive in time for lunch – 'Caviare with crisp toast, then perhaps the chef's stuffed partridge and, to finish with, a really good *crème caramel*' – and how after coffee she'd relax beside one of the complex's five pools while Georges and Brigitte swam. He glimpsed several of the pools while he steered the car between clusters of *cabañas* and past carefully groomed clumps of trees. 'A lively, happy-looking crowd, aren't they?' Madeleine said, gazing at the multicoloured pool surrounds in the late-autumn sunshine. 'Oh, and I see they've built a new shopping centre and restaurant to replace the ones damaged in the Israeli shelling.'

The car slowed automatically as he said, 'You mean this place stayed open all those years – like *this*?'

'Yes,' she said with a malevolent triumph, 'apart from briefly during periods of the greatest damage, that's so.'

The big, white-painted hotel, the parking lot. Madeleine said they might as well eat before starting their search, so they strolled towards the hotel steps and Rick wondered what in hell – apart from her worry about Georges – she was really thinking. *Triumph* over this luxury next to the ruined, bloody heart of Beirut: how could she? At the steps she pointed out how safe and tranquil the whole complex was, and Rick wryly agreed. The search at the gates had included a personal frisking.

The doorman wore (Rick was almost but not quite beyond being surprised) a formal tailcoat with an inevitable bulge on the right hip. The bellhops had similar bulges. The lobby was all blue-white walls and black leather sofas and chairs, tables in wrought iron and glass. Madeleine beside him muttered – yet with, he thought, a certain satisfaction – 'Obscene, obscene.'

The barbecue restaurant, the waiters with their formal dress and one bulge apiece. The huge turning spits along one wall, the black-and-red tiled floor (Rick caught himself thinking, like any Beiruti, 'How practical – blood wouldn't show.'), the cream-topped tables, each with a single red rose. Their table by a window looked out to the immaculate acres of the complex. Beyond the shopping centre and the trimmed bushes and the *cabañas* and pools, he could just pick out the scrub and sand-dunes amid which the airport lay. He pointed them out to Madeleine and she muttered something about kids shooting wild doves there still. Then she said, again with that malevolent edge to her tone, 'You can glimpse the remains of refugee camps too, if you stare. But do you really want to?'

29

I'm corrupted by luxury; since we entered the restaurant my eyes have been automatically surveying one table after another, and when my mind finally asks them, What are you looking for?, they're shocked at its forgetfulness. So my gaze, accusing and caustic, reminds my head, I'm looking for Georges, of course.

The *perdrix* is delicious as it always was, but I put down my fork. How dare I be hungry? Rick leans across, concerned. 'You're ill, Gran?' No, not ill.

So many people, so large an area to cover, and no guarantee that he's here. Yet surely we must come across . . . perhaps not Georges himself, though I'd swear he's been here. The place holds such a strong emanation of life-enjoyment and brute energy and repressed violence, and the odour of all this fits so exactly with what I recall of Georges' physical presence. This is the sort of place he would have fled to first if he had to flee. And Summerland is unique, so there's no question of 'the sort of', this *is* the place. But is he here now? And if not, how can we trace him?

I say, 'We shouldn't waste time eating,' because at this moment he may be driving out of that front gate to return to the city or to go somewhere else. 'We could miss him a thousand times, a thousand ways, in here.' My heart is heavy as if the meal I haven't eaten lies sour inside me. If he were here a buzzer would ring in my head, surely it would. When you care so much about a person surely you'd sense . . . But nothing happens to confirm my straying, passionate wishes. I push away my plate, whose contents are no longer delicious; my rebel common sense has broken the mood in which I believed that we would find Georges. I say, 'We shouldn't have come. A waste of time.'

His transparent face seems ready to suggest that something more indecent than a waste of time is involved in the ethos of Summerland. Of course this place must grate on all his poverty-oriented simplicities. But he's a kindly boy and a noticing one. He leans across and pats my hand, then shoves my plate back to me. 'Eat your lunch,' he says. 'I'm sure we'll find him or some trace of where he's headed off to, then you can rest easier and most likely soon be in touch with him again. I'm betting we haven't wasted our money.' Obviously he's concerned for my physical state, my age and perhaps my apparent frailty and supposed hunger, and for the effect on me that disappointment and effort might have, but all those are immaterial. He says, 'How do you plan we look around this place?' and my hands involuntarily spread in a feeble old-woman gesture: I've no idea, you take over. Meaning – almost – 'I give up.'

But he's developed a resourcefulness, a tough core, these past months. He riffles through the pages of the menu, finds again the map of the grounds and studies it. Past the red-plush menu cover he says to me, 'I could stroll around the ring road, or drive the car around slowly, while you rest up in the lounge here for a while. If I see Georges I'll grab him and we'll hare right back to you.'

'No.' Too many loopholes for all sorts of non-coincidings to happen. And if Georges isn't still here but the priest is (I can't get his nearby presence out of my mind; it's as if the odour of that incense pulls me) then Father Mesrop would be unlikely to let anyone drag him anywhere. A cunning creature he, you'd need to catch the edge of his cassock as it brushed across you.

So we work out a scheme for a mixture of slow sorties on foot and by car for both of us, and while the boy finishes his meal he does his best to cheer me. And — because this place is so elaborate, so glistening and sleek, and is situated a few miles from its opposite, which has become bloodily familiar to him — he starts to make genuine jokes while he eyes the map with awe. 'You could take a sauna while we're here, Gran — aren't you just in the mood for a sauna? Or what time do the night-clubs open? *How* many of them?' And, reverent and repeated as if no other words would do, 'Holy *cow* . . .'

So he teases me, and because he's young and foolish and kindly and I have become — God help us — fond of him, I try to tease back. We — as he would say — kid each other about the tennis courts and a new international bar and Summerland's fire brigade, its taxi fleet and the fuel tanks, the generators, which throughout these years have kept it self-sufficient. Then we stop teasing and fall silent because no doubt he's realising, as I am, the circum-stances, the nearby brooding explosive city that makes these fancy precautions necessary if the place is to con-tinue functioning. We saw enough gutted buildings and splintered walls and charred roads on the way down here to understand what the alternative would be. As if to underline the cruel nature of our laughter, which five minutes ago seemed nearly innocent, a dull, distant crrumpph! sounds from the direction of Beirut. You can scarcely hear it past the chink of glassware and rattle of cutlery and chatter, but our eyes lock and he's heard it too.

I suggest, 'Time to start looking?' and there's no laugh-ter in his face any more; you'd suppose we were search-ing for a corpse. (As perhaps we are, but I refuse to contemplate that.) At the flicker of a fingernail the waiter arrives. I pay (and have a moment's absurd impulse to ask if they've a room free; I'll stay here peacefully for weeks

– absurd, yes, and shameful), then Rick and I go out to the terrace and down the wide arc of steps. We turn our faces toward the remainder of Summerland. To look for Georges.

30

I tell myself that a person's figure, a walk, are unmistakable. Many of these men who lounge or swim or stroll have beards and hair like Georges – so that even a mother might wonder and catch her breath at the first frantic glance – but a walk, a set of shoulders – that's unique.

We drive along at a rate that must agonise Rick, who like all the young has maximum miles per hour pounding through his veins, then he parks the car and we saunter past pools, *cabañas*, and the other, slightly cheaper, restaurants. (But Georges would never use those, he's as much of a hedonist as his mother.) The odd thing is, there's never a moment when I'm relatively sure I've seen Georges (leaving aside the ten thousand brief flickers of wish-fulfilment) but the priest . . . surely I see him everywhere. A ghost, a revenant from some other society, some long-dead era. Whenever a flash of black strikes the corner of my eye or a slightly bald head and broad shoulders fills my vision – there, surely, he is. But closer inspection always shows that he isn't. This place is – apart from any other consideration – not suitable for displaying cassocks; they'd be as out of place as birds of prey in a church. Always it's not him, until . . .

Didn't I say a back is unmistakable? Even when it's lying prone in the quiet paved area set back from the pool's surround, and is naked except for a loosely flung wrap of glaring turquoise and canary-yellow swimming trunks, which don't look priestly either but . . . My hand clutches Rick's arm, I point and whisper and the boy is amazed. I don't blame him. I'm amazed too, and hollowly, terribly, afraid. And how should we approach him? A body so colourfully inconspicuous, amid hundreds of colourful others, has the appearance of insisting on not being noticed. No way of judging which, if any, of the *cabañas* near the pool is his. I draw back into the shade of a mulberry tree and send Rick, who at least is colourfully and youthfully dressed. He fits the scene better than my monotone self.

He picks his way through the prone bodies, bends over the priest and speaks softly. The half-bald head jerks up, then with cautious slowness it turns to survey me. He's afraid; the man is clearly terrified for his personal safety amid this relaxed crowd. That could be the cause of the tight head-turning, but when his eyes meet mine I know there's more.

He slinks beside us to his *cabaña* on the second path back from the pool, he fishes the key from his wrap pocket and turns it in the lock, he pushes the door for us to enter first and whispers as if ashamed, 'Always I'm afraid when I go in here. Always, until I've searched this tiny place and found there's no one.' He points us to chairs; their black-and-white striped cotton upholstery burns itself into my brain, and the white walls with bits of angular black trim, and one hanging picture. Till the end of my life I shall remember the look and chilled-air feel of that room and how the picture – a man in scarlet, balancing on a grey wire or wall in the midst of total greyness – seemed to leer at me. Then the priest shifts on his chair, and nothing else matters.

His bare chest is poking out from the turquoise wrap, and a clump of greyish hair on his torso wiggles as he breathes. Suddenly he hauls the wrap closer round him. He *cares* – at *this* moment – that he's celibate and not fully dressed before ancient me?

I say, 'Tell me what happened.' If he doesn't, and very soon, I'll shake the truth out of him.

But he gets up, mutters, hurries into another room and returns quickly in grey jeans and white shirt, tries to encourage us to iced cola, to fruit juice. I can't stand this. I get up, grip his large hairy wrists in my bony fingers and say, 'For Christ's sake sit down and tell me what happened, or I'll kill you.' A strong old woman still, a remorseless bitch.

He sits down, his wrists slippery with sweat under my grip, and bit by bit from my questions the happenings in the city emerge. 'Georges is dead?' (By now the answer is so obvious that I barely pause to hear it.) 'How, where, when? And − most important − who did it?' My hands may not be young but they must be good for one last revenging. From the swimming pool laughter and shrieks echo faintly. You could assume it's an ambush by some slapstick-loving militia, but this isn't − quite − Beirut.

Mesrop twitches at any footstep along the pathway outside and at the loudening of those shrieks. 'Those people by the pool don't,' he says apologetically, 'realise how it sounds; they're safe here and they've forgotten what the *other* was like. Madame,' he adds, 'you may kill me if you wish but truly I've no idea of the name, the face, that shot him.' (There's almost relief at hearing of shooting: I'd feared most the gleeful carver with a knife.) I say, 'But you're sure he's dead?' (hard as the pathway outside), and he nods. 'I'm sure, Madame − because, you see . . .'

He's reluctant to give details, but I pull them out of him like the exploding gaps in Beirut's streets. 'In an alley,' he says, 'of West Beirut, not far behind Georges' shop: I'd realised, Madame, for several days that there was something awry, some risk to both of us, and so we'd arranged to come here for a while. Quiet, you understand?' I say brutally, 'The two of you had annoyed someone important, had put yourselves in danger.' And he doesn't deny this.

So they'd planned to meet in that alley behind the shop. Georges was going to drive him down here and they'd rented a *cabaña*, this one, which now bursts with a ghost. Instead – Mesrop pokes a finger at his chest. 'A fast, expert job, Madame; it had only just happened when I reached the alley.' 'But,' I say more brutally, '*you're* safe, so it must have been robbery, not politics. Georges and the wad of cash he carried for business reasons, his uncut gems . . .'

Mesrop shakes his head; he won't allow me that relief. 'The wallet,' he says, 'how do you suppose, Madame, I acquired the money to take a taxi down here and to live and pay my way in this *cabaña*? By robbing the dead, that's how.' His large, coarse fingers indicate the size of Georges' wad; yes, it was always that big. 'And,' he says, 'the gems: Georges had discreetly disposed of some beforehand, foreseeing this quick departure, but the remainder . . .' He makes a pouring motion, one hand to the other. Almost I rise up and strike him then because this is the classic jeweller's gesture, which I – and no doubt he – saw Georges make countless times. 'Whenever,' he says, 'you'd like to take possession of them, Madame, because technically of course they're yours, as his next of kin.' He somehow manages to look small and frail as he says this. I'm sure he intended to keep them and sell them piece by piece to finance his continued stay here, but what do the gems matter now?

He sits on the edge of his chair and the sweat pours off him. A drawn blind conceals the outdoors but he glances nervously toward it between every few words. His fingers on his untasted glass of juice tremble. 'Was there' (I ask as my last question) 'reason for this shooting? Any feud or action by Georges that could have precipitated it?' He nods, slow and solemn, as if the precipitating factors are too numerous to mention.

Afterwards perhaps I'll have other questions, or enquiries about his own future (how long will he stay here safe? Where will he go after?), but these questions don't matter now. I return to awareness of Rick; his face is numb with respect and with an embarrassed sorrow for the priest and myself (as if a child watched two adults play Russian roulette and suddenly realised the stakes involved). I get up, Rick gets up too. Afterwards I may reproach myself for a lack of courtesy in not acknowledging the priest's existence, but at this moment he's only a hollow robot. Rick opens the door for me but I turn to the hollow watching form and say, 'You wouldn't have told me, would you? You'd have let me wait and worry for ever. How about your blasted religion now? How about duty and compassion?'

The door is open. Outside there's sun and splashing water and the crowds chatter. That seems incredible. On the drive back to the city Rick starts to speak but I say, 'Shut up or I'll kill you too.' There isn't pain in me but a furious heat, like astonishment – and haven't I a little gun tucked away somewhere?

31

Yes, there's an ancient revolver at the back of my dressing-table drawer, left over from those trips abroad, but there's no ammunition, and whom would I shoot? Beirut keeps its charred, secretive facade, Beirut doesn't speak to reveal who killed this one of its many dead. Thousands were killed here during the Israeli war, hundreds massacred in the camps; I ought to feel ashamed of my pain over this one death. (But, I cry out nightly, it's *Georges*; that makes the difference. An argument that echoes as though it's not valid.)

So a handful of days passes. No funeral; we've no corpse. Rick, the good dutiful boy, visits every evening, mostly without the girl, who's still working. I ask acidly, Does she intend giving birth to the baby at the night-club? and he laughs. Then he recalls there's grief in the house, and he smothers his laughter, but they're young, they can easily pick up the pieces. Even if this were his brother, his father, he'd pick up the bits and go on. (My self-pity is a spider busily spinning, and the more I try to fight it, the more I'm entangled.) Meanwhile Brigitte stays out till all hours; she hardly speaks to me. What's going on inside her? And Seraphite has – I hate to say 'mellowed', but she's found a brusque kindliness toward me as if by my son's death I have half-paid some debt. I long to shout No! The scorpion still has her tail raised, she recognises no debts, she's lethal! I don't shout, but I let my tongue become more insulting, more sharp, and Seraphite gets the point; she cools off again, which is vastly more comfortable. I can't bear to feel *obligated*.

And Helene, my cabbage-brained, potato-shaped daughter in Paris, plans to visit. This news I give Rick on our second evening, wry and brief, ashamed of my incorrect attitude. 'Oh,' he says, 'that's good. Then you won't be so alone here.'

Poor boy, he unfailingly and courteously offers me the exactly wrong words. And I the bitch, the cruel non-motherly, am unwilling to puncture his courtesy by rejecting them. So I say, 'We-ee-ll, of course that's true.' I've no letter to show him: the news came in another of those cryptic summonses to the bank whose phone is more reliable than mine. And there's nothing else to say about Helene. She spoke all the usual bereaved and consoling phrases (how could *she* feel bereaved? She's scarcely seen Georges in years and the two of them were never close) and I assured her I'm well looked-after; I stressed Rick's attentiveness, and Seraphite, and soft-pedalled Brigitte's absences, but no use, she *will* visit. She believes it's the appropriate thing to do, and a Parisienne trained in the old school (and Helene has become more Parisian than any of them) isn't going to let herself be deflected from the routine responses. 'She won't stay long,' I say, and laugh. For the first time since hearing about Georges I laugh, and am devastated when I consider the reason: my dislike of and contempt for my elder daughter. 'Oh Christ,' I say, and bury my face in my musty-smelling hands.

Unfortunately Helene's affection for me has always clung, smothering me. Every time I went overseas to work, when they were children, Helene would weep in a gentle imploring way as if her tears could alter what I needed to do. Brigitte and Georges were much easier: Brigitte would say nothing but give me one brilliant glare, then she'd slide across to her father, eager to clasp his hand and chatter to him about her latest French essay or oboe practice. And Georges would perhaps explode into one of those fits of temper that Seraphite remembers, yet those were always only thunder-showers, soon over with and his laugh bursting through again.

But to bury myself in memories is a luxury I can't indulge when Rick is visiting; this ingenuous boy mustn't be upset. So I neutralise his well-meaning touch by chattering about his girl and that villa – the garden, is it scorched from the summer? Do you find enough time to work in it? He decides I'm brave, I see that, and perhaps am hard also. Should a mother adjust so easily? However, he answers as if this were a game the two of us play; obviously the garden and its plants do genuinely interest him, yet underneath there's a sadness.

'And she doesn't share your love for . . . well, that's natural. Of course she'll soon be busy with—' But he gets up and begins to pace. When he pauses in front of me the pale tapestried lady with her unicorn and medieval land-scape frames his head – but clumsily, not smooth-fitting as she did Georges'.

'The truth is,' he says (slow so that I'm reminded of priests and confessionals), 'I doubt if she'll stay there for long after the kid arrives. She's made arrangements to have the baby adopted as soon as it's born, and I told her that whatever she wanted—'

'You're so soft. What do you expect to get out of life?' A fragment of my ambitions for dead Georges, my fury and pain at his fate, gets into the question.

He turns from me and paces again. 'I've dropped all that sort of notion. My motto nowadays is, take it slow.' He paces back and picks up the little stone cherub-with-dolphin from its nest among my silver ornaments. 'I'll drift,' he says. His index finger delicately traces the curves of cherub and dolphin. 'My job isn't fancy, but they can use me. As for Solange—' He sets the

cherub gently down on the table. His hand is not quite
steady.

'I only hope you're not wildly in love with her.'

'Oh no,' he says (casually, as if he's had affairs with all
the girls in the world), 'my motto with girls nowadays is
take it slow, too.'

Yet I've watched the curve of his arm, its pressure
around her shoulders, when the two of them visit, and
the extra deep and soft tone in his voice when he talks
with her, the way his eyes drink her when he thinks no
one is watching . . . slow, indeed!

We talk again about the villa; it's a fairyland to both of
us. He asks whether I'd like to see it again sometime, but
I'd rather not. To him it's an impersonal and beautiful
anachronism, but to me it's populated by ghosts of varying ages and degrees of painfulness. He tells me about the
abandoned exotic plants there – as ruinous, in their way,
as any Beirut street – and I from my store of subtropical
experience advise how he should prune and treat them,
what aspect they'd prefer. It's astonishing how much I
remember, a whole world I'd deeply enjoyed but closed
off. And, he says, at the far end of the garden there's
a pile of weathered stone blocks as if a building . . .
'But not destroyed in the fighting?' he says, and looks
puzzled.

A bird tower. I hurry to my bookshelves and pull
out maps, diagrams, all of them faded with age – but
those stones are vastly older. His eyes glow as a boy's
should (with a sense of all the world waiting for him)
when I explain that those weren't dovecotes – nothing so
domestic – but waystations on the courier pigeon routes
established eight hundred years ago by the Caliphs of
Cairo. From Basra, Cairo, Constantinople, to Beirut; from
Damascus and Palmyra, too. 'And along the Little Desert
route—' For the first time in days my voice sounds like an

alive woman's: warm, excited, passionate. 'Every fifty miles a tower.' The shaped sandstone blocks rise before us, the romance and silent, nervous excitement of those desert flights.

'But why?' he wonders, and I answer, 'The roads, the cities, were dangerous. Eight hundred years ago——'

Yes, that broke the spell. No 'crrumpph' sounded from outdoors to underline my words, but Beirut's silence is itself ominous. His hand covers mine and for a moment we're a family. He has sense enough not to prolong that moment; soon afterwards he leaves, but there'll be other evenings. He's my grandson and we're both glad that's so. A friend too, which is much more.

The next night I found the priest's body.

In the ruined cinema, an undramatic sight. Lying tidily on his back in what must once have been the foyer, with one neat hole in his forehead and a revolver lying conveniently beside his outstretched hand. Suicide, or a murder arranged to look like? There's no way of knowing which. He wore his cassock, a last defiant statement either to God or some assassin.

I'd gone out from our back door – not able to sleep, and Brigitte wouldn't be home for hours yet, if at all – and hadn't courage enough to try the Line, but the cinema should be safe. Walk there till you're tired, old woman, then go home to bed. So I paced. Much of the roof has fallen recently, not from more shelling but decrepitude, and the silvery interrupted light fell like a series of promises. I was thinking about Rick and his garden, and how a new baby is an astounding bundle of flesh and bones – and there the priest lay, quietly conclusive amid the moonshafts. The hole in his forehead scarcely disfigured him. He was cold but serene, not seeming to have suffered. Perhaps during his priesthood he prayed for the grace of a good death as we were taught to and I never did; why should one waste time brooding on such distant matters? (That was before death came and sat beside us and offered a continuous running commentary.)

Of course he'll need to be buried. No doubt Rick and his cohorts will help if I summon them officially. And the priest will also need . . . other arrangements. So the next morning, before Rick arrives, I take a taxi to the nearest Maronite church that is still open – far up the quarter, towards Qarantina. The priest's lined face and grey whiskers, the tilt of his cap and smear of paint on his cassock, remind me that Father Mesrop had his moments of warmth and humanness, perhaps more of them than I noticed. 'A month of Masses offered, please,' I say, 'for a departed.' Surely Masses nowadays are always 'for a departed'?

'A month.' He makes a note in his book, and then I remember Georges. Did the little gold crucifix mean anything? I never felt able to ask him that. So, to be on the safe side, 'No, two months. One month for each of two people.' I pay his stipend and leave.

Naturally I don't believe a word of all this. Tomorrow I'll be cold toward it as I am toward all sentimental manifestations, tomorrow I'll laugh at myself. Tomorrow Helene arrives, and soon Solange's baby will be born. (I'd swear she's almost due.) Sometime I'll stop wondering why Father Mesrop came back to the city where he would be in danger: he had money enough to last for weeks longer. (I didn't search his body. If he still had the jewels, let the rats choke on them.) Sometime I'll stop wondering why he died here, so near us. Were we his final refuge? And what, if he really believed in heaven and hell, did he in that last instant suppose would happen next? At this question my mind spins like a wheel torn from its axis, careening lopsided into space. I go home, I wait for Rick and the other set of useful muscles, I concentrate on the physical corpse in the cinema. A corpse – not related to oneself, not belonging anywhere – that's ordinary, that's comprehensible. Anyone can understand such a corpse.

32

Rick and his driver arrive with an ambulance and take the corpse away. That's one funeral I shan't attend. Mesrop is gone; he'll be posthumously shriven and then buried but for me he's already finished with. He may or may not by some word or action have inadvertently led to Georges' death, and the residue from that death most probably led to his, but the two deaths have happened. What point would any post-mortem by me serve?

On the next morning – the day of his funeral, the day of Helene's arrival – I sit in that downstairs room which used to be a chapel. The oddments of his religion still lie around: the candlesticks, altar vessels, his threadbare vestments. Brigitte puts her head round the door and I say, 'What shall we do with this equipment?'

'Throw it to the seabirds.' Her face has a brittle, bright glitter. 'Had you forgotten,' she says, 'we must drive to the airport and meet *that woman*?'

Helene, her own sister . . . no, I hadn't forgotten. I get up. 'It's time?' Something about the brightness of her face makes me put my hand on her arm and say, 'You don't mind her visiting? It'll only be for a week or two.'

My house: why should I ask this daughter's permission? But I've a sudden sense of the need to, of urgency. She says (the glitter bounces back my question, my concern, to me), 'Why should I care?' The taxi is waiting at the usual place; we go.

On the way to the airport (a taciturn driver and lowering grey clouds) she doesn't speak. I make smalltalk about how long since Helene was here last, about what we might do and what shops we'll visit if the city remains quiet (Helene will be nervous anyway) during her visit. Brigitte says nothing. Only, when our taxi has passed all the airport security barriers and drives up to the terminal building, she bends and kisses me – hands clasped behind her back, everything except her lips aloof. 'Nothing I might do can hurt you now,' she says, 'not any longer. Can it?' And my own sense of urgency flares out into the open to meet the eruption of urgency in her question.

I must guess that she plans some sort of farewell; what else could she mean? My urgency pulls her hands from behind her back. I clutch them while I say, 'You wouldn't do that – you're too alive.' She takes my meaning instantly and laughs unrestrained as a teenager at my ridiculous idea.

'Not to kill myself – really, Maman! Don't you know me better than that? Suicide is stupid. To give up *living*?' Then she begins to fuss (watching me all the time) about the plane being due, the slow speed we made from the city, how we ought to be waiting inside the terminal (and her gaze, like a needle stitching, watches me every moment). She helps me from the taxi, her fingers cool on mine. We go inside.

Helene looks trimmer. She looks – though never elegant – good. A businesswoman, you'd assume, travelling for some dull but well-paying firm. Her suit has the authentic Paris cut (St Laurent, surely); its chiselled curves neatly enclose her figure. (My mind, shocked at my interested, appreciative eyes, says, 'Georges is dead!' So he is, and there ought to be nothing left of me except pain and hatred, but these damned *ordinary* interests keep waking up; I can't smother them.)

So Helene kisses me, routinely but warmly on each cheek, and my noticing eyes maunder on. She looks vastly more impressive than I'd remembered: neither

Brigitte nor I could wear that light beige – we've the wrong skin tone and too flamboyant a nature – but it looks right on Helene; in it she has the cleanly faceted appearance of a paleish topaz. And the jewellery she's wearing . . . very nice, nothing as low-priced as topaz. Georges himself would have approved the flamingo brooch in pink and white diamonds, and the white diamond earrings: very nice indeed. Under my gaze she fusses with her handbag, drops a glove and complains in her quiet, level voice, 'Maman, you stare so! I've always tried to dress well, to make an effort.'

Yes, why have I remembered her as a cabbagehead, an unsalted potato? And she talks, while we drive back into the city. She makes conversation that is warmer than mere politeness, talks about Paris and Europe and opera and newspapers and her husband's work. Can she possibly be a happy woman, contented in her marriage and intelligent? I listen to her and am genuinely interested, roused. I comment and retort; once in a while – possibly not by coincidence – we smile together. And chunks of preconceptions that I've avidly harboured for years now fall away: she has the feel of being fully alive, fully loving.

During the drive Brigitte speaks only when spoken to, sardonic little nothings barely this side of impoliteness. We'd be better off without those. Helene tactfully refuses to be prodded. She asks after my health (disgustingly good) and after Rick, and her side-glances at the ruined city are no more appalled than you'd expect. 'How long since—' I say, and she calculates on her fingers (a habit of hers which used to annoy me, but now I find it endearing – her husband's a stockbroker).

'Eight or nine years,' she says. 'After the fighting started but before—' Before the Israeli invasion and the shelling? 'Oh yes,' – relieved that she's allowed to show her horror at what she sees – 'before all *this*.'

I still imagine there's a death-smell in the ruined cinema, amid the rat-droppings, but that's a private discovery which I keep to myself. I've searched and there are no other corpses. Brigitte inserts her key into our back door and says casually over her shoulder to Helene, 'Why don't you take her back with you? You must have enough room.' As if I'm a package she's disposing of, and Helene no more personal than the mailbox.

'I'd like to persuade her,' says Helene equably, so unsurprised that she must independently have had this idea too. But she gives me a look which indicates that I'm human and that she's concerned about my living amid these ruins. She even puts her arm round me and squeezes as if she and I are really, meaningfully, mother and daughter. I don't recall Helene being this demonstrative before. Maybe that's because the 'this' which was myself then isn't identical with my 'this' now? I return her squeeze to show that my answer doesn't intend rudeness – because of course, being the person I am, there's only one possible reply.

'Couldn't think of it,' I say firmly, 'never, not possible. I'll die here and count myself happy.' And I realise they'd expected no other answer: Helene with her gaze full of concern and Brigitte with her gleaming hard glance both accept, they don't argue. True, Helene says, 'We'll talk about it again before I leave,' but that's merely a form of words, to save face. Her tone lacks conviction.

Late that evening, when Brigitte as usual is out, Helene questions me about where Brigitte spends all her time, what she's up to, does she never think of settling down and getting married? Helene's face shines, past the skilfully applied foundation cream and touch of pink lipstick, as if marriage were the greatest rapture in the world, and I realise she's deeply, positively, happy in hers. That's something else I was wrong about. She's worried about Brigitte; I'm worried too. She's not mentally abnormal exactly, but there's a *willed detachment*, especially since Georges' death, which is chilling. If Brigitte is this way with everyone, she's got trouble. We agree thus far about her; we can't suggest any way of approaching her. We drop the subject and chat about how pleasant it is that there's no violence for this, Helene's first evening back in the city.

I unlock the door between living room and smashed wall, and she's duly horrified by the scarred tunnel which is the Line. The last bout of violence singed the young trees and burned the grasses so that the long ruined street looks bleaker than ever. Then I take her up to my bedroom and unfasten the shutter; the two of us lean with arms on the windowsill and survey this our home city. The collapse of various ruins has left gaps where, past the tower blocks that remain, we can glimpse the mountain-tops, ochre and amber and rosy in the evening light. The sky is clear, the sun has dipped to the Mediterranean and vanished. The stars appear with a rush above the unlit Line as if they're frantic to beautify the ruins' sharp outlines. No moon tonight, only the fragile glow of stars and, a mile beyond the Line, the lights of traffic and apartments in the occupied part of the city. The evening babble of talk and vehicles comes to us fragmented, in brief washes of sound. I miss Rick a little – his evening visits have become a habit – but it's thoughtful of him to give Helene and me this evening alone together. Unexpected – he didn't mention it last evening when he visited as usual (respectful and baffled about the morning's event, awed as he still is by our sudden deaths) – but it's a kind thought; he's like that.

He doesn't visit next evening either, I enjoy Helene's company but I'm a little impatient with him, and piqued, because I want to show him off to her. He's presentable, not of my shaping but a grandson I'm proud to have. After supper Helene and I take a taxi for a brief trip to

Raouche where, now that the violence has stopped again, the fishermen sail their shallow boats inshore amid the rocks and the damaged piers. I must tell Seraphite to buy some octopus from up the coast in the market tomorrow. Some of the boats use gas lanterns but a few still brandish the flaming torches of my childhood, and the shouts, the swish of water, the torches' flare, fall through me like drops of warm rain. My cold dark undercurrent says Georges is dead, he's dead, but above it in spite of myself move these warm happinesses.

We left a note on the back door in case Rick arrived while we were gone, but when we got home the note was undisturbed and no Rick. 'He'll come tomorrow,' I tell Helene confidently, 'he hates to push himself in and always goes to the opposite extreme, but he keeps a close eye on me and of course he's anxious to meet you. He'll certainly come tomorrow evening after he finishes work.'

So when, the following evening, a knock comes on the downstairs door I say, 'The silly boy's mislaid his key, I'll let him in.' I hurry down so that I can bring him upstairs and introduce him to this calm warm daughter I love – but it's not Rick. A man with black straight hair, swarthy, a thin moustache, no beard. Broad-shouldered, about forty, certainly Arab though he addresses me in French. For an instant I think, Two women alone in the house, an Arab – a thief or murderer – then I remember where I've seen this man before and heard his polite greeting of me. The priest's corpse stiffly in the cinema; this is Rick's ambulance driver. In his fluent but accented French he asks, 'Is Rick here?' No, he isn't. 'But,' says the man Jameel, 'he hasn't come to work for three days, and no message from him. There's a rumour that he's been taken hostage.'

33

Dear God no, not kidnapped. Surely he must for some reason be staying out at the villa? Perhaps the girl is there ill? No, says this Jameel, polite but worried, she's still working at the nightclub; we checked with her and she claims to know nothing.

Arab, but he's human. That faintest stress on 'claims' is a secret he's letting me into, and I'm grateful. And furiously afraid – because if the boy's not at the villa nor with her . . . I say, 'I'll get the truth out of her.' I'm outside in the yard before he or Helene can move.

He has a little car and offers to drive me to the club; I'll get a taxi back. Helene insists on coming too. Her profoundly suspicious glances at him reveal that she has no antennae, no judgement. It's obvious that this man is sincere. A co-worker and friend of Rick's, therefore he must be a friend of mine. Helene hurries after us clutching my outdoor shoes and umbrella. To my surprise weather still exists – a thin, cold rain. At the nightclub entrance he lets us out. I thank him and promise he shall have news by next morning. If the girl won't talk I'll shake her teeth from her head, and if she really knows nothing I'll try the villa – yes, tonight, in the dark; why not? Fear for the boy knocks in me like a pulse.

On this street a handful of the overhead lamps work. The silver facade of the club glitters beyond them like a bunch of devils' eyes. We enter past a doorman in dark trousers and braided jacket with a sort of képi on his head. The restaurant: glass tables, each chair a transparent curve. A gilt-framed lift down to the nightclub.

Half-dark, lit with tiny grey lamps. The girl sings beside a piano on a low stage; along the walls stand imitation antique statues as if they also wait to hear what she'll say. Helene holds me back, drags me to a corner table and sits me neatly down. Someday I shall withdraw my concentration from the girl and hate Helene for causing this delay. 'You can't interrupt her act,' she says, and orders drinks for both of us. The word 'wait' has lost all meaning.

The girl wears a sequinned top, a floaty and concealing black skirt. Her face amid that dusky tumbling hair could be a prisoner's too, emotionless, having forgotten how to care. She sings, of course, about 'amour' and 'folie' and 'juaqu'à la mort'. Time after time I start to get up but Helene restrains me. At my insistence we send a scribbled note via the waiter. He slips it into the girl's hand between songs and she glances at it but doesn't look toward us. After her last number she bows her head to the pitter of applause, she walks into the shadows behind the band and is gone. I get up, probably I speak; people stare, they murmur and laugh; but that's immaterial. I tow Helene behind me and push a cowed waiter ahead, guiding. There's a scruffy pale green corridor, a half-open door, a tiny room. Peeling walls covered with old show posters: a sepia woman in square sunglasses with mouth wide open, a bald fat man in crimson with sword, a Berlin cabaret poster all top hat and grin. A cluttered rickety table full of little pots and jars, a miniature striped flag and a used coffee cup. Two chairs with brown plastic slats. The smell of creams, lipsticks, a drenching sweet perfume . . . Beyond the glaring table lamp (scratched metal with a dirty parchment shade) a woman's voice says, 'What do you want?' It's the girl.

'Him, of course.' Helene holds me back, or I'd choke

this creature who's refused to tell what she knows – and mustn't whatever's happened be in some way her fault? I get as close as Helene's arm and the girl's retreat will let me, and say, 'You've left him lying somewhere ill. Or he's given up his job and done God knows what in despair because he's frantically in love with you and – *what have you said to him?'*

She warily eyes Helene's grip on me, then she pulls one of the slatted chairs towards her and sits. 'They took him,' she says, 'the morning before last, in the street. I've no idea where he is.' I break free from Helene, go to the girl and lift her chin. Dull as a beautiful jewel in an unlit place she regards me, but the mouth quivers like that of a child who's afraid of being inexplicably punished. 'You know how these things happen,' she says to me, like an apology that she and I alone can understand.

'*Who* took him? Where to? You've called the police?'

A flicker passes across her face as if she's amused at this last impossibility. I'd forgotten that the police haven't resurrected their forces since the last spate of violence. But she speaks to me again as if briefly she feels generous; she doesn't smile. 'I've no idea who,' she says. 'You must have seen these incidents before? Four men wearing—' A shudder runs the length of her body, almost it seems strong enough to force out her unborn child. 'Wearing black plastic hoods, as usual.' She lifts her open, generous face toward me as if this ordinary fact might be significant, and she spreads her hands, which are a little swollen; she must be very near her time. 'You'll have seen these happenings before,' she says. 'I have too. Like an arranged meeting, as if they're escorting him to some business conference.' Again the slow shudder takes her; it rocks her hands to her face and away as if the dramatic gesture were an impossible understatement. Helene leaves me and goes to her, but the girl says, 'No, I've seen such things often, so they don't upset me. It's only because—' Not quite a finger-flicker but as if the child in her womb were the one with a conscience, a conscience that the girl would gladly disown if the child weren't a separate being.

I remember what Rick told me about how they'd met, the small spurt of blood from the man who'd been escorting her. At this I push Helene aside and shake the girl's shoulders. 'Where did they take him to?' I say, fierce, but the girl repeats, 'I've no idea.'

I stand back and look at her: she hasn't an evasive air. More shocked, and when she flings back her hair and cries at me, 'He was *kind*, damn you! Otherwise I wouldn't care at all,' my mind says relieved, This is bone-honest. While Helene – poor puzzled Helene, ready to referee our fight – stands between us.

My knees shake at that memory of blood. I pull the other chair and sit down. 'Which militia?' Quietly, because at least the girl cares too. She'll try to run out and leave me holding all the emotion, yet she does care.

The dark long curls fall across her face again. 'Damn you, how can anyone guess? Jeans and a black loose shirt and the black hood.'

'A car?'

An ironic curl of her finger, a studied elaborate gesture. She's already trying to distance herself. 'A Mercedes, of course, with all the extra radio antennae and gadgets. The sort of car any militia would use.'

'And they picked him up where?' For one swift moment I'm busy deciding that I'll get all these details and hand them over to Georges; with his contacts he'll soon discover . . . then I remember he won't. But I'll get the details anyway.

'The corner of Hamra Street and Boulevard de Verdun. He'd driven in for work, and I'd come too because I was working that evening. I usually spend the mornings with friends.' She gives these details in a toneless voice, unemotional as if the child in her were dead and this its carved last message. 'He'd see me to my friend's block; that was our routine. We'd walked half the distance – there was never anywhere nearby to park – and they took him, just like that. Like a sudden wind blowing.'

While she talks my eyes automatically take in further details of the room: a spiky gilt headdress (imitation flames) dangling from a hook next to the mirror, a faded pink curtain across the corner, half-concealing a chipped stone sink. The multitude of little pots and tubes, an orange showercap with her dark hairs caught in it, a floaty dress of lilac and purple hung from a nail. The girl's voice and face have flattened now, like exhaustion. I remember how draining the last weeks of pregnancy are, and into her monologue I say, 'You shouldn't be working.'

A flash of pure astonishment on her face, then she rallies. 'I'm fine, Madame.'

'You have other friends who can help you?'

She nods. 'Plenty of friends.' A mocking simper drags her lips down. This isn't the child in her womb speaking, this is some smear that life has laid on her since.

Then I startle the girl, I startle Helene and myself, but Rick wherever he is would want me to make this offer. 'If you need anything . . .'

Her generous response surfaces and then disappears, but it did exist. 'I shall be fine.' The simper returns, ugly but what can you expect? She reminds me, 'This isn't my first.'

'You've made arrangements—'

'For adoption? Yes, as soon as the brat's out of me it goes away.' She pulls a plastic hand-mirror toward her and freshly outlines her lips. There'll be no more softening from her. And she and I have lived close enough inside each other, during these past minutes, for me to accept that she's speaking the truth about what happened on the street the day before yesterday.

I say, 'I understand,' and perhaps I begin to. At least she looks confused and afraid. I get up, towing puzzled Helene with me; we leave.

Outside on the pavement, while we await the taxi that the doorman has called, Helene says, 'She's a hard little piece; can you trust a word she says?'

'Oh, I think so.' Am selectively sure, in fact, but the language in which the girl and I understood each other – that wouldn't translate readily for Helene. The taxi pulls up, Helene gives our address and we drive home. She's tactful enough not to say, Now what? and for this I'm grateful to her. I believe the girl's description of what happened: they stole him and took him away. Whichever *they* were involved.

'You expect she'll search for him?' says Helene softly with a nervous glance at the taxi driver.

'Dear God, no!' Helene has lived out of this country for so long, and Lebanon has corrupted itself so during those years. It and she no longer have any common ground. 'No, she'll grab such safety as she has and try never to think of him again.' When Helene stares at me shocked and disbelieving, I reinforce this, because my certainty of it is absolute. 'Beirut corrupts, my dear; like a plague victim it breathes on you or you touch it and . . .' One gasp, a toxic swelling or two and within hours you're dead; that's Beirut. Guns not bacilli, but the principle's the same. Beirut, our beautiful city, corrupts absolutely.

34

Since the discovery of the priest's body his sense of danger had deepened; it clamoured in his head continually and not even the busy shifts nor Solange's warm embraces could mute it. Georges was gone, the priest was gone. Rick feared for Madeleine and was thankful that this daughter from Paris, who sounded to be a person of solid common sense, would be staying with her mother for a while. He planned to check on them extra-frequently. The one person it never occurred to him might be in danger was himself. He was a part of the scene now, yes, but much of him still held back and observed, marvelled, couldn't take for granted. He didn't judge any more (except when forced into it, as by the luxury of Summerland), and all his earlier judgements sounded to him like the simplistic babblings of a child. A not very bright child, at that.

So on the street, while he walked Solange to her friend's, he was recalling the previous night and the peace of the villa which so ironically surrounded the squabbling, bickering, intermittently loving pair of them. He wasn't calm Rick any more, Solange could pick quarrels but he could become irritable too, and more than irritable, a sort of desperation to which he couldn't assign a focus. As if she, and their life together, were scouring him out emotionally and there were caverns in him, winds blowing, he'd never suspected before. He hated to become so conscious of these violent emotions in himself, but Solange kept – so it seemed – deliberately provoking them. When he tried to lose himself in any distraction such as working the villa garden, she stirred up some argument which brought him back to his unhappy self again.

There on the street they had one of their brief moments of closeness and clarity. She pointed out to him in a shop window a dress she coveted (which meant, was determined to have) and they laughed together over her clothes passion, her likeness in this to old couture-mad Madeleine. The two of them started to walk on again and suddenly men were around him, shoving her away. They'd thrust him into the back of a car and it sped off before he could believe what was happening.

He lay pressed to the floor by someone's feet and a thick rug, which smelled of dust and motor oil. His mind was dark with fear and although he tried not to panic he could think only: Where'll they take me, how long will they hold me hostage? And, above all, Will I come out of this alive? He did try to keep track of which direction they were taking him in, and a faint surprise pierced his terror – because they weren't driving the twisty route into the slums of south Beirut, where rumour said hostages were usually held, but on a longer journey without many corners. It could be the old highway which led south-east towards the mountains, the Damascus road that eventually climbed the Lebanon Range and led into Syria. A long way: this journey didn't last that long.

Past the roughly tied blindfold and the stinking rug he could see nothing, but when the car stopped and they dragged him out he smelled what was surely mountain air. They shoved him forward between a couple of them and his feet stumbled on steps leading upward, not down. That at least was a relief. Freed hostages had described in gruesome detail how they were held in cellars sometimes, with cockroaches, huge spiders and maybe rats. There'd be no light anywhere, no air except a thin fume-choked stream of it which an ancient generator reluctantly dragged in. So it was almost a relief to stumble with his guards along an upstairs passage and through a doorway into a space that echoed hollow. A room? His two guards wrenched him sideways and he came up against a wall; metal chinked and a cold, hard circlet closed around his ankle. One of the men spoke for the first time, in terse Arabic phrases that Rick in his fear could barely follow.

'You must stay here. We bring you food. You keep this' – a tug at the blindfold – 'on always when we come in, or we beat you. Understand?'

Rick summoned a shaky acceptance. Anything to get away from their close physical presence. They shoved him up against a sort of metal bed (he felt the coiled springs, the edge of a thin mattress) and left. The door closed, a key turned, footsteps muffled by dust went along the corridor. Cautiously he raised the blindfold a half-inch to make sure he was really alone. Yes, and needles of sunlight glittered past the window's iron shutters. He listened but heard no sounds. True, the shutter would block some of them off, but for sure he wasn't in a town of any size. His legs suddenly weakened and he sat down on the side of the bed, laid his blindfold carefully beside him and tried to think.

Solange had seen him snatched away, so what would she do and who would she tell? She'd make sure Madeleine heard about it, for sure. If by any terrible chance she couldn't – if seeing him grabbed had given her such a shock that it brought on the baby's birth – well, word would still get around pretty damn quickly. In Beirut it always did. And Madeleine was well-known, respected. Yes, someone would tell her or pass the news through Brigitte. For damn sure Brigitte wouldn't lift a finger to help him get free, but Madeleine would do all she could.

Trying to reason all this out had calmed his mind slightly but, when he heard feet returning along the corridor, his whole body and mind jittered and he was back in the state of pure panic: he must get free – he couldn't endure any of this. He forced his hands to pick up the blindfold and fix it in place. He could still feel their fingers on him, shoving him and bruising the flesh, and more than anything else he dreaded physical violence. He'd gladly do or say whatever they wanted, for always, if only they'd stay clear of beating him.

'I come in now,' said a gruff voice at the door, this time in English. 'I bring you food, Coke and a jug.'

Rick muttered, 'Okay. Thanks.' He sat hunched on the bed until the man had gone again. The 'jug' turned out to be a urinal: there was a sort of horrible slickness to their actions as if they'd done this to other men, plenty of times before. He looked at the beans and can of Coke with loathing, but the shock of hearing English spoken had loosened his bladder so that he barely grabbed the jug in time.

Afterwards he tried to force down the food and drink. His throat seemed to have closed up, but there was no guessing when they might bring him anything again. While he ate and drank he raked in his terrified thoughts and tried to marshal them: the basic act of eating made this a little easier. Okay, Madeleine would be notified by someone – and what would happen then to persuade these men to hand him back? Enough hostages had been taken and released, during these fifteen years, that the whole process had developed a sort of routine. He and Madeleine had several times watched its stages during the news bulletins on television.

No use approaching the American Embassy; in fact at this point worse than useless. The embassy had never succeeded in getting other hostages released until whichever militia held them was ready to let them go. And sometimes official prodding had been followed by the execution of a hostage at his captors' hands. No use approaching Chehab or anyone else in the States, since pleas by the President himself had failed in previous cases. No, the only course to follow was the usual one: approach the various militias – politely, ready to offer a bribe or tell whatever lies might be necessary – with a photo of the hostage and ask if they'd seen him or heard any gossip. A Western journalist had been kidnapped several months before, and his buddies at the news bureau drove around all over Lebanon, showing his picture at every checkpoint and asking if that militia had seen him. The method hadn't freed the man, but at least it confirmed where he was and which militia was holding him – which could be important, because sometimes the militia responsible would take months to confirm a kidnapping. Only when the basic details were known could slow, patient and wary talks begin. But Madeleine, an old woman: how could she do any of this?

Hours passed, the splinters of sun shifted and went. The chain fastened to Rick's ankle allowed him to take a couple of steps beside the bed but that was all. He paced this tiny area for a while, then sat and, fighting his rising panic, tried to think again. He couldn't think of anyone but Solange and Madeleine – Solange who must have been as shocked as himself by his capture, and Madeleine who, with her long knowledge of the city, must be able to start the process to get him free. Surely as soon as the right militia was approached they would free him? He wasn't a journalist who might have offended someone or have valuable information, and for goddam sure he wasn't a spy. These men had searched him for weapons but hadn't taken away the money from his wallet, so he couldn't believe money was their motive. No, they must have taken him for some political reason and in mistake for someone else. Surely they'd soon realise that.

At dark footsteps arrived again, a different voice this time but guttural English again. 'You cover eyes now.' A clash of metal pans, then the steps went. A loaf of the flat round Lebanese bread, slices of cheese, another Coke, an empty urinal to replace the full one. Rick told himself that he was less scared than at first, but his hands shook and were icy. A musty blanket lay across the foot of the bed; he lay down, pulled it over him, and listened to the silence.

End of his first imprisoned day.

35

So I embark on another search through the city, although this time I don't explore the ruined buildings along the Line: hostages are kept alive for several months at least, and the basements bordering the Line are too wrecked for useful prisons. No, his captors are holding him in some cellar amid Beirut's slums. So I traverse on foot the whole centre of the city, both East and West Beirut. Daily I tramp unheeding across the sectarian dividing lines and ask any man who looks like a militia member, any bearded face or rifle or military cap, 'My grandson – this is his photograph, have you seen him?' They recognise, these Palestinians or Sunni or Shi'ite Muslims, that I'm theoretically their enemy, but also I'm an old woman wandering and unsafely grabbing these strangers by their shirt-sleeves, accosting them, so they decide I'm insane. A dementia, therefore harmless. They glance at the photo and because I'm old and insane they don't bother to lie. In their faces I clearly read the technical interest they take in being free to tell the truth for once. 'No, haven't seen.'

Seraphite gets genuinely angry at me and threatens to lock me in the house, and Helene (who is so out of touch that she hasn't understood the danger until Seraphite shouts its details) resolutely supports her. But I'd defy the two of them and all Beirut, only after eight days something unexpected happens – my body won't obey me. A pain that prevents my left leg from bearing my weight. Helene drags me forcibly to our family doctor, whom I haven't bothered to visit for years, and he confirms it. Rest, he says, and if he weren't such a well-meaning little man, nervously putting on and off his silver-framed glasses while I rage, I'd curse him to my last breath.

But he can't be suspected of any ulterior motive, and Helene and Seraphite act more like fire-breathing dragons towards me than is human (their fear breeds fire), so I rest. Damn the leg and the doctor and the two of them and the whole city, especially damn the filthy types who've stolen the boy away. I rest, I rage, I curse all militiamen because there's no violence, been very little for several days before he disappeared, so why would anyone grab and hold him? No sense to it. Then I remind myself that Beirut never was a place of sense. Abrupt, meaningless contrasts, yes: slums and luxury flats, Paris fashions and rags. And that stupid boast, God help us, about our snow and sea – visit both in the same day! Who'd care? Who'd choose to? There was no sense to that either, just as there's been no sense to the alternations of violence and calm since. No sense to whatever abruptly starts the fighting each time (varying tribal or clannish causes), no sense to the way in which it gradually subsides. No sense to the so-called logic of any of us Beirutis, including myself who loves and hates simultaneously.

On the fourteenth day after his snatching, my leg pains me less and the swelling is down. I say to Helene, 'Call a taxi.' When she shakes her head firmly I pick up the phone myself; fortunately it works. Seraphite's day off, so there's only one guardian to fight. I hate to overpower Helene's will so brutally – this must remind her of the most stringent disciplines of her childhood – but something urges me on, a necessity. We walk out through the ruined cinema. My leg moves stiffly, cramped, but at least it doesn't refuse. The taxi waits.

I give the address of Solange's nightclub and Helene says, 'But this is afternoon; she won't be there yet.'

'They'll know where I can find her.' She must have heard something by now. With all her contacts some rumour or helpful whisper must have reached her. I'll force her to share her information with me. If I have to put my hands around her throat and squeeze, I'll force her.

The nightclub is tawdry by daylight, the silver eyes of its facade tarnished; the restaurant is open and busy. A waiter finds the manager for us. This is an expensive man too, oily-skinned, oily-mannered, with a face closed over secrets. I ask for her address and my tone of voice makes clear that he can't bully or refuse me, I'm determined. He undermines my hectoring by showing a surprising respect: God help me, it's on account of my name. Since the streets have gushed blood, and bomb-blasts shrivelled the trees, I tend to forget that in a previous era my husband's family (and mine too) were *someone*. Rick would cringe and fade at this discrimination in his favour, but I seize it with a thirsty glee; it'll help me find him. 'Madame, she's away for a while.'

'But you have her address.' I'm so tight-concentrated that I've forgotten her pregnancy, the swollen preparedness of her fingers and belly, the tired, expectant face (and my conviction that she'd lied to Rick about the due date). I haven't forgotten the villa (it hangs in my mind like a cruelly pinned butterfly) but she was tired of the place, and in Rick's absence she surely wouldn't go there. So she'll have a city address; I'll force him.

'The baby,' he says with that absurdly respectful manner, 'a couple of days ago – I believe she's still in hospital.'

'Which one?'

He tells me, the American Hospital. The best-equipped; somebody's paying good money. Did Rick arrange this beforehand? I'm already turning away when a thought strikes me. 'She's all right? And the baby too?'

'Yes, Madame, I understand everything went quite normally.' Dismissive, with the faintest of smiles, as if this is an afterthought for him also, as if he realises that for women of position such as myself, women from old-established families, this rootless promiscuous girl's welfare has no real importance any more than it does for him, her temporary employer.

'She'll come back to work here eventually?' I mustn't lose touch with my only slight link.

'Oh yes, Madame, her little *chansons* are quite popular.' Which firmly limits her talent. He adds, as if he and I share a sardonic small joke, 'I believe she is going to stay with − ah − a *friend*, to convalesce.' Which pegs her love life equally firmly and dismissively. And cruelly for Rick, but no doubt the boy expected little else.

I nod, a dignified acknowledgement from a *grande dame*. He rushes (glistening with respect) to hold the door open and I think, You ridiculous relic, Monsieur; even I have more sense than to think I'm important nowadays. Back to the waiting taxi, to the American Hospital.

She has a private room. Yes, money was involved here; useless to wonder whose. And money has become unimportant. I'd gladly lose my fortune and go begging, to find Rick. I march into the girl's room with all the dignity my hobbling leg allows, plod up to the bed and confront her, creamy-peaceful in her creamy setting. (I'd expected her to have tossed the baby to its adopter at once, but it's still here.) 'You must have heard something,' I say.

Possibly not the right greeting to a new mother, but she understands; over the baby's ignored head she gives me the same faintly conspiratorial smile as did the manager. Saying, 'New life isn't important, only you and I and our concerns matter.' Her gaze weighs me up; she doesn't speak.

My brain has been probing every possible angle, so I say, 'He has no capital of his own – if they stole him for the fortune, he can't touch that for several years yet. And these people may have a frightening patience, but surely they wouldn't wait that long.'

'Probably they wouldn't.' Her faint smile persists; it goes past me to a man who withdrew from the bedside when we arrived. He now sits by the window with its protective wire mesh and its extensive view of shattered West Beirut. His pallid European face, cocooned between sleek golden hair and grey business suit, regards me calmly, without interest. The girl murmurs to me, 'A new friend of mine.' Beside me Helene draws a sharp breath, but that's ridiculous. This is no time to worry about the girl's morals.

'Will he be able to help find the boy?'

'He'll put out feelers.' The girl lies back on her creamy pillows, tired but not swollen; she'll be all right. And the child looks normal; between the two of us the small mouth gapes in a sleeping yawn. A dusting of dark hair, dark eyes too, when for an instant it opens them. 'Feelers,' the girl repeats, 'he has some useful contacts. Fixers and the men who pay them.' She yawns delicately like the baby; she's a pretty creature. No wonder the men flock.

'It's been two weeks,' I say. 'He's not used to rough conditions. I can't bear to think of him imprisoned in some cellar—' The baby wakes and waves its fingers, but I keep well away from it: the clutch of their tiny hands at one's own . . . no. An eel, a worm, a primitive life squirming: I'm strong-stomached but that's too raw a happening for me. A new life thrusting. Perhaps that's why I fear them. They're unpredictable, and born to our unpredictable streets. 'Boy or girl?' I say.

'Girl. And Rick – perhaps he's tougher than you think.' But she says this absently, as if she has practised weaning her attention away from his predicament. Then she adds hastily, automatic, 'Of course we must keep trying, but he may be standing it well, getting used to—'

'It will crucify him.' There are dimensions she's not aware of. That big bland country where he grew up, and his secure life there, were the worst preparation for this. 'He wasn't living here through the civil war,' I say. 'It's different for you; you grew up with the fighting.'

She accepts this with the faint, unsurprised smile.

'And this brat—' I jerk my head at the man by the distant window and mutter, 'He's not the father?'

She laughs, an honest belly-gurgle. 'Sacré, no!' Then, with the faintest hint of mischief and allure, 'Not yet.'

I could deeply love this girl, but I shan't get the chance. The man clears his throat, shifts his feet, glances at his watch and at us. We're taking his precious visiting time. I say, 'You'll let me know as soon as you hear?' (Not 'if' but 'when'.)

She pulls the creamy bedjacket close and her smile fades. 'I'll do my best, Madame,' she says. I'd swear that somewhere in her there's genuine feeling toward Rick, but not, I fear, enough to keep the two of them together. 'I fear' for Rick's sake, not for hers. She'd survive anything. I prided myself that I'd had an adventurous youth and escaped so many of the conventions, but this girl leaves me miles behind.

Helene nudges my elbow and I realise the girl is saying goodbye. Her boyfriend has returned to the bed and stands there passing a hand across his gold hair and shifting his feet at us. 'Goodbye,' I say. The baby opens its mouth and produces a wail of astonishing power. Solange lazily cups the infant in her arm and the wail stops; that stabs me back to Rick's total lack of security.

The taxi: my leg hurts but I tighten my lips against the pain. We go home. Where I must, cursing, prop my leg up and accept Helene's ministrations, and wait.

36

In the daytime he could sometimes control his mind, and the guards' comings and goings meant that he needed to be alert to what was going on around him, but at night his dreams skidded wildly so that when he woke, each morning, cursing and covered with sweat, he had trouble remembering where he was. In those night hours Chehab sent him to Beirut all over again and Rick yelled furiously that he wouldn't go. Not because of Josie – even in his dreams she belonged firmly in the past; he'd no time for her any more. But there was some obscure reason why he oughtn't to go to Lebanon. He'd do better to join his mother in that commune of hers . . . no, she'd been dead for years, so he couldn't do that either. The delights of life in the States rose in front of his eyes, those casual laughing times when life had been so good he'd not realised *how* good.

Baseball games: he was no great player but he loved to watch. Vacations at other kids' houses in the mountains or along Puget Sound. One unforgettable week at a cabin rented with other boys near a forest of tall redwoods – not like trees, more like standing giants with their thoughtful, silent heads way up above the world of people. Barbecues on one or another beach. And, once, a nervous laughing ghost-hunting night with classmates in a big old creaky house overlooking the water, on Bainbridge Island. From these pure episodes he woke, with the smell of salt in his nostrils, to the door of the bare room grinding open, the need to grab his blindfold and put it on, the drearily predictable food and the joshing or anger of the guards. Sometimes they spoke to him in Arabic so fast and fluent he could scarcely grasp a word of it, but more often they used their own version of pidgin American, always spoken with irony or anger as if to say, We know what country you come from and we hate you most of all for that.

Sometimes too they beat him – not often, but each time it was intolerable. They used a hefty stick or their fists or open-handed slaps; once in a while they kicked him also. Every time, he chewed his lip and tried not to cry out under their blows, then he cried out anyway and they jeered. He pleaded with them to stop, but they laughed and finished only when they'd a mind to. Afterwards, lying on his bed too exhausted to sob, he'd try to figure out what he'd supposedly done wrong *this* time, but he could rarely come up with an answer. They were like no men he'd ever met before: they were laughing and angry at the same time, cheerful and yet terrified of their bosses in the militia, that shadowy bunch none of whom ever visited him. He did gather that the guards who brought him food and beat him had mostly come from backgrounds of grinding poverty; they'd probably had plenty of family bereavements too. Sometimes, in an evening, one or other of them would come into the room and lounge around asking quiet, brief questions about the States, but always after a few minutes their derision and scorn leapt out. Rick couldn't begin to understand or make friends with any of them, even the quieter ones.

He discovered that the only way he could live imprisoned and stay sane was by dismissing his dreams and thoughts of living people as soon as he woke up. Any memory of people in the States – dead or alive – or of Madeleine and even Brigitte or dead Georges, tried to loosen him emotionally so that if he gave into it he'd have no control left. Especially this was true of Solange. His mind winced away from picturing her or saying her name. He could only handle this captivity by the most rigid control.

The guards were totally unpredictable, and this he couldn't get used to. Adequate – if dull – food some days, near-starvation others. Kicks and blows, then for days on end no contact except the bringing of meals and the twice-daily trip to a hole which was the toilet. Suddenly the gift of a radio with detailed instructions on which programmes he was allowed to hear. The equally suddenly removal, several days later, of the radio although he'd obeyed (hating himself for his servility) their orders. The hours, days, weeks, alone were achingly hard to take. Why wouldn't they at least put another hostage or two in with him? He tried to recall which Western hostages were still held, and by which militia, but although he'd heard those news bulletins with Madeleine the details hadn't stayed with him. Time stretched itself out unbelievably long, but no one except the guards showed up.

37

During the next few days I can only sit with my leg up; it slowly heals and I brood. I answer Helene in monosyllables, I stare at my meaningless collection of silver ornaments, at the stone cherub who has survived while so many real people have died – some of them no doubt young and helpful and generous – and at the walls of this windowless living room. I stare at my favourite tapestry, the wistful woman with assorted flowers and unicorn.

The grass around her is neatly shorn, not coarse ragged tufts like Beirut's ruined streets, and her sky blooms within flowering vines: a happy picture, you'd say. But something stirs in my mind about that legend . . . and couldn't those pale blobs poking from behind the bushes be faces? Then I recall what the legend was.

That she's a decoy. The hunters are really chasing the unicorn, and only the presence of a young innocent will enable them to take the glorious creature alive. And the unicorn – this puzzling mythical animal – is . . . no, I won't accept that.

Seraphite pokes her head in (I persuaded Helene to try a new hairdresser's on the Rue Emile Edde this morning. She'll be gone for hours and the primping session will have the same idiotically cheering effect on her as it does on most women) and says, 'Lunch. Or do you intend to sit there for ever, depressing yourself about the future?'

Our future – that mythical puzzling animal. And the young innocent is sacrificed to those who, armed and active, are hunting the animal . . . no, no. I heave myself up and say, 'Of course I'll eat.' I shake off her brusquely offered help. There's nothing wrong with my leg that another day or two's rest won't cure, then I'll go searching again, badgering, asking questions, gripping people's throats.

Stuffed courgettes, then honey cakes. I'm not in the mood but while he's missing I never would be; I force the food down. Seraphite, instead of polishing or cleaning elsewhere while I eat (since he disappeared, she invents chores so that she doesn't have to stay around me) stands beside the stove, hands on hips, swarthy face inexorable, and begins. Yes, Seraphite, I already realise all this. You needn't put into words what my conscience has been shouting. But she does.

'Whose fault – who put him at risk?' Yes, Seraphite. 'And you *knew*, didn't you, Madame? Knew the danger in advance, but nothing would satisfy you except to push him in among the wolves to search for your precious Georges.' Yes, Seraphite (says Grandmother Wolf). 'And, going further back than the boy,' – I tell myself she won't dare, but she does – 'that son of yours, Madame – who put those ideas in Georges' head, eh? Who encouraged him and stuffed him full, from his cradle up?' God damn you, Seraphite, yes. 'And your daughters, what kind of an upbringing—' Shut up, Seraphite, you're stripping me naked. Finally I yell at her, 'But the boy, damn you! The boy!' and we face each other, both breathing heavily, across the width of the kitchen.

She recovers herself first. 'Yes,' she says, 'when such things happen it hurts, doesn't it?' She goes back to the stove and picks up her polishing cloth. 'It always hurts when it's too late.' That's her epitaph for me. I'm laid away, buried, with my corruptibility and selfishness an integral part of my tainted flesh: she and all decent people have pronounced sentence on me. She goes out of the room and her straw house-shoes heavily climb the stairs.

In the room that was Rick's, and which Helene is temporarily using, her rustling footsteps pad around, polishing the taint of me out of there.

I finish lunch, then take my siesta, which consists of staring at the bedroom shutter and making plans for when I'll be more active again. I'll sup no more self-pity than I must. And after Helene returns, our evening . . . yes, the hairdresser did a satisfactory job, but this isn't Paris and Helene is getting restless; she'd like to go home before much longer. Yet from her poking little remarks it seems that she feels, foolishly, an obligation. So while she sits, with neat hair and charcoal-grey dress, laying out another tidy but insoluble game of Demon Patience, I try to put the matter clearly. 'Leave whenever you want to; no one's detaining you here. I'm grateful you came, but you're not *necessary*.'

Thus Grandmother Wolf spits out the chewed fragments . . . Try as I will, I can't put things tactfully. The card in her hand quivers as if I've deliberately jabbed her. But she's well-mannered (how can a daughter of mine have grown up *polite*?); she abandons her game, earnestly faces me and speaks quietly, restrained. 'The truth is, Maman, I'd like to take you back with me.'

'A holiday? But I don't need one.' There have been times when I've enjoyed roaming the Paris boulevards, window-shopping or prodding a seam or button in some couturier's fitting room, but there's no point in her carting me there for a few weeks to pander to a vanished part of myself. 'Really,' I say (and attempt to soften my tone), 'it's kind of you, my dear,' – that awful dismissive 'my dear' of Brigitte's – 'but I'm a hermit crab nowadays. And anyway I couldn't leave Beirut while Rick is—'

'After that's settled,' she says. How easy it is to dismiss the boy when you've never met him. She becomes crudely realistic and adds, 'Or if not – you can keep in touch. Surely the girl or Seraphite can—'

I say firmly, 'No, I couldn't enjoy a holiday till he's found,' but she counter-attacks.

'Not for a holiday, Maman, but to live with us permanently. Wouldn't you like that?'

'*Leave Beirut?*'

She picks up the pack of cards again, but her fingers are dealing wrong; they forget to count or select. 'Maman dear, be reasonable. This house is bigger than you need, and with ruins all around and the lack of safety in the whole city . . .' She gets up and crosses the rug to me. 'I've worried about you, all these years. Naturally you've enjoyed having your own home but—' She drops a kiss on my forehead and goes back to her chair hurriedly as if I'd bite. 'Daniel quite agrees,' she assures me, sitting down and hastily dealing the remains of the pack at random.

Daniel, that forgettable husband of hers. But for years I regarded her as very forgettable too. Will I never understand people? And will some of them never understand me? 'Leave Beirut and this house?' My ears still can't believe what they've heard.

'Maman . . .' She hesitates and into this pause I can dump Georges and probably (according to her reasoning) Rick, too. 'There's no one but Brigitte here with you, is there? And Seraphite in the daytime. This boy – when he shows up again, he'll rush back to his girlfriend. And Brigitte's out most of the time. What do bricks and mortar really matter?' Her hand twitches in a dismissive gesture and splays the cards across the rug between us.

As she bends to pick them up I say, 'Your game wouldn't have come out right anyway.' Say it clear, decisive, with finality. She straightens with the untidy pack in her hand. Did her face always have this hesitant sweetness? Surely not; I would have noticed and been kinder to her. Or more angry, because to be sweetly begged for what I absolutely can't give is infuriating.

'Bricks and mortar,' I say, 'can be trusted more than people.'

'*Here*?' Surely the smashed house wall and smashed city fill both our minds, but I'll call her bluff. I fling out my arms at the intact furniture and tapestries and pictures and the three intact walls that enclose them.

'Here,' I say. 'We survived, didn't we? And the worst is over.' A statement that would make any true Beiruti splutter with laughter into his 'araq, but Helene has become so separated from us that she can't judge.

'But still,' she says (her sweetness hurts so that it makes me cruel), 'Maman, when Brigitte leaves home there'll be no one—'

'There'll be myself.' And Rick somewhere, and somewhere the bones of Georges. And presumably, somewhere in the city, Brigitte. Probably too the girl Solange, who ought to mean nothing to me without Rick. And in the city there exist some beliefs which I once held: they're shredded and mangled, yet the flavour of them is the flavour of myself. I won't promote them again but I can't avoid being what they are. I'm this city, I'm the walls that enclose me, these crumbling walls of stone and mortar. Those old tremulous people – Michel's parents and mine – and this house, the *objets d'art*, the city they loved, the city I've loved too, the city I've taken the colouring of . . . 'No. I won't let anyone carry me out like a readdressed package.'

No doubt the words, the tone, are wrong again. Helene goes on trying to persuade me to Paris, but in a plaintive, hopeless tone. I shake my head and turn away. Her gentle, unhappy voice trickles on while Paris in all its liveliness and diversity rises before me. Yes, I used to be very fond of Paris. One could live there pleasantly enough with money and an attentive daughter. You could spoon up an ice at a pavement cafe without being surrounded by the mental stench of someone having been

certainly shot there, the stench of another death in preparation for that same spot. Oh, I know they've their
terrorist troubles, but those are headline-makers, difficult
and tricky exceptions, not unavoidable events woven
through the fabric of even a retired old woman's life. A
bateau-mouche trip on the Seine would be easy for old
legs. The bitter odour of the chestnut flowers and the
croak of the jackdaws that infest those quays – it takes no
effort to summon them back. The grey squared roofs
above the sedate grey buildings, the numerous little
balconies like tiny jokes . . . how strange it would be to
see so many balconies all intact. How strange to imagine
leaving Beirut and this house, how impossible.

Helene says with her terrible soft kindness, her air of
trying to neutralise my guilt, 'Is it on account of the boy
that you won't leave, Maman? Because surely—'

'No. Yes. In part perhaps. I couldn't leave while that's
unresolved. But even afterwards – no, my dear.' This
cruel, uncompassionate, varied city and my identical
self . . . 'Thank you, but no.'

It must have been several nights after that – my leg had
almost healed – when Brigitte came home early, stood in
the living room doorway and with her voice high-pitched
and eyes brilliant told us that she was moving out, that
she was getting married in two days' time. At a mosque,
to an Arab.

There are moments blind as lightning. Brigitte leans at
the door and talks; continually she watches me. The
mosque, she says, is the one on the Line near this house,
the mosque where from my bedroom window I saw the
sapling growing in the wall. While Brigitte talks, Helene
fidgets nervously: she's learned a certain amount of
libertarianism from Paris and her husband, but apparently not enough to encompass this. When Brigitte
finishes her explanations my right hand, of its own

volition, holds itself out toward her – the most unlikely gesture she, and perhaps I too, could imagine.

She comes forward dubiously. Above her ivory dress she wears a black-and-silver wrap spattered with silver ferns. Soon she'll be too middle-aged, too haggard, to wear her hair loose, but in this dimly lit room the dark rivers of hair flow and entwine and form the only possible setting for her unmoving face. Composed, but the hand meeting mine trembles.

'Fireworks,' I say (my voice, like my hand, has taken a path outside my control), 'you expect those from me, don't you?' So calm – can I have understood what she said? An *Arab*? My hand pulls her down to a stool beside me.

'Naturally I do, Maman.' She sinks gracefully to the stool and tucks her long legs away. Brigitte would be graceful and composed on the edge of the grave.

'You truly want to do this?' I ask her. She'd started to speak again but checks herself, surprised. I'm surprised too at this unpredicted sure current which rises from the deepest centre of me.

'Of course,' she says. She studies my face and then gives me a mocking smile that excludes Helene. This mocking rivalry – this most painful intimacy – has always been restricted to the two of us. 'I love the man,' she says, and as soon as her lips have finished shaping the words the mocking smile returns; it plays so lively and concealing that I've no idea whether she does care for him. Past us Helene, with heavy throat-clearing, tramps out of the room: tactful or – God help us – another bruised ego to salve. 'You're furious,' Brigitte says, 'aren't you?' She sounds disappointed, bereft.

'Yes, I'm furious.' Poor child, if my anger is the only gift she values, she's welcome to it. And no doubt when my numb incredulity thaws I'll be furious indeed. I examine the hand of hers I'm holding: the long fingers with a few choice rings (some perhaps brotherly gifts from Georges and some from other men), the smooth back of the hand – young-looking for her age – and the palm . . . you'd say soft, vulnerable, if this weren't Brigitte. 'Desolated,' I say automatically, 'and angry – how *can* you do this?' The elegant fingers, the young back of the hand, the soft-seeming palm, refuse to answer. One of her rings is an emerald, a square-cut gem in a setting of twisted silver roses. 'You wouldn't marry this man if Georges were alive.'

She snatches the hand away as if I'd stung her. 'Yes, Georges gave me that emerald; why shouldn't he? We had to find our affection among ourselves when you were overseas and Father was busy. A succession of nurse-maids . . . You'd say this is special pleading,' she says lightly, and her eyes glow in the composed face. 'That we were well looked-after and I've nothing to complain of? Why don't you send me to bed supperless for defying you?' She tucks the hand away safely with the other.

I'd like to ask, Will this man make you happy? but the question, in connection with Brigitte, has no meaning. She probably reads my silence for the anger she sought. She begins to tell me the details that a mother would long to hear if we were a normal mother and daughter and this a normal wedding. 'Of course,' she says, 'I'm converting to Islam. Not that I've any belief, but it'll be convenient.'

She watches me, past the emerald that dead Georges gave her and past her young-seeming hand. I've failed more deeply than I ever realised. Not because of this whim or brute act or cry-for-help of hers; Brigitte would have been Brigitte no matter what. No, I've failed in ways as delicate and necessary as the fern tracery that holds her wrap together. 'Convert then,' I say, 'damn you.' Shall I never find the exact words to reply with, the necessary ones? 'The blasted war did this to you.' But while I say it I realise it's not true of Brigitte. And she makes me momentarily very happy (an amazing warm delight) by agreeing.

'No, Maman, that's too easy an alibi. I would intend to cut loose ferociously – and would carry it through – no matter what.' For an instant her face flashes again with mockery. 'Didn't you always train us, when we were children, to cut loose from emotion and make up our own minds?'

But, as she's said, I was so often abroad that the direct training of them was usually undertaken by others: nursemaids, tutors. And, importantly, by my husband, of course, when he was home from the bank. She reads my mind now, this new fierce Brigitte who almost frightens me.

'Voluntary absence is a form of training too,' she says softly. 'You taught us more in that way than you'll ever admit. Our papa loved us but he was so busy and—' The words 'How could you leave him so often? What kind of a marriage do you call that?' tremble on her lips, I'll swear they do, but my glare keeps them unsaid. Michel and I had a real affection for each other, we both wanted to marry and I understood that as a businessman he wished for children. So we had two sons, two daughters; that seemed to be enough. We could afford to pay whatever staff were necessary for their care, and Michel never objected to my travelling or doing the work for which I'd been trained. He knew I would be impossible to live with if I felt trapped.

I say none of this to Brigitte; it really isn't her affair and I suspect that any attempt I made to explain it would be disbelieved by her. But she gazes past me and her face softens as if she's forgotten my presence. 'The child in the mental hospital,' she says, 'the child who was driven mad by the shelling and will never recover – he's one of the few with a genuine alibi. He could truthfully blame the civil war.'

235

'Yes.' She brought the photograph home for me to see; it was at the start of her career and she was truly shocked. Not openly moved – Brigitte doesn't display emotion – but a stern righteous fiat that such things shouldn't be. The twisted body with the cluster of flies on each sore, the eyes that never closed unless a nurse forcibly closed them . . . of course he's not the only one. And we delude ourselves if we take pride in thinking that Lebanon's happenings are uniquely horrible. I tried to discuss that photograph with Father Mesrop once but he wouldn't play. Sensible man – he knew his and God's limits.

'You're not listening,' she says. This seems to alarm her more than if I kicked and screamed.

'Perhaps . . .' My traitor hand starts to steal out in spite of me to tangle itself in her dark long hair, but I haul it quickly back. 'This is such a shock,' I say. 'When I get my breath again I'll hate you as much as anyone could.'

She relaxes and smiles triumphantly. 'The wedding is the afternoon after tomorrow, Maman. You'll be able to see us from your bedroom window.'

'Yes.' How carefully and with what complexity does hatred make its arrangements, but how unpredictable is the human response. I don't feel the anger that I ought, therefore my identity is shattered. 'I'll try not to disappoint you.' I manage to sound resolute.

'Ah, dear Maman!' She leans forward and claps me on the shoulder. 'There for a moment I was afraid – but you're yourself, after all.'

I ask small, unimportant questions because silence is too revealing. She obviously takes my flat tone for fury and is delighted. And she enjoys boasting about the influence her fiancé has in the Shia community, how he's been able through his contacts to get the mosque partly repaired and opened for this one occasion only. She even pulls a small vial from her handbag and waves its red droplets in front of me. 'Red dye,' she mocks, 'for our sheets on the wedding night, to prove I'm a virgin.' And she laughs – God, *how* she laughs! After the wedding they'll live mostly in Iran, where he has a good job and much influence. She tells me in short, unrepeatable phrases what she thinks of Beirut. And of this house, of my family and her father's, and of me.

Yes, that's what one might expect; she's a jar of venom such as should be locked away in some laboratory. But like myself she's a woman: am I a vial full of venom too? And less human, I sometimes think, than Brigitte. She has a genuine liking for her photography and there was a deep affection for Georges. I say again – the words force themselves out like pressure into a vacuum – 'If Georges were alive you wouldn't—'

The flat of her hand, which seemed so soft, strikes my cheekbone and the force knocks me back into my chair. She stands over me and I wonder if she intends murder, but probably she's only checking that I'm alive enough to hate her. No blood runs from my cheek but the emerald ring has bruised it. 'Mesrop,' she says, 'is his damned chapel still intact downstairs?' I nod and she says, 'They all die like rats; can't you imagine a Giant Rat somewhere laughing at them?' She remembers to add, 'I've no doubt your blasted grandson died that way too.'

At once we're nose to nose, eyes to eyes, crouched and gripping each other. 'If you've heard anything about him you'll tell me.' But she wilts and gives a terrified, obedient headshake, blind and honest as a trapped animal's. I release her and she scrabbles to the door, her dignified saunter forgotten. At the door she straightens her hair, her wrap, then she says shyly like the child she never was, 'You *needn't* watch the wedding.'

The wrap and her face are carefully arranged; she blows me a defiant kiss, she goes.

Helene comes back into the room and I turn my face so that she shan't see the bruised cheek. That's the last –

perhaps the most important – secret Brigitte and I will share. Helene allows herself a little, affectionate triumph. 'Now you'll change your mind and go to Paris with me!' No, I obscurely feel that there's more reason than ever not to.

The day after tomorrow, when I watch Brigitte enter the mosque, I shall rage and my mind will flare in anger. Please God *then* I shall feel angry.

38

They started shifting him around from place to place; at some point he realised he was back in the city again. Still not in a cellar, and no useful gaps in the shutters, but Beirut lay (he was sure) outside the window. The frequent changes of place had tried to unanchor him further, but Beirut was known; he'd worked and had family there. Something of a solid base to life returned.

They stopped kicking him around too, in fact they ignored him except for meals and toilet times. Bit by bit he pulled himself back together into being a human again, but he knew he wouldn't ever be recognisably the same person he'd been before: such huge gaps had opened up. Hours or days of pure panic solid as metal, when he felt sure they'd shift elsewhere and not take him, would have lost interest. He'd be left here, shackled, to starve. Gradually he dared to remember the lives that must still be going on beyond the shutter: Solange and the coming (or arrived?) baby, the country villa and the house on the Line and Madeleine. She was probably blaming herself for his being captured, which was ridiculous because what had happened might have nothing to do with the priest or the death of Georges. You couldn't attach any logic to the events of Beirut and certainly not to the actions of these gunmen. Anyway he'd freely undertaken the enquiries about Georges and the chaperoning of Madeleine out to Summerland. He wouldn't do different if the situation were arising again now. (Yet every part of him, body and mind, screamed that he would; next time he'd refuse, out of cowardice, to get involved.)

Some mornings he was allowed to shave (even in this they were erratic) using an ancient razor with a blunt blade which could be a relic of some previous inmate. The shaving, because it was thought to be a delicate operation, was allowed only under the supervision of a guard, so Rick scraped away at his chin and peered into a fragment of mirror while the guard stayed out of the mirror's range, in a corner behind Rick. One day, while doing this, Rick caught sight of the healed wrist scars and he almost laughed out loud at the irony of his mood in those days and his opposite mood now. But laughter here could be misinterpreted; moreover if he once started to laugh he might not be able to stop. Another time he shifted his position accidentally while shaving: he caught sight of the militiaman behind him and for a moment couldn't be sure which of the dark-haired, dark-jawed faces in the mirror was his own. As if he were a ghost, a dead brother of these identical men.

Then the militiaman peered forward and said, 'Why you stop? You hurry now!' and the spell broke. But in that instant Rick had been Lebanese, sure of that fact and of that only.

One day in a sort of nervous boldness he stopped the guard who was taking the empty meal bowl away, and said, 'Why? If you'd only tell me *why* I'm here?'

Perhaps the guard was tired of not speaking with him too. At least the face behind the mask seemed to smile thinly and the unrecognisable voice said, 'Because your dead brother.' The man turned to leave again. 'Contacts.'

'My dead—'

'Or whatever he called himself.'

'My uncle Georges?' No one could be hurt by his using the name now.

'Whatever name he was going under at the time.' The

man left, locking the door behind him as always, and Rick was left to wonder whether there had been the faintest flicker of surprise in the voice at the mention of Georges' name, whether indeed they were talking about the same person. Whether Rick's kidnapping mightn't have been an error in identification from the word go.

More days – or was it weeks? – of waiting, of imprisonment, more shifting around from one dingy hole to another. When the man came to him after an indefinite period of this and said from behind the mask, in his usual flat tone, 'We move you again this afternoon. Nice move, you like very much,' Rick couldn't work up any interest. They were teasing him in their usual unpredictable fashion? Very well, he had no choice but to go along with them physically, but in other ways he simply wouldn't respond.

39

The next day passes silently; we're all bemused. In the evening Helene tests the edge of my thoughts, like a mouse dubious of the flavour of this piece of rind. She says, 'You won't watch from the window tomorrow – please don't, it would upset you too much, we'll keep busy with other things and . . .' No. Tomorrow my younger daughter is marrying a man I ought to hate. That makes the day special and I'll mark it somehow, indelibly.

Then Helene, seeing that I'm immovable on this, swings to the opposite extreme. She says, 'I'll go to the mosque if you'd like; if they won't let me in I'll wait outside. That way I'll get a closer view and can report to you . . .' Good God, no. Helene, what are you thinking of? To enter a Muslim place of worship or go anywhere near one, on the excuse that I'll necessarily have a *voyeur*'s curiosity about what they're doing . . . 'Do you plan to convert too?' I say sardonically.

'Maman, of course not . . . only I want to prevent you from being upset.'

This makes me decide that she must leave for Paris soon, as quickly as possible. I'm grateful for all she's done here and tried to do, but 'not to be upset' is a condition of life that I can't endure. I say, 'Don't you realise I thrive on these conflicts?' And that would have been bone-true once. There were years when hatred, argument, the fighting of our faction against others, were bread and wine to me. That was before what happened to Georges and

Father Mesrop, before whatever's happening to Rick. But even if my blade gets blunted yet more in the future, Helene's notion of a quiet life would never be right for me – although of course for her it is. I lean forward to where she sits opposite me, and touch her cheek. 'Your husband will worry,' I say. 'You really must go back.' Beirut and I mustn't break this couple's peace. 'If you don't phone the airline tomorrow about your ticket, I will.' My dry hand cups her cheek in a way that feels absent-minded, but she takes the hand and stares at it as if she's never seen it before.

'How can I leave you here?' she says theatrically. Poor woman, she has no gift for expressing herself in a way that could convince. She varies between a staid, genteel and well-mannered suggesting and, when she's upset, this unfortunate and rather repellent melodrama. My irritation gives me rudeness enough to remove my fingers from her grasp and speak brutally. If that's the only mood of mine that will send her back where she belongs, I'll use it.

'You can easily leave me. Did you suppose you're essential here? Because—'

She gets up abruptly and paces away. No doubt there are some things that even tranquil easy-going Helene can't bear to hear. 'No,' she says, 'don't explain any further, you've made yourself clear. People of your sort never mellow, they crumble away as gritty and acid as ever.' She stands over me. 'A battle-axe,' she says, 'aren't you? And always will be. You'll live to be a hundred and fight your family till your last breath.'

'A charming picture.' This crabbed ancient female cursing on her deathbed . . . but if that's the picture Helene needs to have of me in order to preserve her own security and her marriage – very well. She paces away again and says over her shoulder, 'I'll phone the airline first thing in the morning. You needn't throw me out; I can certainly take a hint.' She stands at the door and without our ritual goodnight kiss she says, 'I'm going to bed now. Are you going too?'

'Not yet.' She clearly takes this as a further sign of my cantankerous nature; her mouth tightens and she goes. But there's valid reason for my delay (no, not brooding over the future: I'll fill the hours and years ahead with whatever becomes available and accept any empty spaces, as I must). No, the truth is that Brigitte left something with me – and wasn't there a meaningful emphasis in her look, her tone, when she told me to use this something *soon*? Her eyes, her voice, pressed so deliberately and closely on me that when I now open the drawer of the side table and take the *something* out, I am full not of curiosity but of fear. A key: she pressed it so hard into my hand that it made a round-headed mark on my palm. The key of her darkroom. She said only, 'I won't be needing this any more. I've taken out the stuff I'd like to keep from there – I want you to have what's left. A present from me to you.' Harmless words? but I know my Brigitte.

I wait till all is quiet upstairs, Helene is in bed and possibly asleep. Then I go noiselessly in my felt slippers downstairs and along the stone-floored passage. I unlock the darkroom door.

Yes, I should have expected this. The poor child. The poor, hurting, cruel child.

She must have spent hours, some night when I was asleep, sticking these photos up on the walls. With murderous care she's hung them all at the exact level of my gaze. After the first glance I shut my eyes and stumble around the room blindly tearing them down; I'm terrified of discovering that one of the men is Georges. Her own brother . . . but it's very likely. I've seen enough already to know that there's a number of different men, mostly one at a time but not always. And the woman, from my hurried glimpses, is always herself. Of course it would be. To see any other woman in these poses wouldn't hurt me except in an abstract and distant way, and Brigitte never does anything at random.

Handful after handful of them. I stuff them with their blank backs uppermost into plastic rubbish bags which I must keep locked in here until Helene has left and then burn in the back yard: I can't risk even Seraphite seeing these. I knot the bags' tops together, put them in a corner and relock the room. The empty walls seem to sneer. It'll take a while to exorcise this ghost. Perhaps she'll never be exorcised – because mustn't I have done something grossly wrong to her, to receive this in return? It's as if she were saying, *This* is my gift in return for what you gave me. As if I were the venom-producing spider and had moved quickly with my sac to kill her, and the venom spurted back . . . Exactly that.

Afterwards I ought to lie awake and continue my remorse, my inquest; instead that night's sleep is like a dead woman's. The next morning, when I wake, the photos stand in the front of my mind, glaring and accusing me, but no doubt that's something I must live with. They won't be forgotten but will rise up to bludgeon me whenever I try to claim that I really wasn't a bad or uncomprehending mother. *Uncomprehending*: that's what hurts. I'd accepted that Brigitte was always difficult – but this violence of hers comes from a place in her whose existence I'd never suspected.

Meanwhile, on the afternoon of her wedding I watch discreetly from behind the edge of my shutter. The few women of the wedding party wear long dresses in blue or red or yellow, with half-veils covering their hair. The flowing fabrics mute their gait so that I recognise Brigitte only because she wears the full face-hiding veil, extending to her ankles over a dress of the same hot pink. The other members of the party surround her; they adjust her clothes and move her this way and that as if she's a possession, a thing belonging to them: indeed I suppose she is. God knows how her future will be. Her new husband looks older than her by several years, well-dressed in a white suit with gold-threaded long scarf and hat. He looks solid. Perhaps he'll be able to give her some of what she wants; perhaps their customs and traditions will allow him to. The rest of the space inside her, probably no one can fill. I'd anticipated that she would wave brutally up at me, but I realise now how self-centred and unlikely that half-wish was. Naturally she doesn't want to offend her new in-laws. She doesn't glance up or sideways, she steps into the car with her new husband and along the narrow cleared strip they drive away.

The next day Helene, on my definite order, leaves. I say to Seraphite that afternoon when the plane has gone, 'Well, this is it. Just the two of us.'

'You're a fool,' she says, 'you could have a comfortable life with her and buy the fancy clothes and trinkets you love and forget all the mess this country's in. A stubborn old fool.' But she doesn't rush away, furious at me, to polish elsewhere; instead she scrubs unnecessarily at the kitchen table and says, as if she's really worried, 'I shan't be here at night, you know, nor on my days off. What'll you do then?'

'My leg's well again, I've another twenty years before I need expect to be helpless. My father died at ninety and I should be able to better him by a decade or so.' I look at her sideways. 'There's been no shooting for quite a while; you should be in a good mood.'

'Madame, you expect me to be happy because no fresh graves are being added to the ones already there?'

'Ah, I'm sorry, Seraphite.' And I mean that. But I'm impelled to add, with a bitterness equal to any she could produce, 'A part payment.' And when she stares, 'I mean the boy. It's not my side who are holding him or have done something—' So our conversation breaks down like one of the city's abandoned vehicles, empty and rusting at the roadside.

Between my fruitless searches in the city I often sit, during the next days, in the so-called chapel where Father Mesrop's ecclesiastical bits, like relics from some incomprehensible civilisation, lie dusty. I look at them and say, What did anyone hope to achieve from those years of fighting? And the men who're holding the boy, do they pray? It's frightening to realise that they may believe in the justice of their cause too; it's a space without breathing, a gap in possibilities, because if they're acting in good faith . . . No, I won't dwell on that. But I sit in the chapel and stare at the chalice and paten as if their curves could bring some solution, as if some geometric formula that was used in their making could form the blueprint for an inevitable and permanent ceasefire. Meanwhile, out on the Beirut streets an occasional skirmish is reported, but nothing much. This uneasy, stomach-churning calm continues.

Apparently Seraphite has decided that my sessions in the chapel are for prayer; at least she treats me with a sort of reverent annoyance after each one, as she would a person struggling to recover from some self-induced illness. But the formulae of prayer mean nothing to me. The chapel is closed away from the wind and rain of these winter days, and my chair there is no more uncomfortable than any other. So I sit and wonder what all those prayers he muttered meant to Father Mesrop; I wonder uselessly about the reason for Georges wearing a crucifix. I assume that Rick, like myself, still has no religious belief.

Sometimes during my wonderings I doze. One late afternoon a package or something thrown against the back door wakes me with a start. Serephite upstairs

40

He's not dead, though for a moment I feared it. Nor badly hurt – he moves his arms and legs and stands up with our help (Seraphite came running at my scream). We take him indoors. Whether he fell alone at the door or was thrown there we'll never know. Upstairs: Seraphite hauls a bucket of hot water from the stove for his bath; when she's sloshed it in I send her out to buy (discreetly) new clothes for him. He steps into the bath unaided but the scars – especially a half-healed one across his face in front of the ear – make me wince. When he's scrubbed off the thickest grime I say under my breath, as if his captors might hear us, 'You escaped?' But he shakes his head.

'They let me go free.' He speaks with gaps as if words are unfamiliar, as if human beings are, too. 'Said they'd gotten the wrong person. Chucked me.'

No logic to this, but there never is in Beirut. 'Who were they?'

He scours the last strips of dirt from those bony shoulders. 'Toughs. Bits of this uniform or that.' I'd welcome even the ghost of his old grin, but of course it doesn't come. 'They didn't give me their names, Gran.'

Seraphite crashes up the stairs with her packages. She's panting and the smile on her face is a real one. She says, 'Oh yiehh! Look at that dirt!'

He stands up and, nearly asleep on his feet, says, 'I'll clean the tub, Seraphite.' She answers in Arabic and his face flickers almost like a real person's. '*Lovely* curses,' he says, swaying.

On the way to his bedroom (she and I on each side) I ask him, 'Who put that wound on your face?' Too late I remember tactfulness and add, 'Of course it won't leave a scar but – I'll kill him.'

'I don't doubt you would,' he says, his eyes closing, 'but truly, Gran, they were only voices and hands in the dark. In a room someplace. I've no idea where or who. So you'll never be a murderer.' With that he falls on his bed and sleeps, sleeps, sleeps.

But worse crimes than murder sit on my conscience now, because there are refinements of torture that can be worse than death, and each of our militias has learned – along with its bludgeoning techniques – plenty of refinements. I go down to the living room, put my face in my hands and rock to and fro in the classic position of mourning. Seraphite comes in and says, 'What good d'you think that'll do?' but I can't stop. Somewhere there are men who've hurt his body, but the biggest criminal towards him is in this house, this room, here. Myself.

He sleeps till next morning, then walks into the kitchen where I'm eating breakfast. He wears the new jeans and T-shirt with its purple-and-white pop logo, but even his walk has changed; the assured amble has become a sideways-glancing nervous tread. How much I've robbed him of – and, I don't doubt, for ever. As he sits down at the table I say, despite Seraphite's warning glance, 'Georges. It must have been connected with that.'

'Who knows?' He shrugs. I'm mourning the fact that they've drained all interest and enthusiasm out of him along with everything else, when he suddenly raises that unrevealing gaze from his plate and says, 'I've not gotten in touch with Solange yet – must do that right away.'

'Eat your breakfast first.' And thus postpone his disappointment for as long as possible. 'An easy birth,' I say distractedly, 'and they were both well the last time I checked.' (A brief phone call to the hospital before their discharge.) He must discover for himself how baby and mother have since scattered and what other people they're now committed to.

He spoons his yoghurt and crumbles bread. 'They fed you?' I say idiotically, and his gaze is no longer unrevealing; he looks at me out of a place I've never imagined. No, of course they scarcely fed him; if they had, how could he be so thin? The politeness, which that big bland country bred into his bones, has cracked across like the crazing on a worn plate.

He says, 'You know how these things go,' and I'll never dare ask anything about his captivity again.

After breakfast he asks for the phone number and address of the friend Solange is supposed to be staying with. I give them and he makes the call from the living room, in my presence. I'd walk out to give him privacy, but he apparently doesn't care. A short conversation, strangely glowing and illusioned. He's speaking with her personally, but doesn't she at least warn him she's found a new man? Seraphite, from the doorway, glares at me again, but I didn't intend to disillusion him: that's strictly between him and the girl.

When he's at last gone out to meet the girl, Seraphite says, 'Let him make his own mistakes.' Yes, Seraphite, I've learned that much wisdom. And, 'You suppose he'd believe it from you?' No; why should he believe anything from me ever again?

Seraphite attacks the housework as if she's demolishing a barricade; she's pounding away with a vacuum cleaner on the stairs and cursing the weak electric current when he returns. He doesn't quite bound in, but there's a startling happiness to him.

'All fixed,' he says glowing, 'and I checked with my job too. They'll give me a couple more weeks off, then I'll start work again. Gran, we'll come by and see you one evening real soon, but we do need to rush out to the villa now. There'll be so much to do there, clearing up after these weeks it's been empty, to make the place livable again.' His eyes shine; his taut skin shines with happiness too. 'And for the baby we'll need to get the place extra clean.'

I can't believe what I'm hearing. 'Solange is well?' But I don't mean that. 'She's going with you? And the baby too?'

'Sure,' he says, 'what else?' His face softens till he looks as drowned in emotion as the little Pompeiian cherub on my table. A single arrow would smash through him and he'd never breathe again. 'She's missed me,' he says, 'been waiting and hoping . . . I never thought she'd stay after the baby was born, but now she says . . .' In a daze of what I'd call calf-love in anyone else he collects his few belongings, kisses me (with lips which, as my dazzled mind notes, must last have kissed hers) and goes.

After the back door closes I say to Seraphite (who as usual was listening from the kitchen), 'What do you make of that?'

'The things you've said about that girl!' she retorts angrily. 'You can't ever realise that people might really *care* about each other – can't trust them that far, can you?'

I could stretch my imagination far enough to trust the capacity of some people, in some relationships, but not that tender boy who's just hurried out of the door – and not, especially, the girl he hurries toward. But there's no point in my saying so. Seraphite, while she works, begins to croon those sliding Arab melodies again, not probably this time in an attempt to irritate me but simply because she sees Rick's future as contented and stable. Despite all her personal bitterness and griefs she still believes in the possibility of happiness. I huddle in the living room and pretend to be reading a magazine. Whatever happy domestic relationship you pleated me into, I'd break its threads and entangle it. Even this boy whom I do love – see how I've messed up his life? It'll need his own integrity, and all the kindness of which that amazing girl is capable, to ravel away a fraction of the damage I've done.

Seraphite sticks her head in at the door and says, 'Finished for today – but I hate to leave you alone.'

We go through this every day. Past my magazine I mutter, 'Haven't you learned by now that I'm happiest when no one's bothering me?'

'Well,' she says, irritated too and doubtful, but she does leave. After a while I hear noises out front, where the Line is. Not fighting noises but casual, unfamiliar chatter, footsteps not belonging to a militia. Then I seem to hear the click of a camera. I get up, go to the front shutter, throw it open and expend my fury and all the curses I can muster – on a strolling party of, God help us, foreign tourists.

41

Solange's welcome drowned him in delight. They fell into each other's arms and – at least for the first few days – it seemed that much else bound them together besides body meeting body. She was bubbly, laughing, warmly concerned for him as she'd never shown signs of being before. In bed she traced the lines of his scars and grieved over them till he, longing to look to the future and shut away the past, reproached himself silently because her grief seemed so voluptuous; almost she bathed in it.

At least the baby was there to prod Solange also toward the future. In those first days back at the villa he helped take care of the infant. He'd never known a tiny baby on a day-to-day basis before, and every detail of its life fascinated him. He had dreams at night, of course; he'd expected to: quite the wrong sort of dreams for this idyllic place and her and the child, but you couldn't expect to escape those missing weeks easily. He often woke biting his lips and rigid; even in nightmare he'd been afraid of disturbing Solange. But the daytimes, with her and little Nur and the garden – at first there was nothing wrong with those.

He visited Madeleine often, in the evenings while Solange worked (she'd rushed back to work sooner than he'd hoped, but he, who'd not been around when she most needed him, felt he couldn't suggest or criticise). A genuine bond, he told Madeleine reassuringly, between Solange and myself now, and of course the baby . . . a real family. This wasn't exactly so. He was becoming aware of the many subtle ways in which the three of them weren't such a family, but he couldn't at present come up with solutions or even find exact words to describe the new cobwebbing difficulties, so best to say nothing to Madeleine about them. Yet as the weeks went by, her shrewdness prodded harder and meanwhile the idyllic nature of that life increasingly fell apart.

Almond blossom, he would say, did you know the first flowers are already out? Madeleine's eyes held nostalgia but so much else, too. He could deceive Solange as he never could . . . then at the notion of in any way deceiving Solange he was appalled. Yet something of that sort, a twisting away from truth, was happening to their relationship. The bird tower (he went on telling Madeleine) so peaceful, those stones where the fighting's long gone and only a lizard or, at dusk, cicadas . . . Geraniums, they'll be in flower soon too. And beyond the villa apricot trees, then beyond the highway and a swathe of giant purple thistles, the sea.

He told her this one night while from her bedroom window the two of them watched the prickling small lights of inhabited blocks beyond the black gash of the Line. When he stopped talking there was silence, then – as if answering his doubts rather than his words – she said, 'How can you measure emotion?' Before he had time to get an evasive reply ready she went on, 'And your work, you're happy again in that?'

Nervous, as he'd never been nervous in the job before, but that was understandable, and the other drivers and crews had reassured him all they could. 'It's work that needs doing, and I have some qualifications.'

'Cannon fodder,' she said. Then with another of those leaps which made her such a dangerous poker into his mind she returned to the topic of Solange. 'Of course I'm glad for you but surprised. I never thought she'd stay.'

'Me neither.' His gaze wouldn't meet Madeleine's. To cover his confusion he said, 'There's been other men while I was gone. She told me honestly about them. After all, no one knew if I'd ever come back.' He tried to believe that she'd been wholly honest with me about what she was doing, and he tried also to imagine himself in her position. Those chasms which had opened up in his personality during imprisonment gaped at him again and he said, 'I'd most likely have done the same myself.' Because he couldn't any longer be sure of what he might do under pressure.

'There's been other men since you came back too?'

'No,' he said, 'oh no.' He couldn't prove this; in fact he was beginning to suspect there were still others. Her many absences, her brittle evasions when he dared to question her, and her wild gaiety sometimes when she came home . . . But if there were others, he wouldn't blame her. His own behaviour could, he felt, provide plenty of reason for her unfaithfulness. 'I've changed,' he said, 'you've no notion, Gran. I'm not the same person as I was at all. The first days after they freed me, I was excited and happy to be with her again, and she seemed happy too. We were both riding on an unreal hoping, I guess. But all of a sudden the bottom fell out of that: she seemed to get restless and my fatigue caught up with me so I couldn't make the effort to coax her into calming down any more.' He spread his empty hands wide. 'She and I haven't quarrelled lately, we've drifted. Oh, sometimes things are still good, and when they're not the fault's most always on my side, because I'm so goddam *tired* and I don't seem to care about anything any more.' No use trying to explain to Madeleine how evenings without Solange brought their own peace and reassurance, how staying alive had become his major preoccupation. In the evening a book or some half-witted radio programme was enough to satisfy him; they didn't need effort or the sort of emotional attachment he now seemed unable to make.

Madeleine snorted and said, 'Porcelain illusions,' and he couldn't be bothered to tell her that the truth was so different. Anyway he still felt a certain loyalty toward Solange, if nothing more.

After six weeks of this, his increasing disquiet at the charade that the villa life had become pushed him into speaking more frankly. Madeleine's shutter was open to the spring darkness; he and she stood at the window and while they talked his finger mechanically picked at the framework, sending rotted bits of wood down to join the grasses and sprouting trees of the Line. 'You've no notion,' he said slowly, 'what I'm really like nowadays, Gran. Corruptible as all hell. I discovered that in their damn shuttered room.'

'Acquired it there, you mean.' In the dark he couldn't see her face but her voice was accepting, supportive; he couldn't have that. No one must excuse the capacity for not merely sloppiness but evil which he'd discovered in himself.

'Discovered, Gran.' The night breeze blew with a million warm spicy scents on it out of the charred reaches of the Line, and he went on explaining to her how during those imprisoned weeks he'd come to believe he would do anything for freedom – his personal freedom; he'd stopped caring about any wider – and for immunity from pain. 'If I'd had a chance to betray someone I thought I cared about, and then walk free out of there, I'd have taken the chance at once. When they beat me up I got terrified at first, yeah, but after a while if I'd had the chance I'd have beaten any of them into the floor gladly. I'd have enjoyed doing it.'

'You can't be sure,' said her old defensive drone, 'it never came to the point. You can imagine, but—'

'I can be sure enough. And this life of ours at the villa – somehow the heart's gone out of that. It's gotten kind of hollow and unreal.'

'She's tired of it too,' Madeleine said, with a certainty that startled him.

'Well, I'm not that sure – I guess she finds it convenient still in some ways.'

'I see it all,' said her prophetic croak out of the darkness. 'When you first came back she tried, for whatever peculiar reason, to make the relationship work, but she's given up trying. She's more bored and frustrated than your calm nature can imagine. At any moment she'll explode.'

He listened to his voice replying; yes, it did give the impression of calmness. What he felt was something quite other, a sort of turning his back on them all because he was at bottom still mortally afraid. 'No,' said his voice, 'I doubt that. She comes and goes there as she wants, and her quietness when she's there lately seems like a sort of proof—'

'That girl? But I've seen her passions blaze in her face. She'll grow to hate you.' He wanted to shut his ears to the croak, but it persisted. 'Perhaps she'll use violence to you or the child or herself. Don't take that risk.'

'The child,' he said, mildly interested but without emotion, 'now there's another odd thing. I've always liked little kids, enjoyed playing with my friends' young brothers and sisters back in the States, but this baby . . . She's a fun kid, and she doesn't yell a lot or anything, but you know how I feel about her? Damn-all, that's how I feel. And with Solange I'm hollow, scraped out, nothing except politeness left.'

Along the Line in the dark a couple stumbled, male and female. Their voices murmured and a guitar that had lain discarded briefly twanged. A woman's laugh, smothered by the night; tiny sucking sounds; then the stumbling steps receded into the dark. He said, 'Let's close the shutter.'

Madeleine switched on her bedroom light and said, 'That wasn't her; the timbre of voice wasn't—'

'No,' he agreed, and couldn't be bothered to point out that on another night, with another man, it might have been.

'What will you do?' Madeleine said. She looked old and shrunken among the satin draperies of the bedroom.

'Go on the way we are, what else is there to do? I won't rat out. It's not her fault if I'm different than I was.'

Not your fault either, Madeleine quickly insisted. But he shook his head.

'You haven't grasped it, Gran. Since those weeks they held me, there's nothing I'd feel incapable of doing. Crime or whatever. If it's cheap and convenient and there's not much risk, a part of me wouldn't mind grabbing at it. That part must've always been there.'

He said goodnight (she told him tartly, 'You kiss me as if you have a dozen grandmothers and I'm the last in line') then left to return to the villa. Driving back out there alone (Solange was spending the night with a supposed 'friend' in the city and he'd pick up the baby from its minder when he reached the village) he recalled how Madeleine had reminded him that evening of his long-ago dream for rural living. 'Yeah,' he'd answered, 'but I guess someone called my bluff on that. After all, countryside's only countryside, isn't it? When you come down to the bumps. Only trees and bushes and birds and flowers.' Driving home, he remembered the ruins of the stone bird-tower and the butterflies that had fluttered around it on the day of Solange's christening. For an instant the fact that the tower was ruined meant that pigeons were no longer needed because the roads were now safe. Then he laughed at this idiotic fancy.

42

After he's gone I reopen the shutter at a distant spluttering noise and see a shower of sparks breaking over the city, breaking like red and green and white mistakes. In the old days this tracer fire signified a wedding, a happy social occasion, but its rare appearances since the fighting began have mostly signalled a ceasefire. I watch the evanescent pretty sight till the Line and the sky fall dark, then I close the shutter and shut Beirut out. My laughter sounds as unreal as Rick's mood, as those coloured bullets, which exploded and vanished. Which of the many factions are deluding themselves that they've stopped fighting this time? I lie in bed trying to calculate how long since the last ceasefire (as in another country an insomniac might count sheep or lovers). Must be a while. These rash illusions of hope have, like Rick's pastoral dream, ceased to inspire belief. In the night I seem to hear someone niggling at the back door, like an appeal; I think unsurprised, 'Father Mesrop,' and almost I get up to let him in, then I remember. The next morning shows only a drift of leaves and twigs from one of the Line's trees; some vagrant eddy must have swept them over the house to fidget at the back. Where did Mesrop get his eggs? What tree have the leaves blown from? How soon and in what way will Solange finish with Rick?

Seraphite when she arrives says, 'You're snappy this morning,' but she's grumpy too. She admits to seeing those flying coloured sparks and they've set our teeth on edge. 'A waste of money,' I say neutrally, but what I really mean is, 'A waste of hope – let's not begin that again. It's too painful.' I add in conventional excuse, 'I'm worried about the boy.'

'The fools,' (she's not referring to Rick), 'won't they ever learn?' And in my ancient dingy kitchen we laugh, Maronite and Arab laughing together for the first time in years. Our cynical disbelieving laughter unites us in an ironic warmth.

43

The Line throbs under the spring sun and once in a while little groups of tourists spawn among the broken stones. Bright-coloured foreign shirts and expensive cameras, loud polyglot voices. In my shady room I seethe against the tourists, I brood about Rick's tired politeness and the much too quiet girl he's living with. Finally, on an evening when earth and sky shine clear as primal innocence, I pick up my phone (miraculously it mostly works nowadays), I call a taxi.

During the ride my sense of compulsion and necessity remains, but when the taxi has dropped me and the manager with his inappropriate reverence has shown me to that poky little dressing room, I stare at the girl as she sits in a scarlet wrap at the cluttered table creaming her face – and I say nothing. Because wasn't I ready to interfere again? I've rushed hot and furious to order her for Rick's sake to leave him, let him be free to pick up his pieces . . . but at the sight of her bland, composed face I realise that the boy's stumbling flat statements may not, for all sorts of valid reasons, exactly reflect the truth about either himself or her. So instead I mutter about passing by and hadn't seen her for a while, wondered how the baby was. While the words leave my mouth I'm getting ready to hobble away.

'She's fine.' That smooth, unrevealing face . . . She creams her forehead thickly, turns the glistening mask to me and says, so expressionless that the surface of the cream scarcely moves, 'It's all right, I'm leaving your grandson.'

'That's not what I—' She pulls a chair forward and I sit; her unsought surrender has stunned my legs. My sense of intruding propels me into, 'Is it because of anything I – but you've been together there all these weeks, why now?' Is it because Grandmother Wolf has arrived and stands in front of you baring her teeth, so that the children run screaming?

The girl's forefinger delicately explores the pallid countryside of her face, then the finger pauses and she leans at me. '*You're* asking me why?'

'Is it because I've interfered—'

The finger resumes gliding across the calm plains, the rounded valleys, of her cheeks and chin. 'You?' she says. 'When did you ever make much noise about us or we take any notice? Old women like you . . .' The young, supple finger meditates further along the smooth skin. 'No, I meant because you yourself when you were young . . . didn't you?' She adds wistful, 'I did hope you'd understand. He's going to need *someone*.'

I realise she's not accusing me of a sexual expediency like hers, she's finding in me a more general likeness to herself, a ruthlessness perhaps. 'Yet you did go back to him, and took the baby.' Not accusing, only puzzled.

Her forefinger makes deepening circles in the cream just above her left eyebrow. She'll need to redo the make-up there for a smooth effect. Tiny remorseless circles till the bare skin shows . . . 'Not love,' she says, 'that's a word I don't accept.' The finger circles like a hawk hunting.

'A tenderness?'

'God, no! That would be worse than love. No, but there was always a – an openness in him toward me. While he was a hostage I thought, "We'll break this off easily; I'll just disappear," yet when he came out the sound of his voice, the familiar sight of him, sent me walking toward him and in through the door of his openness. But these past weeks at the villa – that was a grind from the start, trying to twist myself into a shape I wasn't meant for, and it gets worse every day. So I'm leaving. You see now why he'll need you? He'll be so unhappy—'

'Is he happy now?'

Her finger stops circling and she turns her astonished face to me. 'Of course,' she says. 'With me there, why wouldn't he be?'

'And you cancelled the baby's adoption?'

Her finger visits the cold-cream jar and carries a dollop to fill in that hole above the eyebrow. 'Ah,' she says, and through the mask I detect her mischief, 'I did a little manipulation of the facts on that. Expediency. Don't deny, Madame, that you've used expediency in your time too. In the same way as I altered the due date. I hoped Ricki wouldn't realise how far along I was and guess I was desperate for a prop.' The finger deposits the dollop of cream and starts to smooth it in. 'No,' she murmurs, 'there never was a friend willing to adopt, no one so convenient. I hoped something would turn up, but it didn't,' – as if she still believes in the instantaneous transforming magic of fairy tales – 'so when Ricki re-appeared and I was still saddled with . . . A family,' she murmurs, creaming the last traces of the hole away; it's impossible to exaggerate the cynicism of her tone.

'There's another man, of course?'

She chuckles and her creamed finger indicates the room. A new row of little pots and a flagon of Paris scent, a hanging dress with subtle green and blue folds and a canary diamond ring she'd taken off to do her creaming: its chilly glitter sits triumphant before her on the table. 'He's generous,' she says. 'The same man you saw in the hospital.'

'Ah. He's not the baby's father?' (As I asked then.)

Her throaty laugh echoes across the little room. She's already escaped from us all in spirit. 'You're so conventional,' she says, 'at bottom, aren't you? Such a wild old witch, and yet you'd like everything to be neatly tied up. No, he's not the father.'

'How soon will you go to him?' The hard slatted chair presses painfully on my thighs; the scented air is stuffy enough to choke on.

She answers gently, as if she pities me, 'Very soon. He's getting impatient. But,' she laughs, how she laughs! 'I was willing you, *ordering* you, to visit me here before I go. Did you realise that, old woman? So that I could explain how your grandson will need—' Her laugh has evaporated. She crumples a tissue between her creamed fingers. While her eyes peer slyly at me she says, 'What a good pair you and I could have made if things had been different.'

'You could have been a grand-daughter-in-law I'd love.' This is simple truth.

Her face loses its slyness and opens up into that sudden generous warmth which could compel anyone's affection. 'Yes,' she says, her gaze bright, 'but you'd eat me.'

'Not any longer.' But her eyes and mouth narrow, and her shove of the cold-cream jar is dismissive.

'Ah,' she says. 'I've met other people like you. Your type never changes.' She applies powder, mascara, lipstick, eyeshadow. You could call the result sharp and wary. But she and I have travelled far beyond those misleading labels.

'This other man,' I say, 'you'll be all right?' I can't ask, 'Will he be good to you?' because she, poor child, thinks their happiness is a matter of her being good to him. Poor child indeed; in another existence I'd have enjoyed the living near her, talking with her. But I've done enough harm for one lifetime, I'm passive for evermore.

'He's got money,' she says, and the wary face becomes lean with expectation. Perhaps she really will be happy. If she can lower her sights so that money and cossetting satisfy her . . . but I'd be disappointed in her if she did. She realises this, for the lean face broadens to that mischievous smile. 'A nice enough man,' she says, 'he's got other assets too,' and I see she's toying whether to consider herself in love with him. Unfortunately it's not so simple.

I don't dare say, What's the baby's future? That's definitely none of my business and she'd quickly tell me so. I get up, but before leaving I kiss her creamily perfumed forehead; she gives me that wide, peaceful smile, doesn't speak. Certainly I hope the man will at least be kind to her. At most . . . but probably she, unlike myself when young, doesn't dare hope for the best that could happen. Whatever she or Brigitte might say, the war has made them cynical; the laughter of Seraphite and myself, that morning after the ceasefire, is by comparison fresh and pure.

Next day the political news becomes crazier than ever – former enemies not merely firing coloured tracers but grinning alongside each other, arms linked, in newspaper and television pictures, and making elaborate plans for rebuilding the city (where do they expect to get the money? What foreign government would lend to this armed and reeking dump?). Then, the next day while I listen to the radio, an announcement: there's a proposal underway to disband the militias.

I laugh at this till I choke. When I can speak again I say, 'The *fools.*' Seraphite eyes me sourly. I say, 'I'd better go back to live with the Madagascar tribes. *They* had their wits about them, whereas this bunch of—' And it's true: a smoulder of devils in the forest, haunting or shrieking, would make more sense than our militiamen.

Into the last of my laughter an unignorable noise comes from the Line, a disturbance. Seraphite runs and I hurry after; when I reach the window in our cracked front wall she's already got the shutter open. Below us among the grasses and saplings people run, shout, scream; grey-bearded men almost my age are limping, young men leap past the earthen berms. They aim rifles, they fire and various of them fall, but there's no blood. Then I see the film camera grinding along. The director calls for another shot, the dead and injured jump up and run grinning like urchins freed from school; they take up their former positions and the firing starts again. I take a savage pleasure in disrupting this shot by screaming curses at the director and his group. I passionately long to blame foreigners for this intrusion but, God help me, these men are Lebanese.

Finally my voice gravels and Seraphite reaches in front of me to bang the shutter closed. 'Enough,' she says, 'they'll put you on film next. Wouldn't like that, would you?' In the kitchen I tremble and she brews strong coffee; past its steam and my quivering she says, 'Better get that front wall fixed one of these days, so you can open the shutter properly and get a new window put in too. No use ignoring facts.' I find a few leftover curses for her, but her broad shoulder tosses them aside. 'Look,' she says, 'your eyes and ears are as sharp as mine. No use swimming against that current, however crazy a current it seems to both of us.' She jerks her head toward the Line.

I call her the filthiest names I can find. Tears prickle at my eyes but I don't weep, haven't since Madagascar. She stubbornly continues preparing lunch and an hour later, while we're eating it, the film crew packs up and goes away. Seraphite (yes, she condescends to eat with me lately) says past her mouthful of bulgur, 'Now we know what the unemployed militiamen will do for a living — they'll all become film actors,' and we both find caustic grins for this further obscenity.

During my supposed rest that afternoon I visualise

44

Solange left the plane ticket lying openly on the chest of drawers in their bedroom; he was almost surprised she hadn't dumped it on his pillow while he slept. In the middle of dressing he spotted it. He turned with it in his fingers and she said quickly (as if she'd waited weeks to say this), 'You see? It's for this afternoon.'

'Yes.' He laid it back down and pulled on his T-shirt. He felt pity for her because after all she hadn't found this easy to say: her hurried, forced tone told him so. Pity — the one emotion she'd hate and reject — and for himself he felt absolutely nothing. The pain would, he knew, come later. 'I hope it works out,' he said, 'whoever the man is.' And she, with that ruthless determination which made her sound like one of the Line's prowling animals, assured him that it would, it must. His pity for her deepened till it almost overwhelmed him. He tried for dry practicalities. 'Of course you're taking Nur, but you haven't packed—'

'No.' The monosyllable spun him abruptly to search her face again.

'The man is buying new clothes for both of you?' She couldn't, surely, mean anything else.

'No no no.' She slipped from the bed and stood close to him. The familiar scent of her made him long to grab her and say, Surely we've a future, you can't be meaning all this. But it was too late, or there'd never been a chance. 'For me,' she went on, 'yes, he buys clothes. What would I want with anything bought in Lebanon?' She gave him the pure, seemingly totally honest smile she'd sometimes given Madeleine. 'Clothes bought in Beirut would corrode my future. I won't allow that.'

'And the baby?' He still couldn't believe what he was hearing.

'Nur? I leave her here. You may dispose of her as you wish.'

'My God,' he said, 'she's not a damn *package*. You mean you're really opting out of—' The baby in her crib set up a wail as if she knew she was being discussed.

'One life,' she said with a shrug, pulling on a silk wrapper, 'what's that?' She came close to him again and, intolerably gentle, touched his cheek. 'For you this infant is the first time,' she said. 'Not your child, of course, but the first time closely. Yes? But for me—' She turned away, tied the belt of the wrapper and said with a nonchalance in which he couldn't find any tremor, 'I never did claim there hadn't been one or two others.'

Hadn't she? Or had she fudged the explanation? Somehow he'd gotten the impression of an abortion or so, but a live birth was different. What had happened to those infants? He knew he could never ask her, and that if anyone did ask she'd lie like all the world's merchants in reply. 'But Nur – what do you plan is going to happen to her?'

Again the nonchalant tone. 'I make no plans. Between your care and the village woman's I suppose she'll survive.' She picked up a hairbrush and frowned into the mirror. 'Ricki, sweet, we mustn't be late this morning. I have farewells to make in the city. So hurry up.'

'But Nur—'

She turned from the mirror and said, 'Sometimes I really don't understand you. We'll drop her off at the village woman's on our way to Beirut, as usual, and you'll pick her up when you return here tonight. Where's the problem?'

'And you won't be coming back here at all after you leave this morning?'

She laid down the hairbrush and stared. 'How could I? Even if I wanted to, which I don't. Haven't I just told you I'll be in Berlin by then?'

He said brutally (the pain was starting to wake up), 'And what happens when he drops you?'

She began to brush her hair again; the long tranquil strokes took her further from him than she'd ever been. 'He and I marry this afternoon,' she said, 'very discreet. I didn't invite you because—' She glanced round at him and was the purely mischievous Solange he'd known their first few nights. 'He mightn't like, *hein*? Of course he knows there have been other men and I explained to him that the problem of the baby is solved, but he mightn't wish those other men lining up to watch me marry. Ricki, really!'

He opened his mouth to say, Solved, my ass! but there was no point. The space of two continents and a lot of bodies separated them.

He drove back to the villa after work that evening, picking up the baby on the way as usual, but the villa held nothing for him now: it was more torment than pleasure. And Nur's future was his biggest problem. That had got to be solved. He bathed the baby, mixed the feed and fed her, put her to bed, then he sat trying to think. The echoing emptiness of the house confirmed that Solange wouldn't indeed be returning. There must be orphanages in Beirut, and people who'd lost kids in the fighting. For the first time in months it occurred to him that once Nur's disposal was solved he could go back to the States, could put the bits of himself together and make the sort of life he'd previously wanted. The backwoods ought to be peaceable and healing, after Beirut. He'd stayed here long enough that Chehab couldn't object to his return.

The logs on the hearth crumbled and fell to ash; the chill of the spring night moved in. After a while Nur whimpered in her cot upstairs and he automatically changed and soothed her, then he returned to the embers of the fire. He sat down beside them and tried to figure out whether there was anything he really wanted to do with his life, whether he was capable of caring much about anything – or, for that matter, anyone. Which brought him back to Nur and the need for making arrangements about her care, arrangements that would give her a chance of a tolerable future. She was at the start of her life: didn't she deserve a better beginning than to be shoved into some overcrowded orphanage and left there with no one on the outside caring about what happened to her? He remembered his own – much less complete – experience of what life without parents was like. He tried to feel cynical, to tell himself that, whatever, she'd turn out to be as irresponsible as her mother; there was no point in troubling yourself over one feckless woman's infant. After the countless deaths he'd seen . . . and anyway, wasn't irresponsibility most likely in her genes? Nothing to be done about that but accept its happening and then wipe it away, go live your own life.

While he thought, something was trying to happen inside him and he fought it with all the strength he had. Not a warmth, never that, he wouldn't accept that after what he'd been through. Wouldn't or, he told himself, couldn't, whatever. No, but a loosening, a wrenching apart, as if the person he'd learned to be since he came back from captivity was losing little bits of itself, wasn't completely reliable any longer. This shook him profoundly. How could he possibly judge about Nur's future now?

At last the notion came to him: ask Madeleine and abide by her advice on Nur. Madeleine's not the least bit sentimental about babies. She'll tell me what to do.

45

No sun that morning, instead a grey wetness, the last of the spring rains. He stands at the door with the baby in a pink plastic carrier. Silently I hold the door wide, silently he climbs the stairs behind me. The baby lets out a wail as thin as the rain, and I say, 'She left the child with you like a *parcel*?'

He follows me into the living room. There he lifts the baby out of the carrier and rocks her in his arms. 'She wanted to start out new, I guess,' he says. He sounds totally casual and I flinch, because a *baby*, a human infant . . .

But I'm myself, old Madeleine, I haven't forgotten how to match hardness for hardness. 'There must be an orphanage in the city,' I say, 'are you on your way there? A sensible solution.' And I watch to see whether the horror I thrust him into has irrevocably ruined him.

He stops rocking and the child falls asleep in his arms (with that incredible rapidity of infants, which I'd forgotten). 'Is that what you'd suggest?' he says, looking past her at me, and I realise it's myself who's on trial. God forgive my arrogance, I had automatically set myself higher than the boy.

I stall, 'There's no chance of her deciding to claim the child? She won't go back to the villa – change her mind about the baby and hope to find you there?'

'She won't go back.' He isn't helping me to climb out of the cell I've constructed, but why should he?

'She won't come here looking for you?'

'She won't come here either.' He lays the sleeping baby

gently in her carrier. 'She's already left for Berlin,' he assures the tumbled pink blanket, the spread across which yellow elephants plod. 'She's marrying this new guy of hers. By all accounts he's loaded – *and* a foreign job and apartment.'

'Berlin will be safer for her than here.' A city full of spirit and energy, with shops as glossy as anywhere in the world and a tradition of good-time, of rich food and cabaret . . . 'She'll settle happily there.'

'Yeah,' he says, 'I guess so. She always did like varied living.' He leans over the carrier and pokes his finger at the baby's tiny fist, but she's fathoms drowned in sleep. (Her dark fluff of hair is straight; that's one difference from Solange). 'You said there's orphanages?' He sounds casual as ever. Was my insight mistaken?

So, 'Is that what you want for the child?' There's no reason why he should feel a responsibility for her, and less than no reason why I should. The baby wakes, a series of astonishing – would you call them thoughts? – passes across her face, and the little fingers squirm in search of his, which have left her. I say, 'What did you say her name is?'

'Nur. Solange chose it.'

'An Arab name.' I won't, I *won't* bend and touch the child. The tiny strong grip of infants' fingers, any infants', is an imposition. 'Arab,' I repeat, to explain my distancing.

'Oh, Gran!' He chuckles, seemingly untroubled, but he doesn't pick up the carrier and leave. He says in that level, unrevealing voice, 'I can't guarantee that the kid's a good Maronite or ever will be.' He glances around. 'Seraphite's not here?'

I dart into his mind and this time I'm sure: with that acutely searching glance he's laid himself wide open. 'She's upstairs cleaning my bedroom. You hoped she'd be your ally?'

'That's a funny way of putting it.' But his face

twitches, his mouth and eyes are breaking up into uneasiness, despair, dreams falling apart; he's at my mercy. Old Madeleine who had no mercy in her.

I bend, I force my right index finger down to the child's level, to that segment of the world which the child's tiny hand occupies. I shove my finger at the infant and the little tentacles close round it, grip. No, I hadn't forgotten how that grip feels. Above my head the boy's voice is once more unrevealing.

'The villa,' he says, 'it's not practical for me to keep the place on any longer. I'd need to get a woman in to look after Nur, and with the sort of hours I work that'd get too complicated. Then my job can be risky. The city's quiet now but if anything flares up—'

'Yes.' After all, this is Beirut. 'So you intend to give up the villa?'

'Oh yeah, keeping it on wouldn't be a bit practical.'

'Perhaps,' – I'm thinking aloud – 'we could rent another villa somewhere, sometime, for days out.' Or buy one with some of my money, which is sitting barren in the bank. Not *that* villa, if for him it's too full of memories of Solange, but another villa with an overgrown garden and bird tower. Perhaps we could?

He's gazing at me very kindly, as if I'm the infant now. And perhaps I am. 'Yeah,' he says, 'if you wanted to, why not?'

And perhaps one day he might even enjoy working in its garden again, might lose his new, gentle tiredness which makes me frightened for his future . . .

Then he stands up, and as if hope were a piece of luggage he's finally jettisoned he picks up the baby's carrier. 'Where are you taking her?' I say.

He looks down at me, his young face troubled, open, without resentment. 'I'll figure out some arrangement – look for an apartment or a room and set about making a home for her. There must be some way—'

'She *is* home, damn you,' say my uncontrollable lips, my tongue, 'she's as much home here as she would be anywhere. Put the carrier down, blast you, you'll wake her up again. And aren't you late for work?' He sets down the carrier and stares, stunned, at me. I'm stunned too, but those words were urgent and necessary.

'Seraphite,' he says, 'won't she—'

'She's been yearning for my grandchildren for years, complaining that we're an unproductive bunch.' Before the fighting got bad this was true, and old Madeleine catches herself plotting, 'I'll stir her up to feel the same again.' Old Madeleine, squash her down as I may, keeps rising busily up. 'Call Seraphite, would you?' I say. 'You're so expert at subtle hinting nowadays, you've been doing nothing else for the last half-hour; call her and find out for yourself.'

So he calls her, but he doesn't need to put the question. I'd never realised in all these years that Seraphite is a woman who drools over cradles: any cradle, any baby, anyone's. You see such women around; I've known some among my friends. Whether the baby is Arab, Christian or Jew, these women hang over the cradle and coo and croon. So she croons and clucks, she carries the baby off to bathe it and to heat milk; when the door closes behind her I find on Rick's face the same faintly disgusted expression as I feel on mine. I haven't laughed so deeply in years. (But my guilty, cautious observing of him persists, that interior voice which whispers, Perhaps you haven't totally destroyed him – see, he can still smile.)

'Go to work,' I say finally. 'Your bedroom's ready for you and Brigitte's is empty too. Between Seraphite and myself and your free time, we'll look after the child.' Someday, please God, he'll thaw out, then he'll feel the urge to make other arrangements. Someday he'll get involved (I hope) with another girl, a sensible, happy one who likes children. Someday he'll be fully adult and circumstances will shift. (Or if they don't, it doesn't matter; those words of mine were still necessary. Somehow we'll work matters out.)

'I'll do my part, of course,' he says, 'and arrange for plenty of help. Maybe Seraphite would be willing to live in and get a friend to cover for her time off, when I'm working? If not, I'll hire someone else to cover. But don't say yes if you'd rather not.'

It's obvious from Seraphite's cooing that she loves babies even more than she hates Maronites. And suddenly I remember how as a child I discovered the upside-down world, the world seen from between my knees with head hanging. In that world – so much more interesting than ours – the sea flowed upside-down beside the land, and buildings and trees pushed themselves into the blue-earth depths of sky. Almost the curvature of the globe was visible, and certainly we all clung to it by a bare eyelash. The world hung together in an incredibly fragile lacing; we children ran and played upside-down while a tremendous unseen force held us, and the birds flew on the first step of the Milky Way. The immense, scaring force of the tiny, grabbing finger connects with this memory and dazzles me. 'Go to your job,' I tell Rick. 'Who's the expert on babies around here – you or us?'

'I told them I might be late in because I'd need to get things sorted.' He pauses, then rushes on, 'I'll stick with the ambulance work for a while; they can use me and in a way I don't mind the toughness of the work.' The cellar, what men did to him there, hangs like a great rabid bat between us and always will. Probably the worst things that can happen to the boy already have. 'Fact is,' he goes jerkily on, 'I'm thinking about options, but I want to allow myself plenty of time to decide. I might even bend my principles some and use a bit of family money to qualify myself for another job.' And he flushes with the ghost of the raw young embarrassment he hasn't shown for weeks.

'Work in the bank perhaps?' But I'd be disappointed. He's got other qualities in him.

'Not the bank. Fact is . . . I need to think it over some.'

A sudden illumination strikes me that he may mean training to be a doctor. Unprovable (old Madeleine sometimes has sense enough to restrain her questions when she's been firmly told to) but he's always shown this bizarre medical interest and I can imagine him in a white coat with stethoscope. Old Madeleine is so sure of her accurate guess, she can hardly restrain her knowing grin. But she manages to catch it back; is she finally learning caution? At the least it's now clear that his idealism is a stubborn, if dangerous and illogical, root. Beirut's facts and my criminal handling of him haven't yet dislodged it.

Beneath Seraphite's crooning another noise begins, a grumble in the distance, then an approaching roar. From, of course, the Line beyond the house front. Seraphite continues singing to the child (one of those wailing Arab creations – what *will* the child grow up to be?) and Rick unlocks the door to my smashed wall, to the shutter.

A thin grey rain continues and the sky is so bled as to be almost white. The Line southward sighs, waves, hisses, with its thickets of grass and trees; the Line northward – stripped bare, all vegetation swept away. Beneath my window a couple of bulldozers bellow, grey angular monsters. The men on them, the supervisors and tidiers at the sides, wear the grey-green uniforms of Syria, our peaceful army of occupation. While I watch they move on to rip apart a wire barricade in the next block. At the far north of the Line they're detonating ruins – the dull crump and puffs of smoke intersperse our talk.

I say, 'Didn't I tell you months ago how many times they've cleared here and brought the bulldozers through?

And soon fresh barricades go up, the fighting starts again.'

'Sure you told me.' And we recite the litany of dates together. Then he says, with more earnestness than he's shown about anything else except the child, 'They're clearing the ruins now, for rebuilding. Surely they didn't do that before?'

'Well, no, but——' An oildrum from some dismantled barricade has rolled along the side of the street; while we watch, it rolls further and disappears through one of the gaping doorways. A puff of cement dust rises where the drum touched a wall. The rusty end of a connecting rod snaps off; the momentary quiet magnifies these sounds. And I remember Georges – won't I always remember him in these circumstances, these surroundings? Rick puts an arm around my shoulders and I realise that my long battle to stay in this house may be almost over. Not through my death, no. I intend to go on breathing for some years yet. But the city authorities have been muttering, in our times of relative calm, about their grandiose plans for the future of ruined Beirut, how they'll make enormous public spaces and apartments, fancy new shops and arcades, here in the centre of ruined Beirut. One old Maronite woman with a fierce determination to stay in her dishevelled house isn't necessarily going to stop them; they can purchase and throw me out if they wish. Mightn't it be better to go calmly, gracefully, to a villa away from the crowds and the stink of rebuilding? A house where the child can grow up safe and Rick can repair his torn nerves. In Beirut, of course. I couldn't live anywhere else. In Ashrafiyeh perhaps? Certainly one of the chic East Beirut areas not too far from here.

Rick's arm round my shoulders tightens as if he guesses what I'm thinking. With his other hand he pushes the shutters closed and we go back indoors. In the kitchen Seraphite has started on the more cheerful parts of her musical repertoire, which she's not used for years. Water splashes and the baby hiccups. 'You could go back to the States,' I offer to Rick one last time. 'This present peace may not last.'

'The hell I will. Unfinished business here, Gran.' He sinks into one of my brown-and-gold cut-velvet chairs, links his hands behind his back and, unreadable but determined, surveys me. I've no idea which way he thinks our future will swing, but that doesn't matter; he's obviously committed to this city as all of us are. Not politically, not a battling Maronite, but in his own way.

Meanwhile they're detonating buildings, so they must be planning to rebuild. Are we all such innocents that we can believe in the possibility of an agreed peace, even while the death-charged air hangs around us? But can any fighting, any torment situation, go on for ever? I'm amused (and scornful) to find that even I can still believe. So if the city authorities and Seraphite pester me enough – and it would be a sign of Rick's recovery if he begins to pester me too – I will one day make arrangements to move us all to one of Beirut's more civilised streets. Perhaps this time I really will.